D. Rob Norvelle's life-long ambition to write engaging, thought-provoking stories has commenced in his captivating first novel, *Seasons of Freedom.* His career as a novelist began in 2018 when he concluded a successful career as a bank executive for a major financial institution.

Rob's passion for writing is nearly matched by his enthusiasm for travel, Russian River valley wines and Washington Nationals baseball.

He resides in the South Carolina low country with his wife, Donna, and their five ill-mannered but enormously loved Chihuahuas and Dachshunds.

To Donna, for believing.

D. Rob Norvelle

SEASONS OF FREEDOM

AUSTIN MACAULEY PUBLISHERS™

LONDON * CAMBRIDGE * NEW YORK * SHARJAH

A CIP catalogue record for this title is available from the British Library.

ISBN 9781398412101 (Paperback)
ISBN 9781398412118 (ePub e-book)

www.austinmacauley.com

First Published 2021
Austin Macauley Publishers Ltd
Level 37, Office 37.15, 1 Canada Square
Canary Wharf
London
E14 5AA

Many thanks to Michael Jackman for his critical feedback, positive reinforcement, sound advice, and valued friendship.

Part 1
Freedom

Chapter 1

Everything Old Is New, Again

Late Fall 2019

God, I had forgotten how crystal clear the Blue Ridge Mountains are on a cold Virginia morning. 'Cold as a witch's tit', Dad would say every year when the first really cold spell hit the area. The crispness to the air, and the hard freeze to the ground make this little town feel even more frigid and uninviting than it actually is, but only slightly. It's sad to say about one's own hometown, but a return visit to Freedom is akin to paying a call on a worn-out old hooker with rotting teeth and the clap; you will probably get what you came for, but it won't be pleasant, and the lingering effects can haunt you for a lifetime. Take that as gospel from me. I realize that I might be a little biased, but I have damn good reason to be. One family was responsible for this town deteriorating into an ancient whore with tons of baggage. It started well before my time growing up here, was at its worst during my childhood, and still exists today (if one is to believe the town gossip). You can paint her up, and call her quaint...still everyone gets screwed in the end.

From the looks of things on the main route through town, it appears that the aging residents of Freedom have lost interest in even attempting to gussy up this old girl. If one were to integrate a heaping helping of dilapidated mobile homes, abandoned gas stations, closed businesses and poorly maintained turkey farms into a Thomas Kincaid rural Southern landscape, then you would have a fairly accurate portrait of Freedom. The town has a residual grittiness, a greasy film, to every surface that is only magnified by the thin gray morning light filtering through layers of ice crystals deposited in the late November frost.

The appearance of neglect and resignation is validated by the frayed, sooty, white Christmas lights dangling haphazardly from the porch overhang on, what once was, Marvin Cline's barbershop.

Although the holiday season is approaching, these decorations haven't flickered in the more than fifteen years since Marvin succumbed to the bottle. The last remaining bit of flaking, colorless, lead based paint and torn screens in the filthy front windows are the only minor variances from how the old shop appeared a few summers ago when I passed through town.

Marvin Cline, what a piece of work. In the mid '60s, Marvin benefited from being the only practicing barber in town. There were a handful of hairdressers for the lady folk, but only small boys would be caught dead getting their noggin's groomed anywhere outside of Cline's shop. Although, 'groomed' may be a far too generous verb to describe Marvin's trademark piss-pot clip, typically performed in a drunken stupor with an inch of ash drooping like a spent Black Snake firework from the end of his Pall Mall cigarette. Eyes squinted and watery from the R J Reynold's halo cloud wafting around his face, Marvin's creative aptitude consisted of visualizing a bedpan on your head, and trimming around the edges. Even if Freedom's version of Vidal Sassoon lacked the skills to adequately shave a dog's butt, there was certainly no denying that his shop had the best collection of reading material in town. I spent many a Saturday afternoon patiently waiting my turn for a clip in the red vinyl chair next to the corner behind the wood stove, furthest from the prying eyes of the barber's other customers. Unbeknown to those patrons, who at a glance assumed that I was intently perusing a newly delivered, pristine copy of Look magazine with an emaciated Mia Farrow and crooner Frank Sinatra on the front, I had stealthily slipped the well-worn, crumpled October 1967 issue of Playboy inside of the conveniently larger cover.

Lustily viewing the Halloween themed Miss October foldout, half of her nipples covered by a blue flannel shirt and her pubes blocked by a pumpkin sitting on bales of straw, the blond model was a young peckerwood's wet dream. With all of those revved up, newly forming hormones, the front of my pants was jutting out like a coat rack hanger, as I embarrassingly made my way to the barber's chair when called.

In retrospect, at ten years old, you are yearning for the milky-white breasts of Miss October. At sixty, you contemplate why Frank and Mia adorned the cover of Look instead of a newly sworn in Supreme Court Associate Justice, Thurgood Marshall. In 1967, black wasn't news unless there was a Huey Newton Panther involved.

My final perambulation to Cline's barbershop in my youth was a remorseful one, not due to any trendy hairstyle that I would be neglected from donning, but the resulting loss of access to Marvin's soft-porn magazine library. On that particular weekday afternoon, the barber had been partaking of his customary Booths London gin for a significant portion of the day prior to my arrival at his institution of commerce. An hour before the 'old men, shoot the shit, just got off from work' crowd started arriving around 5:00, I was the sole patron in his shop. Class pictures were scheduled to be taken the following day at school, and Mom Armentrout thought that the bowl cut from my most recent visit to Marvin's didn't look awkward enough. Disappointed that I was being deprived of perusing the magazine rack literature due to the lack of other customers, I had been forced to proceed directly to 'the chair'. It was immediately clear, even for a ten-year-old, from the sway of his upper torso and the slur of his speech that Marvin was incapable of slapping himself on the ass with either hand, much less having the dexterity to perform his traditional scalping. Knowing this, while still attempting to respect my drunken elder, young Bubba Armentrout had hesitantly scaled the black, well-worn leather chair and plopped my butt in the barber's seat. I'm forever haunted by the syrupy sweet smells of cologne and talcum powder, but on that day, I closed my eyes and silently recited those few portions of the Lord's Prayer that I had memorized in Sunday School. Finding the passage insufficient, I ended with a brief heartfelt prayer, "Lord, please don't let Mr. Cline poke my eye out with his scissors. He knows not what he does." A moment or two after asking for divine intervention, panic ensued, as I heard the familiar clunk-clunk-clunk and swirling sound of shaving lather being whipped; a service that Dad would occasionally partake of after week long hunting trips. I gave up on deliverance from Jesus when Marvin slapped a steaming hot, mentholated towel over my face, as he reached for the straight razor next to the combs floating in alcohol on his work counter. Hyperventilating from fear and menthol vapors, I jerked the towel away from my eyes just in time to view Cline attempting to sharpen his straight razor on the belt strap dangling from the side of the barber chair. Failing numerous times to connect the shining metal blade with the belt, missing by nearly a foot with each swipe and Marvin unsteadily rocking back and forth like a possessed evangelical at a Baptist revival, I concluded without a doubt that my ass was in deep shit. That crazy, drunk son-of-a-bitch would have accidentally slit my throat if I hadn't flung myself from the barber's chair, and frantically burst through the shop's screened front door, nearly tearing the wood from the hinges in the process. There was zero chance of the door hitting young Bubba Armentrout in the ass on the way out. I had been well past Bennie Gee's Grocery down Old Route 23 before realizing that I still had the wet towel draped over my shoulder, condensation trailing me like steam from a newly dropped cow patty.

Gee's Grocery, it's amazing what a prominent role that seemingly nondescript places and people can play in one's life.

On my last visit, Mom told me that Bennie and Em Gee had been dead for well over twenty years. Even if by some miracle of nature that they aren't, you wouldn't be able to differentiate based on your sense of smell. Those two purveyors of what barely passed as consumable product, as well as their ramshackle store, had less hygiene than a Big Apple homeless shelter.

When I was a kid, you could crawl through a metal drainage culvert under Old Route 23 and traverse from the outside of the one room cinder block Post Office on Jamison Street to the concrete bridge that divided Mill Creek and Gee's Grocery on the other side of the main road. If the water moccasins and broken Schlitz beer bottles didn't deter the local hooligans from making the trek, Bennie Gee would be angrily waiting at the store end of the weed infested drain, shaking his pudgy fists and shouting, "You goddamn kids are gonna get your dumb asses killed, and that ain't the bad part. Fuckin' town will blame it on me, and I'll end up a gettin' sued."

Bennie was a gruff little bastard with receding, dirty gray hair, a three-day stubble of beard and a shitty disposition that matched his overall outlook on life. Because of his small stature, prominent waddle, nasally voice, filthy hygiene and inherent ability to be disliked by everyone, my buddies and I referred to him as 'Miggy the Piggy'. Although totally apt, we were cautious not to call him anything but Mr. Gee to his droopy, pockmarked face. Timmy Wyatt, Davey Grater and I devised the nickname as homage to Miguelito Quixote Loveless; the evil, diminutive villain from the Wild, Wild, West television show that we watched religiously every Friday night on CBS out of Richmond.

Bullshitting the customers from behind the counter in his store, Gee constantly regurgitated a tale, to anyone bored enough to listen, of his heroic deeds on the battlefields of Korea. He seemed to take particular pleasure in describing the bullet that fractured his kneecap, causing a permanent limp, and of the horizontal slant of the Haengju girls' vaginae as viewed from his personal carnal perspective. Now, I have great admiration for those that serve our country, but Uncle Rick, a veteran himself, privately disputed Bennie's claim, noting that he remembered Gee's family from his trips to play Bankston High in football. Rick was certain that Bennie hadn't traveled outside of Rockland County until he was well too old to enlist, and that Gee had knocked up Em in senior high and needed to run a milk delivery route before scrounging up enough money to buy the Grocery with his father-in-law.

For anyone looking, mostly repo guys and food inspectors, you could always find Bennie and his four pack a day unfiltered Camel habit idling behind the counter near the front of the store, contemptuously inspecting anyone under thirty, as if Warren Beatty and Faye Dunaway would burst through his bug splattered screen door at any moment. If Gee wasn't bitching about how the local kids were stealing him blind, then he was on a diatribe of how Lyndon B. Johnson's sole interest in leading the United States of 'Merica' was shelling out money for food stamps and making life good for the goddamn 'coloreds'.

Em Gee, Bennie's wife, was a submissive heifer of a woman, sloven in appearance and bovine in her movement. She spoke with a thick, slow, molasses coated drawl that helped exacerbate her genetically lethargic looks. Although afflicted with severely bowed legs and slightly humped back, Em was nearly a foot taller and twice the weight of Bennie. Her size advantage provided little deterrent to the verbal expletives that Bennie threw her way, Em cowering from him like a whipped pup, and he spewed them often. On rare occasions, she would generate enough courage to argue, spit flailing from the wide gap between her two front teeth, but those public incidents were rare; the bruises that Em attempted to cover the following day weren't.

A moderate amount of the Gee's business was derived from the luncheon meat and fresh cuts displayed in the filmy, fly splattered glass counter near the front of the store. Bennie and Em wore the remnants of their bloody trade like badges of honor on their unwashed garments. Bennie's daily attire typically consisted of an oily, stained tee shirt, elastic suspenders and frayed corduroy pants that failed by two or three inches to meet the top of his cracked, faux-leather loafers. Em lumbered behind the counter in a feed sack sized faded print dress with a portion of the previous evening's dinner of God knows what species of slaughtered animal's grease stains dried on the grimy cloth covering her ample bosom. Without a bra, Em's boobs would have easily dragged the glass counter, providing the first real dusting the case had received in years.

Bennie once plopped me on the crown of my head with a torpedoed can of Green Giant lima beans when he thought, incorrectly, that I had swiped a Tootsie-Roll Pop from the ceramic candy jar near his cash register. I had been lollygagging around town with Missy Prease, demonstrating the fine art of culvert crawling, as I ogled her butt while she shuffled on all fours through the metal drainage pipe under Route 23. Missy had determined that the exertion of exploration entitled her to a complementary treat at Gee's, so she pocketed the candy from the penny jar when she figured that Bennie wasn't looking. I had been perusing the Brownie sodas in the soft drink machine a few feet away, when Missy flashed by me in full sprint through the store's screened front door. I quickly attempted to catch up to her, unaware of the circumstances that had caused her to bolt. That was when the can of beans nailed me, connecting directly behind my right ear, then bounced off the wooden steps leading up to the store. Staggered, and somewhat dazed, I was able to maintain my wits enough to escape into the culvert behind Missy. Although I retained a significant lump below the cowlick near my ear for more than a week, the effort and repercussions were well worth the pink pantie shot that I was granted as Missy wiggled her behind the entire way to the Post Office.

****

Man, it can be disconcerting how once nearly forgotten events, big and small, life altering or inconsequential, can come floating up to solidified cognizance with a minimal number of sensory stimuli. Simply driving through Freedom is dredging up memories that have been hidden in cerebral silt for years. It's as if God, in her infinite wisdom, has determined that, for the most part, time satiated obliviousness is more conducive to long-term stabilized mental health than reality evoked learnings. Except, some memories are too pervasive to be forgotten. You can hide them under the out of style hats, broken appliances and too small coats in the darkest corner of your limbic system closet, but they tend to fall out and clunk you on the head when least expected. Mom's letter pushed that closet door ajar, but I've always known that I would eventually need to throw the door open and start digging. Exhuming long interred experiences isn't the reason for my return trip to Freedom, they are simply a by-product. My primary impetus is justice.

Sure, this visit will entail fulfilling the normal cursory requirements of family socialization and delivering respects, not unlike the national politician campaigning in a remote area of the country to appease their party, even though the impact to constituency is negligible. In one day, out the next, 'wham, bam, thank you, ma'am'. The relationship with my family has remained cordial throughout the years, and there is certainly the bond of love inherent between most parents and adult children. Our 'closeness' became severely frayed when I left Freedom for college, and then work, in the late '70s. After all, from my parent's perspective, anything that you could ever want or need can be found within this little four-square mile plat of heaven and kudzu called Freedom. My ties to childhood friends have been relegated to the occasional notification of upcoming high school reunions or, more recently, untimely deaths.

This trip is different. Mom's note set off a cacophony of bells and whistles that I always knew, one day, was coming. Her words stirred a dormant beast that wasn't forgotten, only caged and tranquillized, for fifty years. I won't assume that my reconciliation with those events of a half century ago will have any significant bearing on others, no matter how strenuous my efforts. The importance, at least to me, lies in bringing the facts to light. After all, sunlight is the greatest disinfectant. If my quest is successful then, hopefully, I can clarify, catalogue and recalibrate the dimensional weight of events that compose a significant drawer in the Dewy Decimal System of Robert Allen (Bubba, in my adolescence) Armentrout's mental library.

****

My parents have called Freedom home for their entire lives, seldom traveling further than a weekly trip to Bankston for necessities, or Charlottesville when medical needs arise.

Freedom, population 1892 and established in 1836, as the beer can pocked sign states on the outskirts of town, has since its inception maintained a cultural and socioeconomic attraction that inhibits greater than fifty percent of the town's inhabitants from ever venturing outside of the Rockland County line. From Freedom's origins as a Post Office and general store that were converted to a Confederate outpost during the Civil War, when the town's name was changed from Peaksville, the small hamlet achieved its heyday when the Rebel soldiers settled and started families soon after Appomattox. One of the first orders of business for the small rural community had been to establish a governing body that would help create ordnances to prohibit the men folk from pissing in the road and keep the local livestock out of the already rutted dirt streets. The freshly named town of Freedom chose a University of Virginia educated young man from a prominent family in the nearby burgeoning city of Bankston as its first mayor. His name was Gaylord Griffin Maynor and, notably, his great-grandson would hold the same elected post nearly one-hundred years later. If not for this appointment in 1866, my current trek focusing on Gaylord's great-grandson, Griffin, would almost surely be unnecessary. Unfortunately, the Mayoral line of Maynors was in the cosmic cards, and Griffin Maynor's transgressions, especially those sins that I was uniquely privy to, have catastrophically impacted our town and our people. For a few, the ramifications were fatal.

Driving past structural relics and childhood haunts like Cline's Barbershop and Gee's Grocery, I'm searching for a synaptic thread that I might tug upon to unravel the burial shroud of memories for any elusive and important fragments that I may have forgotten. What better way to exhume the interred than to re-engage with the past? If all goes as planned, maybe, finally, justice can be served.

****

The building that housed Gee's Grocery, boasting flaking whitewash and a rusted tin roof, is apparently now a second-hand store. Judging from the makeshift cardboard sign propped in the cracked, bird shit-streaked front window, the business is now called Jennie's Antiques and, from the junk littering the grounds, specializes in bird baths, wind chimes, chipped china, throw rugs, desks, dining tables, bicycle tires and a veritable hodgepodge of gizmos and gadgets for use around the house. Through the front windows, mannequins donning everything from a faded Ren & Stimpy T-shirt to a camouflage jacket are visible. The baby stroller and Rollerblades on each of the steps leading up to the door practically shout 'Goodwill Cast-Offs'.

The ancient, concrete bridge over Mill's Creek has weathered the last fifty years significantly better than much of the town. The winter storms and inebriated drivers have accomplished little more than knocking a few small chunks from our town's Stonehenge. On more than one occasion, the bridge had served as a podium for my beer buddies and me to hold a late-night pissing contest. Points were awarded for stream and distance, with the biggest loser required to buy the next six-pack. Quips abounded about the water being cold and deep from the participants perched on the cement rail.

With the construction of the new Route 23 By-Pass in the early 1970s, Freedom residents can now sit on their front porches for periods of an hour or more and not see a vehicle after the school buses run and the townsfolk have left for work. Today is no different; other than an elderly lady dropping a large manila envelope in the overnight bin next to the Post Office and, I assume, Jennie Whoever's vehicle idling unattended at the Antique Store, Freedom is exhibiting about as much activity as a Sorority girl on a Sunday morning.

A half mile further down the highway, Chestnut Hall, a showplace during my childhood, comes into view. The once opulent structure had been the residence of our local monarchy, the Honorable Mayor Griffin Maynor and his socialite spouse, Louise Frederick Maynor. She was affectionately dubbed 'Lady Louise' by those in her circle of friends, 'Mrs. Maynor' by the majority of the town without social standing, and 'The Wrinkled Old Bitch' (just not to her face!) by the kids that she regularly chastised and scolded for drawing hopscotch blocks on the sidewalk in front of her neatly trimmed hedges at Chestnut Hall. Lady Louise, who had spent her childhood and prep school years up North in New Hampshire, exuded every scintilla of arrogance and presumption commonly attributed to affluent Yankee upbringing. She was a dried prune of a woman, externally and intrinsically, where late mid-life had unabashedly surrendered to all the accoutrements of old age. Physical characteristics that as a teen might have been labeled good bone structure and a china doll complexion had morphed into a Rand McNally Colorado road map of wrinkles, with the aforementioned bone structure comprising the jagged mountain ranges. As her appearance hardened, her demeanor and empathy for others calcified to the consistency of granite. These liabilities aside, Louise knew small town politics, how to make and retain money, the most effective manner in working a room, and had an innate ability to fuck over and ostracize anyone standing in her way.

On the flip side of the marital relationship, Griffin Maynor had been Freedom's Wal-Mart version of Aristotle Onasis. Short and stocky, with a head covered in thick, graying hair, the Gold Label Palma Candela cigar chomping Griffin was an unrivaled egocentric and undeniable narcissist. His aura screamed dominant, directive and demanding; his actions only magnified these pervasive qualities. Griffin and Louise were a power team.

As the two approached their mid-sixties, they had become near genetic clones of one another. Unfortunately for Lady Louise, physical attractiveness didn't translate well in the aging Y-chromosome.

Mayor Griffin Maynor ran Freedom in a manner resembling a small child conducting warfare with plastic soldiers; carefully placing each figurine, controlling every movement, shunning external advice and trampling the battlefield when he became bored or distracted with the game. The mayor had his lieutenants, but they were simply that, controllable soldiers that would unquestioningly carry out the orders that Maynor felt would most benefit his town, and more importantly to him, serve Griffin's needs and ego as the General in charge. In the mayor's mind, Freedom was a small chunk of the Big Rock, but by God, it was his chunk, and he would run the town exactly as his father, grandfather and great-grandfather had held rule from Chestnut Hall since the 1800s.

****

Jesus, fifty years removed from the Griffin Maynor era and Chestnut Hall appears to have succumbed to the same destructive organism that has consumed much of the town, gnawing first at the cosmetic façade before burrowing deep into the bones and tendons, precipitating and then enforcing structural rot. The once immaculate, rolling green landscape of freshly cut grass and meticulously trimmed hedges have degenerated into knee deep crabgrass and barren brush that appear to have been neglected for years. The vast, colorful flower gardens surrounding a cherub pissing in a marble fountain, and the edged walkways covered by bright-pink lattice sagging pregnantly with plump, juicy grapes have been reduced to untended, dead vines with plastic replicas of deer and other faux-wildlife replacing the splendid fountain. The ceramic, black faced lawn jockey that had stood guard on the walkway entrance to Chestnut Hall, fashionably attired in his bright red jacket, and the racially demeaning 'yes um' grin on his over-sized lips has maintained his residence in the same location, but his lantern toting arm has suffered a complete amputation sometime over the last five decades, and his once vibrant colors are now washed-out hues of green mildew and indiscernible pigment.

The structure of Chestnut Hall has been ravaged by the cancer that has metastasized unbounded throughout the grounds. The glorious red cedar shingled roof has been haphazardly patched with tarpaper. The white, wooden siding is covered in a bile-colored moss, mildew, ivy vines and decaying boards. The Hall's beautiful black shutters have been dislocated from filthy windows, if they remain attached at all, while lifeless brown hanging plants litter the sweeping front porch that has lost a portion of the handcrafted railing from both the veranda and the steps. The grand dame, Chestnut Hall, has been relegated to a status where even the termites refuse to reside.

****

A mile and one-half from Chestnut Hall in distance, and five decades in travel time, is the venue where the catastrophic events of 1967 began. I'll bet that you can't plug that into your GPS while driving and whistling to the Peppermint Trolley Company. Freedom Elementary, a bastion of childhood education (and I'm not referring to reading, writing and arithmetic), is the nucleus of my return visit. In small towns, education, at least useful practical learning, is primarily garnered from illicit information that your friends are more than willing to share. Some of the information acquired has reliable sources, such as buddies with sisters that have recently started their periods, or older siblings willing to relay life experiences.

Other knowledge obtained has previously been massaged, sprinkled with hyperbole, simply fabricated or made-up, and then served with enough genuineness and commitment that it is taken for fact. Such was the case when Larry Rickle, a kid with a clubfoot and cleft palate, informed me that his parents had recently gotten a divorce, and that the judge had sentenced his dad to live with another woman until he came to his senses. Larry's Mom, in turn, had acquired a live-in man for the same purpose.

Certainly, believable for a naïve ten-year that looks to see the best in everything.

The most effectual and enduring education, both beneficiary and cautionary, is acquired through experience. Freedom, in 1967, was a hotbed of scandal, ignominy and debauchery. I've come back to Freedom, not to relive a joyous portion of my youth, but to provide the past with any assistance needed in reaching its long dormant sprigs towards the glaring light of justice.

Chapter 2
School Days

Late Fall 1967

Magazine photos of Gus Grissom, Ed White and Roger Chaffee cover half of the cork bulletin board on the rear wall of Ms. Huckman's third grade classroom. Prior to the simulator launch fire at NASA in January, which became a current events topic at school for months, every guy in my room had fantasized about becoming an astronaut. The St Louis Cardinal's four-games-to-three World Series triumph over the Boston Red Sox earlier in the fall, fresh newspaper clippings adorning the upper corner of the board, changed most of our minds. Who would want to risk being toasted in a metal tube when you could be famous for hurling a baseball like Bob Gibson? 'Hoot' Gibson, Willie Mays and other ball field heroes are the only Negroes that are invited into family living rooms and business lunchrooms as most folks listen to the day games on radio, where color and ethnicity can be placed on the back burner for seven days in October.

The remaining portion of the bulletin board is designated for World events. Faces of a South Vietnamese family in front of their mud-roofed hut talking to an armed soldier, injured America GIs awaiting transport to a medical facility and children tending the rice fields are all taken from Time magazine photos clipped this month. Ms. Huckman describes the Vietnamese depicted in the pictures as sympathetic, politically manipulated and consumed by an unwanted war. Ralph Morris, whose oldest brother returned home from Southeast Asia in a flagged-draped box, refers to all Asian's as 'slanty-eyed rice pickers' that ain't worth the goddamn shell it takes to blow ''em to Hell'. Ralph said that his daddy, Ralph Sr, told him that the little bastards weren't no different than those Communist Cubans whose missile threats caused such a stir for Kennedy, and forced shelters to be built in Bankston for when Castro decided to bomb the shit outta' the Good Ol' USA. I ain't sure who's right, Ralph or Ms. Huckman. All I know is that the teachers still have us practicing crawling under our desks in case somebody finally decides to drop the 'Big One'.

Fresh spitballs, made from torn Weekly Reader pages and graded homework papers, are splattered across the entire bulletin board. Flicked from halfway across the room, us guys, and sometimes Rhonda Rowl, who is almost a boy, tally points for achieving a direct hit on the photo of the week. Even 'Hoot' Gibson isn't immune to receiving an accidental projectile to the two Cardinals on a branch stitched onto his wide jersey. An immediate visit to the Principal's Office is the penalty for getting caught by Ms. Huckman, so stealth and timing are big factors in staying in the game. When our teacher turns her back to write on the blackboard in the front of the room, a series of slobber-soaked paper missiles fill the classroom airways. Each afternoon, after school, the kid responsible for cleaning the blackboard is also required to remove the hardened, gum-like balls from the photos and the surrounding area.

****

Thanksgiving has come and gone, and the Christmas holiday break is only two weeks out. I had been assigned the role of John Smith in the annual Turkey Day school play held at the combination school auditorium and basketball court. Metal folding chairs were arranged in rows for the event, and the entire elementary school attended. I was selected for the role because nobody else would volunteer, and I was caught making paper airplanes out of my spelling word study guide. I can promise you, it sure wasn't because of any recognizable talent or positive reinforcement for good classroom behavior. All of that aside, everything about the play had ended up pretty peachy. Terri Chandler, the cutest and most popular girl in my class, had volunteered to play Pocahontas. The school skit was OK because it allowed me to ham it up when thanking the Indians, and hugging Pocahontas, for feeding me the corn mush and A&P Grocery bought turkey for dinner. I gotta say that I was a little disappointed that I didn't get to shoot at the natives or dodge arrows, but I did get to hold Terri's hot little hand as we bowed to the audience of laughing and heckling classmates at the end of the show. I also managed to avoid clumsily tumbling off the stage, which had been my biggest fear and a disaster that I had dreamed about the previous three nights. For the next coupla' days, Davey Grater and Timmy Wyatt, my two best buddies in the world, had dubbed me 'J.S.' for John Smith (or, Jack Shit according to Davey). In spite of the ridicule and name calling, I considered the Turkey Day play a resounding success.

As the Horn of Plenty perforated cutouts are transforming into multi-colored Christmas decorations, our entire class is beginning to rev up about our next vacation from school. Since we haven't seen the first flake of snow this year, Freedom Elementary will have a full two weeks without classes over the Christmas and New Year holidays. Like Reverend Spicer preaches at church, that vacation will be more than enough time for idle hands to be the devil's tools. Even the Jewish kid from Mr. Glick's fifth grade class, Abel Abberman, or 'Apple' as he is nicknamed when the teachers aren't around, is wound tight as a tick. The guys and me think that Apple is the luckiest kid at school because he gets an extra week break to celebrate Hanukkah. We don't have much racial or ethnic diversity in the Freedom community. Besides the Abberman family, LeMaster Holmes and his sister, Vesta Lee, are the only non-Anglo-Saxon, white, Protestant people in the whole dang town; well, with the exception of our teacher, Ms. Huckman.

****

Ula Jane Huckman is a tried and true, don't try and screw with Virginia Mennonite. Unlike Apple, who wears his yarmulke on designated special occasions known only to him, Ms. Huckman's lacy, white bonnet with the strings tied firmly under her sharp, protruding chin is a permanent fixture on her tightly knotted, bobby-pinned hair. Davey and me call her the 'Pilgrim' when she is out of earshot, and her look definitely fit the theme during the Thanksgiving week festivities. Ula wears identical long, drab, stiffly pressed, blueish-gray dresses that cover nearly the entirety of her sun-repelling skin. There isn't a single day that she steps foot in Freedom Elementary where she isn't enshrouded in that Puritan-like garb from the nape of her neck to the tips of her dull, black leather, high-top, shit kickin' boots. Dad met her at the local Feed and Seed store one Saturday when he was picking up food for his beagle pups, and I overheard him tell Momma that Ula has the disposition of a sexually deprived Mormon when a sixth sister-wife is added to the clan; to which Momma threw her hands in the air, whispered, "Oh, Arle, you are awful," and left the room.

Ms. Huckman's milky, white complexion is, in part, the result of being protected from the sun by the green, canvas awning covering the horse drawn

26

buggy she uses as a means of travel. That, and Daddy Huckman, sitting proudly on his brand spankin' new John Deere tractor, obviously hasn't used her as field help during the summer hay bailing season.

Ula Jane's family owns a large, clapboard sided farmhouse and barn on the eastern outskirts of Freedom. To hear folks tell it, the Huckman's don't have a television, and only installed indoor plumbing a year or two ago, but by golly, they have a new John Deere every coupla' summers. If you are unfortunate enough to get behind their surrey on Old Route 23 during a weekday, then you can surely count on being late for wherever you are going, and getting a good dose of horseshit smell to boot. The more a driver honks to encourage the buggy to speed up, the tighter that Johnson Huckman pulls the reins.

Ms. Huckman prides herself in being a no nonsense, take no prisoners, her way or the highway disciplinarian. She is as quick to slap exposed fingers with a heavy, wooden ruler, as she is to hold the class from taking recess due to a couple of bad apples talking during the Pledge of Allegiance. There are only two things that can bring a pained smile to Ula Jane's thin lips, and even then, it still resembles an exaggerated grimace. They are, a peek in the classroom door from our school principal, Ester Yoncey, and the afternoon bell dismissing class for the day. Ula makes it clear in her words and actions that it isn't a love of teaching, and certainly not a fondness for the kids, that brings her to work each day.

****

As Christmas approaches, the school population is a honeybee's nest of activity and excitement. I guess that makes Davey and me the wasps in Ula Jane's bonnet. She has been riding the two of us pretty darn hard since she caught us tearing out pictures of naked, African tribal women from the National Geographic magazines during library hour. The class had been assigned time to 'research' maps in the World Book encyclopedias, and determine what country we would choose to report on in the six weeks after Christmas break. Me and Davey found the study of Aboriginal women much more entertaining. Our interest in their ability to stretch their earlobes and lips with dangling decorative weights was surpassed only by our fixation on the women's elongated boobs that resembled the stretched-out animal balloons that clowns pulled from their jacket pockets at little kid's birthday parties. That error in judgment had caused Davey and me (and Timmy Wyatt too, since he had laughed when we shared the pictures across the library table with the other third grade class) to miss recess football for two days, as we remained in the classroom writing 'I must use library time to complete the required assignment and not distract my classmates' one-hundred times on the wall-long blackboard. Not one to leave well enough alone, and to get a charge out of Davey, I wrote, 'I must complete the required assignment that Ms. Huckman gave us because she doesn't like other women with boobs bigger than hers', with every intention of erasing the line well before the class returned from outside. There was only one problem; we were so engaged in the sentence writing exercise that we didn't notice that it had started to rain. When the class returned, twenty minutes early, the three of us were belly laughing so hard that we didn't see Ms. Huckman snarling angrily at the board. As usual, punishment was swift and severe. Ula Jane demonstrated her riding crop skills to the entire class as she beat me, and my buddies, like a stubborn mule with the yardstick that she typically used to draw sentence lines on the board.

****

Late Fall 2019

Reflections

The cacophony of bells and whistles that Mom's letter evoked can be traced to a time period beginning in December of 1967. It's impossible to validate if the subsequent occurrences were coincidence, planetary alignment gone askew, or the misguided plan of an omnipotent being. That Christian God, she can certainly be a jokester. What I am absolutely certain of, without one doubt, is the genesis, the specific moment, when Freedom irrevocably lost its innocence; and a kid named Bubba Armentrout was forced to make some very adult, and life-impacting decisions.

****

December 1967

The 'get your butt to your desk' morning bell will be tolling in about ten minutes...just enough time to shoot the breeze with Davey before settling in for another day of tedious Freedom Elementary education. Man, the days get longer and longer the closer we get to Christmas break. I see my buddy standing by his desk with his back turned toward me, seemingly staring at nothing in particular.

"Hey Davey," I yell, grabbing the belt loop of his jeans and jerking them us as far as his crotch would allow, "wanna come over and shoot baskets after school? Momma is takin' Grannie Bess to get her hair done tonight."

"Dang, Bubba. Don't go sneaking up behind me and crushing 'the boys'," he replies in his typical, good-natured way. "I can't go nowhere for the next coupla' days. Ms. Huckman called the house last night and told Pop that I'd been acting up during library time. He was pretty pissed, and grounded me for a week. At least, for once, I didn't get my ass whipped."

"Yeah, I figured that she might call our house, too," I respond knowingly. "I'll bet she tried, since she called your Pop. Luckily, I cocked the phone off the hook in the basement knowing Momma probably wouldn't notice. She doesn't go down there much 'cept to can vegetables in the summer and get the winter clothes outta' storage in the fall. Scared the piss outta' me when she went to call Grannie Bess after supper. I had to run and hang up the basement phone before she started dialing."

"You're just puttin' it off, Bubba. The 'Pilgrim' always gets her man." Davey Grater is a block of a kid, nearly the biggest in class. He is almost as huge as Wayne Zigler, who is more than a year older than Davey. Wayne failed a grade when his daddy left town two years ago, and his momma moved the family twice to shack up with different relatives...boyfriends, if you hear tell the gossip. Davey's yellow mop of hair nearly covers his sleepy eyes, making him resemble Shep the shaggy sheepdog on 'My Three Sons'.

"Well, maybe she'll forget," I reply hopefully, knowing that is nothing more than wishful thinking. Ms. Huckman has the memory of an elephant, 'cept an elephant can't whup your butt, then call your momma.

"Sure, she will," Davey adds sarcastically, "just like she forgot to tan your hide when she took away your Swiss Army knife for carving your initials on the desk."

Man, that hit a sore spot. Although Dad took off the sharp blade until I get older so as I wouldn't cut myself, the tool has everything that you could ever need. My favorite present from last Christmas is a combination bottle opener, nail file, scissors and screwdriver. The screwdriver works 'bout as well as a knife to carve your initials in wood; which I like to do 'cause it's sorta like old Duke, our bench leg Beagle, who likes to cock his leg on the outside doghouse to mark his territory, and show our other mutts just who is in charge.

"The 'Pilgrim' wouldn't even have noticed," I respond accusingly, "if you hadn't been so dang anxious to grab it from me to pop that scab off your arm."

"Do you think that she'll ever give it back?" Davey asks, genuinely concerned.

"She damn well better," I reply adamantly, "it's been locked in her drawer for over a month."

Rubbing the side of his ruddy face in thought, then shoving both hands in his jean pockets, Davey muses, "I bet that she doesn't even remember that she has it. Why don't you just ask her for it back?"

"Yeah, that'll work." I retort. "After the last few days, you and me are both lucky that we ain't camping out in Ms. Yoncey's office and getting an up close howdy-do with that paddle of hers."

Ms. Yoncey's paddle, Big Baby, is famous all over our school. Supposedly, 'Big Baby' got its name when our principal hung the behavioral modifier from the wall in her office, enclosed in a safety pinned cloth bag so as it wouldn't be immediately recognizable to parents and other guests visiting for appointments. Kids, especially those about to face judgment, would say that just looking at the paddle made you cry like a big baby. 'Big Baby' resembles the business end of a rowboat oar, with a small baseball bat knob attached to the handle.

Legend says that there are ten dime size holes drilled into the face of the paddle, that allow it to cut through the air without resistance on its way to the Promised Land. After doing something at school that I shouldn't, and wondering if I'm about to get caught, I've often thought about Ms. Yoncey modeling her swing after the great Carl Yastrzemski. I can almost imagine her, late at night with one bulb burning in her office, taking batting practice by swinging 'Big Baby' over and over again to make sure that she makes solid contact when game time arrives. I once heard Grannie Bess call Ms. Yoncey a schoolmarm because of her reputation for strictness and her never being married; in my mind, that only gives Ester plenty of time for extra practice on her swing.

"You know, Ms. Huckman wouldn't even miss your knife if you stole it from her desk," Davey offers with a sly grin.

"Well, first off, it wouldn't be stealin' 'cause it's my damn knife to start with. Secondly, how do you figure I'm gonna pull that off being I'm not Houdini, and we ain't got the key?"

A devious look erupts on Davey's face. If I didn't know better, I'd bet my Topp's Batman trading cards that my friend was transforming from Dr Jekyll to Mr. Hyde. "I might not have the key," he chortles, "but I DO know where it is!"

This would be the perfect and prudent time for me to say 'Naw, let's forget these shenanigans and head back to our desks', but, you know, it just ain't fair that Ms. Huckman confiscated and kept my prize possession. Shoot, James Bishop had offered me a bag of cat-eye marbles, a super ball, and one-dollar and thirty-two cents for the knife near the end of the last school year. I flat turned him down, and the value has probably only increased since then.

"So," I prod him, "are you gonna tell me about the key, or are you just shittin' me?"

"I wouldn't shit you, Bubba. You're my favorite turd. And I don't need to TELL you, I'll SHOW you where the 'Pilgrim' hides the key."

Now Davey has captured my total attention. We could wait until another day when the bell for class wasn't about to ring any minute, or for a chance when we've been kept in for poor behavior during recess but, as Granddiddy Tilley is fond of saying, there ain't no time like the present. Encouraging Davey with a small nudge to the ribs, I say, "You better get on the stick 'cause we ain't got much time before Ms. Huckman heads this way."

Ula Jane almost never mossies into our classroom until the last reverberation of the morning bell. My guess is that she doesn't want to see our smiling faces any sooner than is required.

Davey begins to wedge his way through Janet McCutcheon's social gathering of eight girls congregating near the front of the room, and I follow close on his heels. From the snippets of conversation that I hear as we push ourselves by the group, Janet's parents had set up a sleepover birthday party for her last weekend. The little missies that had been invited are cackling like a bunch of barnyard hens about the fun that they'd had, and all of the girlie secrets that they'd sworn not to tell.

Davey slows his pace to elbow past Laura Jenkins, Janet's closest friend, and delays just long enough to churn out an Ol' Faithful size belch, adding an 'ahhhhh' at the end, while waiving his hand in front of his face to spread the half-digested smell of eggs, bacon, and Fruit Loops throughout the group of girls. Janet counters with the obligatory, "Davey Grater, you make me sick," to which Davey responds with a shit eating grin that indicates just how pleased that he is with himself.

31

I take advantage of the brief opportunity to wink at Laura Jenkins, as I slip sheepishly through the gaggle of girls. Laura is always eying me from her desk, two rows over, and once even passed me a flowery, perfumed paper note asking 'Do you like me? Circle yes, or no'. Ms. Huckman had jerked the note from my hand, having seen the paper travel from student to student until it reached me, then had me stand up and read what Laura had written in front of the entire class. Both Laura and me were as red as a Fireball candy by the time that I had finished and sat back down at my desk. Hopefully, it made her proud when I answered, to the room, that, yes, I liked her and that I was lucky to have her as a friend. Now, following my wink, Laura shoots me a quick smile, blushes and then turns back to the other chickens that are currently squawking about having baked chocolate chip cookies and other goodies to put in a care package being sent to a neighbor boy serving in Hue, South Vietnam.

As I finally break free of Janet's posse, Davey's wide butt is already disappearing under Ms. Huckman's broad, oak desk. One of his red, Chuck Taylor Converse All-Star tennis shoes is the only body part visible, as I drop down on all fours and crawl into the cavern-like space after him. I notice that a class brown-noser has left a small package with a bright, blue bow on the rolling chair that we needed to push out of the way to get under the desk. The tag on the gift reads 'World's Greatest Teacher'; ugh, if that ain't enough to make you wanna puke! Sliding in next to Davey, he reaches for a small library card envelope, barely visible in the dim light seeping through the cracks in the wood, taped on a string that is thumbtacked to the back panel of the desk's underside. He grabs and shakes the envelope, and out falls a little silver key into the palm of his hand.

"How did you know where she kept the key, Davey?" I say in amazement.

"Anytime that I see her get in the desk drawers," Davey replies mischievously, "she reaches between her legs first. The key had to be in one of two places, and this was the only one where I was willin' to look." He laughs, then continues with his explanation, "I found the key here before we took our Virginia history quiz."

"That beats all," I say, impressed with his deductive ability.

"Yep," he adds, pausing a moment for dramatic effect, and grinning like the Cheshire cat, "it ain't just your knife that she keeps in this drawer. She keeps all of her test answers and homework assignments in there too!"

"Dang, I wish I'd known that before I got an 'F' on the last English test," I lament.

"Wish in one hand, and shit in the other. See which one fills up first." This is a favorite of Davey's many overused sayings, and it is particularly worse for wear.

Sometimes, what seems like good fortune on the front side, don't always smell like roses on the back end. We are definitely sniffing the tail-end of luck as we hear the screech of Ms. Huckman's voice attempting to rise above the cacophony of sound in the room, "Everyone in your seats, NOW!" Davey and me freeze as stiff as two back of the Frigidaire Freezer Popsicles when Ula Jane's shadow creeps along the tiled floor near where we are stashed. Our classroom sounds like an aircraft carrier that has just received an 'incoming' warning from the Commander. Feet slap across the floor, and metal creaks as kids skid into the seats of their desks. Davey's eyes are as wide and white as the Pygmy in the Bugs Bunny cartoon 'All This and Rabbit Stew' that we watched before the main feature at the State Theater a few weeks ago. There ain't much doubt that mine probably look the same as his! "Holy Mary, Mother of Jesus, what do we do now?" Davey whispers from a face as pale as a ghost, Holy or otherwise.

"Stay quiet," I respond softly, moving my index finger to my lips. "We'll crawl over and sneak out the door if she stands in front of her desk like she usually does to call roll." Although there ain't time to think through the idea, the plan seems as good as any other that I can pull out of my butt in the moment. If we can get outside of the classroom without being noticed, or one of the other kids ratting on us, we can hustle to the office and get a tardy pass. Heck, we might even be able to get off Scot free.

Unfortunately, our hopes crumble when the bottom of the 'Pilgrim's' long, drab dress sweeps the floor near us, directly behind her oak desk. Ms. Huckman is slowly tapping her left foot as she stands impatiently waiting for the commotion in the classroom to settle down. Within seconds, the room is as silent as an atheist at baptism.

"I have a special announcement to make this morning," Ula Jane begins in her typical stern, matter-of-fact manner. Although, this time, her tone seems the slightest bit different. I can't quite put my finger on it, but there sounds like the smallest bit of...joy...in her tough, nails on the chalkboard voice. It's sorta similar to when Reverend Ross Spicer talks about going to Hell for not following

the Ten Commandments; he's just a little too excited about the message to hold back his enthusiasm.

"Class, I will be leaving Freedom Elementary as your teacher after the Christmas break," she announces. "I have been called to serve my church in the spreading of the Lord's Gospel. It is an opportunity that I have yearned for my entire life. I would greatly appreciate if you would behave as ladies and gentlemen over the next few weeks, conducting yourselves in a manner that makes my remaining days with you positive for everyone (I can tell from the exasperated way that she pronounces the word that she wants to say bearable instead of positive). Please make every effort to welcome your new instructor, Mr. Hodges, as you have the opportunity to meet him this afternoon after lunch." You can almost hear nearly every kid in the room exhale with relief, feeling the same joy that Ms. Huckman is trying so hard to hide. As for Davey and me, the excitement is quickly sucked out of the room like a hickey on a prom date when the 'Pilgrim' opens the student binder and begins calling roll. Adding insult to injury, the commencement bell to start the school day reverberates, banishing all opportunity for us to escape without being noticed. Man, why did it have to be today, of all days, for her to arrive in class early? I guess that she couldn't wait to let the good news cat out of the bag.

All I know is, for the two cockroaches hiding in the dark under Ula's desk, nervousness has peaked, and passed concern, on its way to outright panic! Ms. Huckman has called the first few names from the binder, and is currently waiting a 'present' reply from Sarah Gregory. For some reason, known only to her, Ula Jane calls roll in alphabetical order, but with the girl's names before the boys. Sweat is pouring from my pits and down my back, as I try feverishly to come up with a revised plan to get us out of this mess. Ms. Huckman is about to call Kim Zeigler, the last girl name before progressing to Robert Allen (Bubba) Armentrout, when I reach out to Davey with a cold, clammy hand to let him know that the time has come for us to surrender and receive our punishment. Davey's anxiousness was escalating as the girl's names diminished, and he jumps as if I have shocked him with jumper cables attached to a car battery when I touch his arm. His legs reflexively shoot out from under the desk striking Ms. Huckman slightly above the top of her right boot. Thinking that she might fall, I lunge out and grab her left ankle to help brace her balance. Ula Jane, probably thinkin' that one of those demons that she was always telling us captures misbehaving children had mistakenly targeted her, screams 'Lord Jesus, help me!' kicks the leg I'm holding out of my grasp like a mule, catching Davey in the collarbone, and then pisses down the front of her darkening, wool dress. Ms. Huckman throws her roll book straight up in the air, jams her chair under the desk as far as our bodies will allow, and sprints through the classroom door into the hall as if the Devil himself will catch her if she slows down one bit. She leaves Davey lying on his back, grasping his shoulder, with one chair wheel propped on the middle of his chest.

The frenzy inside the room gives me a few seconds to push the chair off of Davey, peek at the knot on his swelling shoulder, and create a plan...no, that's not right; to hatch an excuse.

Shaking his head in disbelief at how our situation has deteriorated, and rubbing his neck and bobbing his head to ensure that it is still attached, Davey keeps repeating, "Oh, shit. We're gonna get killed!"

"It's OK, Davey," I say, trying to assure the both of us, all the while hoping that my heart won't thump out of my chest and land in the piss puddle that Ms. Huckman left on the floor.

"We're only gonna have one chance to come up with a story, and it better be a doozy. Get yourself under control, and put the key back so that nobody knows it's missing."

We are securely back in our seats, and behaving like well-mannered choirboys, by the time that the School Principal's ominous shadow precedes her hefty body through our third-grade door. Ms. Yoncey, posture as rigid as the Washington Monument that we visited on a school field trip last year, exudes foreboding as she angrily stomps into our class. She quickly glances into the cavern that me and Davey had recently vacated, and then steps over the pee puddle on her way to the front of Ula Jane's desk.

Ms. Ester Yoncey is a dang impressive presence under any circumstances, and I ain't just talkin' about her physical characteristics. Authority and smarts practically radiate from her even though she doesn't actively show much warmth and friendliness; to anyone. I've often wondered why that is, and I reckon it's mostly because she's a woman workin' in a man's job. That can't be easy, especially if you hear the fellers talk down at the gas station. They seem to think that any lady workin' outside the home, especially in management, just ain't a real woman and is askin' for trouble.

From my perspective, she can't be all piss and vinegar even if she doesn't seem overly nice. Grandma Bess remembers Ester from when she was a *teenager, and she told me that Ms. Yoncey once rescued a little girl from drowning in the Shenandoah River when she was home for spring break from the teacher's college she was attending in the '40s. Grannie said that Ester damn near drowned herself pulling the kid from the rapids, and spent more than a week in the hospital after developing pneumonia from the water in her lungs. Anyways, don't nobody ever talk about that, which ain't right. The way I see it, the town owes Ms. Yoncey, even if she is tough as shit.*

She and me ain't never had the opportunity to get too close on my occasional visits to her office, but I dang sure respect her gumption. She's like a Real McCoy...what you see is what you get. I just hope that includes a healthy helping of compassion this morning.

"I'm going to give five seconds for the individual responsible for disrupting class to come forward. If they don't, then the entire class WILL be punished," the principal states threateningly.

My drawers feel like they are loaded with cement as I slowly stand, and meekly raise one hand in the air. Davey sorta tumbles from his seat, staggers, regains his balance and then raises his hand as well. Having the two perpetrators of the crime identified, Ester Yoncey moves with the stealth and quickness of a leopard as she grabs my arm, nearly pulling it from its socket, and jerks me over to where Davey is standing beside his desk. She grasps Davey by the collar of his shirt, ignoring his whimpers of pain as it rubs against the swollen nape of his neck, and marches the two of us out of the door and into the hallway. As if forgetting something, Yoncey stops, maintains her firm grip on the two of us, sticks her head back in our classroom, and states gruffly, "If anyone so much as moves or speaks, your bottoms will be too sore to sit down. Place your heads down on your desk, or study your spelling words. I will have a substitute teacher for the room in short order."

Being paraded down the hall to her office, I feel like a dead man walking. Davey has tears welling up in his eyes, and a scared shitless expression on his reddening face. All I can think about is the prisoner condemned to be fried by electrocution on that old episode of The Twilight Zone; 'Shadow Play', I think it was called. I doubt if Rod Serling will be providing the narration for our soon to be execution. The results of an encounter with 'Big Baby' might be too intense for the network television censors.

Reaching the school administration end of the hall, the staff secretary working on forms and oblivious to our presence, Ester Yoncey tosses us into her office and loudly slams the heavy wooden door. The frosted, glass window labeled PRINCIPAL in bold, black letters vibrates in its frame. She is already grabbing 'Big Baby' from the hanging bag hooked on the wall before I can gain my balance and stand at attention.

"Bend over Robert Armentrout," she growls through gritted teeth, her face red with intent.

"Yes, ma'am," I respond, biting my lower lip to both hold back the tears and potentially lessen the beating. The ploy works with Momma when she is about to use a switch on me from the oak tree in our backyard. She wouldn't admit to it, but the more pitiful I look, the harder it is for Momma to let loose on me. "I definitely deserve to get a whippin' for scaring Ms. Huckman, but I want you and her to know that it was an accident." This last snippet of information causes Ms. Yoncey to hesitate a hare's breath, which gives me just enough time to get in a last plea for a reduced sentence. "Davey and me was flippin' a nickel so as to decide who gets the squirrel tail that we found in the parking lot behind Holt's Gas Station. At one time, it was a whole squirrel, but a poultry truck musta' hit it and, lucky for us, about all that is left is the tail. We're gonna take turns tying the tail on our bikes, but somebody's got to be the winner and get first dibs." I take a quick peek from meekly watching the tops of my shoes to see if I am making headway with our plan. Ester still looks pissed, but she has at least lowered 'Big Baby' to her side, so I don't see no harm in continuing. "I dropped the nickel after I tossed it, and it rolled under Ms. Huckman's desk. It's dark under there, and we were still searching for the coin when she unexpectedly came in the room."

"Yeah, and Ms. Huckman is never in class before the morning bell." Davey adds, hoping to verify the story.

"At first, we were too scared to move," I continue with sincerity, telling the only true part of the tale, "but we figured that we had better show ourselves when she started calling roll. Davey nudged her leg by accident, then she screamed and kicked him up side his head."

Davey points to the growing red splotch on his shoulder and neck, and sobs, "Bubba and me didn't mean no harm. We are awful sorry." Real tears stream down his face and begin to drip from his chin onto his sweat-stained collar. If this is an act, Davey should win an Oscar for this performance. For good measure, he layers it on, "I don't know how we'll make it through the rest of the year (sob, sob, sob) without Ms. Huckman."

Ms. Yoncey has cooled down to a more natural shade of pink, so I decide that she is as good with what happened as she is going to get; the proof will be in the pudding. I turn my back, bend over and pray that 'Big Baby' won't swing for the fence in a blaze of glory. "Go ahead and lay it on me, ma'am. Hopefully, Ms. Huckman doesn't think ill of us, at least not until we can apologize."

True friends come through in the toughest of times, and Davey proves that he is as loyal as a Collie pup. He walks over to Ms. Yoncey, stands up straight, juts his meaty jaw, wipes the snot dripping from his nose on the back of his over-sized paw and declares, "No, Ms. Yoncey! It was my idea to crawl under the desk going after the coin. Bubba was followin' because I asked him to. He said that we were gonna get in trouble, but I still went ahead anyways. I'm the one that should get the whippin'."

Silence follows Davey's confession as Ms. Yoncey pauses in thought. Then, she does the unthinkable. Ester Yoncey drops 'Big Baby' back in its cloth bag, and hangs the paddle on the metal hook. "You boys DO realize how close that you came to getting your backsides tanned, right," she scolds. Davey and me nod emphatically that we understand perfectly. "And I'm still not certain that the two of you aren't feeding me cold slop from the sow's pen. Consider yourselves fortunate that you have been given an early Christmas present. Go STRAIGHT back to your room and keep your big mouths shut to the rest of your class regarding your punishment; or lack thereof. You will stay after school and clean blackboards in all of the classrooms for the next week after apologizing to Ms. Huckman for scaring the bejeezus out of her. Am I perfectly clear?"

"Yes, ma'am, Ms. Yoncey," we chime in unison, already inching towards her office door.

"And I would highly recommend that you take classroom time, even before and after school, to study your lessons as opposed to deciding how to divide a rodent tail."

Davey appears about to argue that it wasn't no rodent, it was a squirrel, when I grab his arm and pull him past the school Secretary's desk. If Ms. Yoncey said more, it went unheard. The back of our heads would be all that she could see as we bolt down the hall towards our classroom.

****

The two of us cleaned blackboards in each of the twelve Freedom Elementary classrooms this evening, two rooms for every grade, and we consider ourselves lucky. We were able to dodge a bullet in avoiding 'Big Baby', and it appears that Ms. Yoncey is pretty well satisfied with our explanation of what happened; at least she didn't say that she was going to call our parents.

Ms. Huckman, fresh off of her big announcement and saturated undies, had immediately left the classroom in the hands of a substitute teacher, June LeVay. Mrs. LeVay is the mother of a second grader, Lennie, and regularly fills in for any teacher absences. We met Mr. Hodges after lunch, but he won't be our permanent teacher until after Christmas break. As expected, Mrs. LeVay hit the road within seconds of the 3:00 dismissal bell to grab little Lennie and dutifully head home before her three teenage kids arrive on the bus from Moncross Junior High School.

Seeing that luck is obviously not a stranger, I ponder if today still might be my best chance to retrieve my knife from the departed Ula Jane Huckman's desk. I mean, once the new teacher takes over, who's to say what happens to anything remaining in the desk.

Davey left on his bike, heading for home, immediately after helping me clean the boards. He told me that the last thing that he needed was to get in deeper hot water with his dad, or have his grounding extended. I hadn't let him in on my plan for fear that he would demand to stay behind and help me retrieve my knife. Davey had already helped me get off the hook once today, and this job will probably go smoother if I pull it off alone. I'll need to wait until Ms. Yoncey leaves school grounds around 5:00. After this morning, I can't afford for her to catch me in Ms. Huckman's desk drawer.

Things are good on the home front, too. Momma is taking Grannie Bess for her weekly hair appointment, and Dad won't arrive home before 7:00, even if he doesn't stop by the Moose Lodge for a game of poker, and a bourbon on the rocks. All that I'll need to do is stay out of sight until Ms. Yoncey leaves, unlock the desk drawer and grab my Swiss Army knife, maybe take a peek at our next Virginia history quiz, then sneak through the library and out of the non-alarmed janitor's door at the back of the school. Shoot, I will be home with my bounty and a coupla' hours to spare, and nobody will even miss me.

With my plan devised, and ready for deployment, I slip quietly into our classroom's coat closet, keeping the door slightly cracked so that I can periodically peek out of the window on the far side of our room. That's the window that provides a full view of the teacher's parking lot. Ms. Yoncey is always the last person to leave the school, so once her car is gone, I will be home free!

****

My plan has gone to Hell in a hand basket. At 5:10, Ms. Yoncey's 1962 Plymouth is still parked in its normal spot in the lot, and other vehicles have begun to provide it company in the spaces nearest the rear entrance to the school. Unfortunately, for me, it is clear from the makes and models of the cars, even before I see recognizable faces of familiar townsfolk, that this evening is a meeting night.

Town Council commences once a month in the Freedom Elementary library to discuss the usual topics; fund raising, suitable dates for the spring lawn parties, the upcoming Minstrel Show in the school gymnasium and the troublesome bacteria growing in the town's septic system. The Council members and guests enter through the utility access door in back of the school, move by the phone and electrical boxes attached to the walls in the closet-like utility room, and then proceed a short distance down a hallway to the library, which is adjacent to the Administrative Office and sixth grade classrooms. After school hours, there is only one way in and one way out of Freedom Elementary, for the Town Council members and for me. So, my path to freedom (pardon the pun) requires me passing first Ms. Yoncey's office, and then moving through the library to the utility room access door.

As School Principal, Ester Yoncey is a mandatory participant at the monthly meetings, where she reports on school doings, building repairs, upcoming academic events and student needs.

The bulletin board posting next to her office provides the monthly meeting agenda, and her report is almost always scheduled last. Even if that wasn't the case, Ester wouldn't leave until Mayor Maynor pounds his gavel to close the meeting for fear that he would have her heading some committee or town project in her absence. Momma says that the mayor takes advantage of Ms. Yoncey, what with her being so committed to her work and all.

Well, as it stands now, there ain't no decision for me to make. It probably wouldn't be received too well if I moseyed through the library, waved and grinned at Council, told them that they had my full support, and then walked out the door to head home. I don't have a choice but to wait out the meeting in Ms. Huckman's class coat closet. Since this is the December meeting, with the hustle and bustle of the holidays, maybe the old geezers will finish up quicker than normal. Shoot, it would give the men folk time for a little last-minute Christmas shopping at Woolworth or Roses in Bankston before retiring at home for the night. Heck, even if they don't finish up their meeting until the typical seven o'clock cut-off time, I can still beat Momma and Grannie Bess home by twenty minutes or more.

Yep, I'm thinkin' that everything is still going to end up peachy-keen. Man, I couldn't have been more wrong!

Chapter 3
Council Coupling

Late Fall 2019

Reflection

Once the memories start percolating, they flow like black coffee on a workday Monday. Sitting on the bumper of my Lexus parked next to the new baseball field, directly adjacent to a modernized Freedom Elementary, I can remember that night of the Town Council in 1967 as if it occurred last week. The sequence of events seems like they happened to someone else, with me auditing the details from a remote studio behind one-way tinted glass. I only wish that I could reach out and provide some hindsight guidance for Robert 'Bubba' Armentrout, advise him to wave the white flag, admit his error in judgment, accept punishment and move on happily ever after. Sadly, ifs and buts ain't candy and nuts, so these were lessons that I needed to learn on my own.

****

The Verner brothers had been the first Council members to arrive at the school that I recognized. Stu and 'Lump' were prominent dairy farmers in the area, owning nearly seven-hundred acres of prime farmland, and two-hundred head of cattle between the two of them. Their connecting farms had been in the Verner family since the town of Freedom was in its infancy, and every male child in their clan became inherent dairy farmers (tit-tuggers in the local vernacular) the same as their fathers, grandfathers and great grandfathers before them.

Stu had two of the finest looking daughters east of the Blue Ridge Mountains, teenage bombshells with boobs like grain silos and rear bumpers that you could bounce a quarter off of. Born a year apart, the girls could pass for twins, but physical resemblance is where the similarities ended. Allison was a wholesome, cookie baking, bible toting, God fearing angelic being that set the moral standard (at least from a parent's perspective) for every young lady in Freedom. Lou Anne, on the other hand, was the yin to Allison's yang. 'Bounce', as the population of male slobbering infatuates at Moncross High labeled her because of the frenetic action occurring beneath her bra-less Herman's Hermits tight pink tank top, was free spirit defined. She smoked Viceroy Cigarettes in and away from the designated school smoking area, guzzled Blue Ribbon beer with the guys in the beds of their pick-up trucks at Friday night football games, and sold reefer that she grew herself in a hidden rear corner of her father's cornfield. 'Bounce' would, from time to time, sit for me on those rare occasions when my parents eloped for a dance night at the Moose Lodge.

Oh, how I cherished those glimpses into what post-puberty held for me. When 'Bounce' was keeping an eye on me, we would consume frozen Swanson turkey dinners, the ones with the tangy red cranberry goo that stuck to the tinfoil covering, on fold out trays in front of our solid state black and white Zenith television to watch 'Chiller' horror movies starring the likes of Bela Lugosi and Boris Karloff on a fuzzily received WTTG station out of Washington, DC. She would use a church key opener to poke holes in both ends of her Blue Ribbon can, allowing her to shot-gun the frothy liquid, fire up a joint, and rap about the Dylan concert that she planned to crash when she could hitch a ride to some faraway Eden named Haight-Ashbury the following summer. Hippie Hill was calling her name, and she had every intention of answering. 'Bounce' symbolized my conception of the world outside of Freedom, a land filled with wonder, and she was my pagan goddess. You know, I can think of poorer role models.

Ernest was the more challenged of the Verner brothers, but only in the physical sense. He had been tagged, appropriately, with the nickname 'Lump' due to a baseball size knot on the right side of his head. 'Lump', as a teenager in the early 1940s, had fallen from the loft to the cement barn floor as he stacked hay bales at the family farm. At the time of the accident, according to what Grannie Bess told me, his doctors believed that the embolism caused by the fall (or more accurately, the impact with the floor) would result in 'Lump' not living more than a day or two. At best, the family could only hope for him to survive in a permanent vegetative state. To everyone's surprise, and dispelling his prognosis, 'Lump' managed to recuperate with only a slight stutter, a definitive limp, an unflattering but apropos nickname, and an uncanny financial acumen that helped make his business ventures the envy of other county entrepreneurs.

Jack Lipsay's robin egg blue Chevrolet Chevelle was the next vehicle to arrive in the school parking lot. Jack sold advertising time for a local independent television station that broadcast out of neighboring Bankston. With a girth and beard that resembled Santa Claus, and a jovial extroverted personality to match, he was beloved by his customers, kids and anyone else who crossed paths with him at his local haunts. Often quick to smile, and always full of shit and Shinola, Jack would settle down on the bench outside of Gee's Grocery on summer Saturday mornings, hand out promotional Channel 2 baseball caps to me and my buddies, and take bets on that afternoon's televised wrestling matches with a few of the gullible locals and anyone else that he could entice that wasn't from Freedom proper. He consistently possessed a wad of fives and tens that he had gentlemanly pilfered from aforementioned rubes by betting on combatants carrying names like 'The Minnesota Wrecking Crew', 'Crusher Lisowski', and 'Dick the Bruiser'. Late one Saturday afternoon, after everyone had disbanded from the benches in front of Gee's, tails between their legs and mumbling about the luck of that sum-bitch Lipsay, bets collected with a few paid out to make the process look above-board, Jack and I had been sitting alone in front of the store. He confided in me, after a sworn promise that I would never reveal his secret, that the 'live' Saturday afternoon wrestling matches were filmed in a studio contrived to resemble a field house on Thursday evenings, and that he had significantly more than a little insight into which behemoth would take the belt on any given week. Jack was making bets on matches that he had viewed in the Channel 2 studio, as tape edits were made on Friday nights. Needless to say, I thought that Jack was the cat's ass, not simply because he could take the local goobers for a little extra pocket cash, but because that he entrusted me with the skinny of how he accomplished the deception. More than a few times, I had a week's worth of lunchtime ice cream coin to spend that I had won from nickel side bets with buddies visiting Gee's for sodas while the adult population was distracted.

By the time that Leonard Byron had pulled his new 1967 midnight black Lincoln into the parking space next to Lipsay's Chevrolet, the few remaining elongated shadows of the day reflected through the thick glass of Ms. Huckman's class windows were beginning to dissipate. My belief that Byron was the figure approaching the rear of the school was confirmed when the recently lit florescent light above the back-access door illuminated his flashy hand-tailored three-piece suit and black Florsheim penny loafers. Byron had been just another local yokel until a New Jersey pharmaceutical company purchased a hundred acres of his land near the Shenandoah River and built a massive plant. The drug company had primarily hired the locals for the lower paying jobs, janitors and office secretaries, while bringing in experienced corporate men from up North to fill the management positions. With the land transaction, the pharmaceutical company had made one local, Leonard Byron, the wealthiest inhabitant of Freedom and, likely, the richest man in Rockland County.

Time can blur a memory, as distance obscures the intricate details of a remote object. But, the sequence of events that occurred in December of 1967 are neither blurred nor obscured. These memories unfold now with intense clarity because, in large part, those events, beginning with the Town Council Meeting, drove my actions and decisions, manipulating my life for much of my childhood.

If Betsy Mae Byrd had peered to her right at the catty-cornered L-shaped wing of Freedom Elementary, the area enclosing Ms. Huckman's third grade classroom, she might possibly have seen my freckled nose pressed against the glass, straining to recognize the council participants as they arrived in what had progressed to full-fledged December early evening darkness.

Seeing her mystically appear under the florescent light over the utility access door had caught me by surprise because I hadn't seen other car headlights bounce into the lot since Leonard Byron arrived a few minutes earlier. The evening had seemed far too chilly for her to walk the mile from her home, across from Cline's Barbershop near the bridge, especially since she was attired in an ultra-short, skin-tight, beige miniskirt and red high-heeled pumps that she had squeezed into for the meeting. Whatever faux animal fur that she had draped around her bare shoulders couldn't possibly have kept her warm with so little polyester between her 36-Ds and the evening's declining temperature. Betsy Mae's breath hung cloud-like in front of her face, as she had knocked and waited entry into the school.

Betsy Mae Byrd had been voted Homecoming Queen at Moncross High School fifteen years earlier and, that night, had clearly plastered all available easy, breezy, Cover Girl makeup to her sun aged face trying to retain a semblance of that once youthful look. Even with her well-deserved reputation as the town siren, she had clearly gone over the top in preparation for the evening. Betsy Mae would have fit in perfectly as a hick starlet, escorted by Uncle Joe, on the red carpet at the Hooterville Academy Awards. It had been all that I could do to suppress a yelp when she had started to turn towards my voyeur location, and I cracked my funny-bone on the heat radiator, as I dropped below window level to avoid detection.

James 'Jimbo' Byrd, Betsy Mae's less significant other, was a Town Council member as well. Built like a line-backer and sporting a Score lathered crew-cut, Jimbo was a blue-collar guy that had held the position of Freedom Volunteer Fire Chief; the title that gained him a seat on Council. Slightly dense and extremely reserved, his no-nonsense approach served the town well on the rare occasions that a crisis actually occurred. A catastrophe in Freedom was typically limited to a bush-hog amputation or a wood stove fire. As a quarry foreman at Sherando Brick and Block, Jimbo's primary employer, he didn't fit the town elitist mold of his Council counterparts. Although prohibited in the town by-laws, Mayor Maynor had made an exception to the spousal rule so that both Betsy Mae and Jimbo could serve together. Dad once remarked that the mayor wanted Jim's bulk and Betsy Mae's ass, and wasn't willing to sacrifice either. Few could deny that Betsy Mae Byrd was a whole lot of hair and not much dog in regards to intellectual substance, but that perky butt of hers, Dad had said, helped to make her the best damn fund raiser in any town in the County.

When I had seen Betsy Mae arriving alone for the meeting, I figured that Jim must have been kept late with his job at the quarry.

The next arrival had been anticipated, and was fashionably late, as always. Having recovered from nearly paralyzing my lower arm on the radiator, I had peeked above the windowsill just as Mayor Griffin Maynor slipped through the utility access door and into the building. My assumption was that Griffin either had a key, or someone had been near the door awaiting his arrival. Unless there were going to be invited participants, his presence completed the normal attendee list.

I remember wondering if the mayor had driven up to the school in the minute or two that it had taken for me to get the feeling back into my hand, and the courage to take another look out of our classroom window. It had seemed strange, even to a youngster, that both Maynor and Betsy Mae had arrived within a few minutes of one another without observed transportation, in declining temperature, for either.

The answer became clear later that evening but, at the time, I simply pondered the question as I slid back into the coat closet to wait for the dignified town participants to wrap up their meeting.

December 1967

There is a faint, barely audible noise coming from somewhere...ring ring ring.

I think foggily, 'Ugh, can it be time to get up, already?'

Opening the one eyelid not buried in the covers, I determine that it's still dark outside and drift back to sleep.

Ring ring ring. My heart jumps up into my throat, igniting my pulse like a rabbit at a racetrack.

'Holy Hell, that's a phone ringing. It must be Ms. Huckman calling Momma. Why is she calling so late? I gotta get to the phone! Clothes hangers rain down on me as I flail my arms and legs, finally realizing that I must have fallen asleep in the third-grade coat closet. Bumping my head on the hard, yellow, plastic bucket that contains the orange sawdust Janitor Breffton uses to clean up puke is more than enough to bring me back to my senses.

Whoever was calling on the phone in the administrative office down the hall that I had dreamily mistaken for home must have realized that nobody was going to answer and decided to hang up. One dim light between the fifth-grade classrooms, and the faint glow of the red emergency exit sign at the front entrance of the school are the only illumination penetrating the darkness that has enshrouded the room where I have been waiting for the Council meeting to end, and that's only enough light to barely see the outline of the room across the hall five paces away. Geez, it could be midnight judging from the silence of the building. Only the popping of the radiators and the occasional grunt from the boiler in the bowels of the basement provide any indication that the world hasn't been blown to Hell with me being the last survivor on Earth. That just might be a preferable outcome because if Momma and Grannie Bess are home (and God help me if Dad is too), then they'll be out lookin' for me, and my butt is in for a major strappin'. Well, one thing that won't help, and that's to panic; I'll just have to come up with one whopper of a story on the short trip home. Better to worry 'bout first things first, and I can't get outta' the school until I find out if everyone has left the building for the night.

*I slither over to the windows, small ice crystals starting to form in their corners, and cautiously take a quick look outside into the cold, December night. Crap...it's way too dark to see if any cars are still parked in the lot. The good news is, and I need all that I can get, there's no sign of life near the access door. Thank God for small favors. I shuffle over to where the muted light reflects the outline of the doorframe intending to peek around the corner, all the while **praying** that the Council members are gone...but, not gone for too long. Through my growing panic, it occurs to me that I am really stretching my relationship with the Holy Spirit, and I ain't done much to warrant the divine consideration.*

Swiftly bobbing my head out of the classroom and into the hallway (like Hoss and Little Joe do when they're thinkin' that there might be a shootout with intruders at the Ponderosa Ranch), the only clue of anyone still being in the building is a dim light shining through the clouded glass of Ms. Yoncey's office door near the end of the hall. Next to her office, and the last room before the utility area access door, is the Library where the Town Council met. Other than a minuscule reflection from Yoncey's office light off of a silver, Christmas ball hanging from holly over the Library door, the room is as dark as my hopes of avoiding a butt beating.

My choices seem pretty simple; wait on Principal Yoncey to leave (and heck, that could be all night if she is already gone, and leaves the light on for Janitor Breffton to clean), or risk being caught sneaking by her office on my way out of the school. And there's other considerations too, not the least of which is if I can push the metal bar that opens the access door without calling attention to myself. But, my first priority is just making it that far! Peering out one more time into the hallway, the dark rooms, staircases and drinking fountains remind me of the time that Momma, Grannie Bess, Aunt Marybelle and me had gotten locked in Legion's Department Store in downtown Bankston. The surly old cashier in the women's lingerie department had irritatedly warned us that the store had closed five minutes earlier, but Grannie Bess had insisted on digging through the piles of girdles and bras in the discount bin near the back of Legion's looking for one last discount. Evidently, either the clerks forgot about us, or had reached a point where they didn't give a shoot, but in the short time that it took the store staff to turn off the lights and lock up for the night, we were way too slow to get to the front of the building and attract their attention. The four of us had been stranded in the pitch dark for nearly an hour, feeling and fumbling our way through the aisles while holding hands so as not to get separated. We finally found a phone at the checkout register of the Layaway Department and called the police, who in turn called the Manager of the business to come and unlock the store door. The school gives me the willies just like I had that night in Legion's Department Store, except tonight, I'm all alone. Every object seems frozen, shadowy and lifeless as if the teachers and students are the blood of the school and, without us, this old relic of a building would collapse to dust. I mighta' watched one too many horror movies, but I wanna' get the Hell outta' here before it crushes down on me. Sitting against the classroom wall, knees pulled up to my chest and head resting on my crossed arms, still pondering my next move, I hear what must be Principal Yoncey's office door open. That solitary sound in the dark is followed by the click, click, click of her heels as she moves down the hall. Problem is, I can't readily tell what direction she is headin'. Before my brain can tell my butt to haul it and find a hiding place, the clicking fades and I hear the metal door loudly slapping closed at the rear of the school. You could hear an ant fart in the impending silence. Man, what a relief that I didn't break for the door before she left the building.

Scooting on my behind over to the classroom window, afraid that if I stand Ms. Yoncey might catch a glimpse of me, I inch my way up the wall until I'm on my knees, hoping that I can quickly glimpse her finally leaving for the day. Hesitant to bob my head above the sill, relief floods over me when the reflections from her headlights sweep across the blackboard, as she pulls out of the school parking lot. Maybe Grannie Bess is right and there is somethin' to this praying thing. The last of the reflection from the retreating light illuminates the ancient Westclox above the board, and the bold, black hands on the yellowing white face of the clock tells me the time is 7:07. Well, it ain't good, but it ain't midnight like I thought that it might be. I might still be able to make it home by the hair on my chinny, chin, chin and stay in everyone's good graces.

After waiting a minute to ensure that the principal is well on her way home before sliding under Ms. Huckman's desk, I unlock the drawer and retrieve my knife, return the key to its envelope, and tiptoe out of the classroom into the hall. Even having seen Ms. Yoncey leave, I still don't want to take any chances, and Janitor Breffton could show up at any minute to turn back the boiler now that the meeting is over. Creeping stealthily along, hugging the wall as I work my way to the library, the distance seems about a mile to my destination instead of just the six classrooms and the administrative office. In the quietness of the building, the plopping of my Chuck Taylors and hammering of my heart sound, to me, like they should be performing in the school band. Heck, if Elwood Breffton don't catch me tonight, he'll probably find me tomorrow morning, as he comes in to turn the temperature back up to 72 degrees, dead as a doornail from a danged heart attack. I can see it now, drool dripping from my lifeless mouth onto the pea green tile floor, with my Swiss army knife protruding from my pocket, and a drying pee stain on my pants. That ain't a pretty picture, but it's probably what I deserve.

Halfway down the hallway and starting to truly believe that my ticker just might make the journey after all, my optimism is crushed when I hear a key scraping a lock, and the swish of the metal access door that the principal passed through minutes ago. Adrenaline freezes me as streams of questions gush through my mind, making a plan of escape nearly impossible to formulate. Could it be Janitor Breffton on clean-up duty after the meeting? Had Ms. Yoncey forgotten something in her office? Did she somehow know that I was still in the building and had come back to root me out? As unlikely as the thought seems, I guess it's possible that she saw me peeking through the classroom window. No, that can't be, I saw her headlights on the blackboard and didn't look above the window sill. If it's the principal, why did she drive off and then come back?

My anxiety of being caught is stirring up a raging white-water rush of panic, as I am finally able to make the decision to dart into Mrs. Squire's fifth-grade classroom. This is one of the few rooms that have a television and projector where we watch reels of tape from metal cannisters about health, hygiene, and how to stop, drop, and roll if we are ever unfortunate enough to catch on fire. None of the skills that I've seen in those movies are worth shit in helping me to get out of this predicament.

Slipping behind the door, so that I can view activity in the hallway from a crack between the hinge and the frame, Mrs. Squire's room is pitch black, and should provide cover so long as no one knows I'm here. Moments after hunkering down in my position, Ms. Yoncey bursts through the library and into the hall with her head cocked sideways and her fists balled. The way she is leaning forward, nearly tipping over from the extreme angle, the principal resembles an angry bull preparing to impale the red caped Matador. Yoncey is definitely on a mission as she stomps into the sixth-grade classroom closest to her office. I see light reflect out of the room momentarily, and then flick off just as quickly. Holy Jesus, I don't know how she knows that I'm here, but she is going to search every room until she finds me! Appearing even more agitated from not discovering her *prey in either six-grade class, she rushes into Mr. Lanier's room directly across the hall from where I am hiding. As before, lights on, lights off, slapping the switch plate hard enough to dent the metal, followed by a Tasmanian devil-like creature, eyes reflecting the fiery depths of Hell, erupting unrestrained into the Freedom Elementary hallway. Crap, she is scarier than that rabid fox that chased Mike Macintosh and his sister down Langston Road a couple of years back. I had been at Glen Mitchell's house playing Strat-O-Matic Baseball on the porch when the two Macintosh kids ran by. I heard tell that Mike's daddy needed to cut the animals head off just to pry its teeth loose from his sister's leg. Hell, the way Ms. Yoncey looks, I'll bet that she would keep on gnawing even after being decapitated.*

As the principal begins her trek across the hall to where I'm hiding, scared shit-less, I realize that my only hope of escaping detection is the coat closet situated in the same corner of Mrs. Squire's room as it is in Ms. Huckman's class.

Hopefully, Ms. Yoncey won't decide to dig through the toboggans, gloves, hooded coats and other assorted junk since she hasn't in the other rooms; at least on her first pass thorough. As I quickly turn the closet doorknob a few feet to my right, and dive under the mass of outerwear littering the floor, I realize that I'm too far away to close the closet door. Then, an even greater discovery crashes down on me like a blazing meteor...I'm not alone in the friggin' room.

An odd, slurping, suction noise, that reminds me of the sound the plunger made when Dad unclogged our poop-filled toilet after the town sewer backed up, is coming from the back of the class.

A soft purring, similar to a satisfied cat rubbing against a couch leg to relieve a persistent itch, compliments the bizarre symphony that momentarily distracts me from my predicament. With no time to consider the origin of the noise, I cover myself with a random piece of clothing that smells to high heaven of dirty gym socks and mothballs. With my luck, the head lice that have recently run rampant throughout the school will all have decided to make a cozy home in my current hiding place. I guess that's the least of my worries!

Before I can take a steadying breath, Principal Yoncey slams the light switch on as she blows into the room where I am hiding. The inertia of the charging bull stops, and suddenly she becomes a still snapshot, almost as if time froze and the film snapped while watching a theater movie. Yoncey squints, like a blinding light is framing the action occurring where she is focused at the back of the class, and her jaw drops wide in an expression of total disbelief. The Incredible Hulk becomes green as he transforms in my comics, but he has nothing on Ester Yoncey. Her pallor is a kaleidoscope of color, first changing from red to white, and then to a darkening purple as she begins to comprehend what she is watching. I quietly shift position in the closet just enough to get an angle to view what is causing this metamorphosis in Principal Ester Yoncey.

Mayor Griffin Maynor's back is to the entranceway of the room and to Ms. Yoncey. More accurately, his ass is pointing to the entranceway. Maynor's heavily creased pants and stripped boxer drawers are draped around his ankles as he stands facing the far wall. His lily-white buttocks and bony, fuzzy, gray haired legs are in sharp contrast to his unbuttoned navy-blue dress shirt that hangs loosely from his shoulders.

Betsy Mae Byrd, on her knees directly in front of and facing the mayor, is bobbing her head up and down below Maynor's waist like an engine piston, and whatever she is doing is causing the suction sound that I heard before the light came on. For a moment more, Griffin has one hand tangled in Betsy Mae's beehive hairdo, guiding her head back and forth, as she goes about her task with undivided attention. Her glittered red panties hang limply from the mayor's fingers that aren't preoccupied with her nest of hair. The two of them are so engaged in their activity that it takes a second or two for them to realize that they are aglow in florescent lighting, and that their little rendezvous has been interrupted by one Ester Yoncey. That ecstatic obliviousness ends abruptly when Ester takes two long strides forward, shakes her fist violently in the air like Jesus addressing the tax collectors at the Jewish temple, and screams furiously, "YOU TWO-TIMING SON OF A BITCH. I SHOULD HAVE KNOWN THAT IT WAS THIS COCK SUCKING LITTLE WHORE THAT YOU'VE BEEN SCREWING AROUND WITH!" Both Griffin Maynor and Betsy Mae Byrd react like the second Ice Age has engulfed Freedom Elementary, frozen in time as if not breathing would render them invisible, two Neanderthals locked in a compromising embrace forever. Betsy Mae's waded panties dropping from Griffin's hand to the tile floor is the only movement in the otherwise still room.

That is until Ms. Yoncey reignites her tirade by growling, "If I hadn't driven by the gym to see if those goddamn kids were parked and tossing beer cans again, I wouldn't have seen that shitty Cadillac of yours hidden next to the building." Ester is shaking like a dog shittin' razorblades as she contemplates what to burst out with next. Finally, having made her decision, she points her index finger and shakes it vehemently at Mayor Maynor, then states with firm resolution, "I'll bet that Louise will be damned interested to hear about this fucking tryst...maybe even more so when she learns that you've been banging me in the back seat of your Caddy too!" Having made that proclamation, Principal Yoncey appears to try and gain composure, fails, then abruptly turns and stomps angrily out of the classroom.

No longer being chastised from behind, the previously statuesque Maynor quickly swings around toward the door, and unsuccessfully attempts to cover his stiffly erect 'little Griffin' with two cupped hands. Betsy Mae appears to remain in a state of stupor on her hands and knees, shock causing her mouth to remain in an 'O' shape like the blow-up dolls in the back of Cline's Barbershop magazines.

With his pants and boxers still around his ankles, the mayor lunges to follow Yoncey, trips and falls flat on his face onto the tile floor. Scrambling back to his feet, a trickle of blood dripping from his nose onto his blue shirt, he jerks up his pants and runs from the room yelling, "Ester wait! Ester, please wait, it's not what you think. ESTER ESSSSTEEERRR!" Maynor's pleas echo down the hall and diminish only slightly as he chases after Yoncey into her office. The thick glass in her door vibrates as if it is going to explode when he slams the door shut behind them.

The commotion generated by the principal and the mayor has evidently broken the trance that Betsy Mae has been mired in. She quickly gets to her feet and, with no apparent humiliation, packs her boobs back underneath her strapless top. She grabs her panties from the floor where Griffin had dropped them, and stuffs them in a small black purse that she scoops up from the seat of a nearby desk. At last, possibly grasping the gravity of the situation that she finds herself in, Betsy Mae Byrd bolts like lightening from the room, and shuffles as fast as her high heels allow towards the Library at the end of the hall. She has disappeared from sight as I stick my head out of the fifth-grade classroom to see if the coast is clear. Behind her closed office door, Yoncey is still screaming at the mayor, scolding him with profanities and threats, as I follow Byrd's course down the hall. Rushing by Ester's office, and through the Library and utility room, I stop long enough to crack the access door and glimpse outside. Now ain't the time to throw caution to the wind, and I want to ensure, however unlikely, that Betsy Mae didn't decide to wait on Mayor Maynor. After verifying that she is nowhere in sight, I burst into the night air, oblivious to everything *except hauling ass through the Freedom Elementary parking lot, around the school bus loop, and onto Schoolhouse Road. Although extremely grateful to be free of whatever it was I just witnessed, and I have a pretty good idea from Marvin's magazines and my after-school conversations with my buddies, my biggest concern now is beating Momma home.*

Chapter 4

The Fire

Momma's vehicle is pulling into our open carport as I jump the hedge and duck under the clothesline strung between two pine trees in our neighbor's, Ms. Wanda Leity, backyard. Hustling across our cement patio that Dad spent all of last summer perfecting, I barely avoid a head on collision with the two-by-four hoisting my basketball goal, as I bolt into our screened-in back porch. I hear Momma's car door close and the porch screen creak open while nearly tripping over Dad lying asleep, snoring, on the living room floor. Johnny Cash's 'Folsom Prison Blues' is blasting from the wooden RCA console phonograph in the corner next to the cabinet that houses his record collection, and the metal stand that holds his most played favorites. When Momma yells, "Hey guys, I'm home," I'm already on my bed cracking open the seldom used unabridged Miriam Webster's Dictionary that I've pulled down from my dusty bookshelf.

Most everything that I know about sex has been gleaned from an infinite resource of everything bawdy; Timmy Wyatt's older brother, Jeff. Timmy has been my neighbor and best friend for as long as I can remember. His family moved next door, well, a vacant acre lot owned by Sherwood Toms and then the Wyatt house, when me and Timmy were still poopin' our diapers. Timmy's got two brothers, Jeff and Ben, and a pretty brunette sister named Beth. When Beth, who turned twelve last spring, announced proudly that she had got her first period, Jeff, at our prodding had shared his substantial knowledge of the birds and the bees as only Jeff could. Jeff Winegard is really the other Wyatt boys' half-brother from their mother's previous marriage, and seems to always be stirring the pot with Timmy's dad by getting into minor scuffles and, sometimes, bigger trouble with all types of authority. Jeff is a sophomore at Moncross and definitely puts the HIGH in High School. During his freshman year, he had gotten stoned at a party, had some buddies drive him to the high school, and broke into the cafeteria through a low window. When cafeteria workers discovered him an hour before school the next morning, Jeff was asleep, clad only in his skivvies, on one of the lunchroom tables with half eaten bags of Lays potato chips and Cheetos scattered all around him. His stepfather's pull as a local contractor that Moncross relies on for maintenance and repairs was the primary factor in keeping Jeff from being sent to Reform School. A few weeks of community service picking up trash from the side of the road with other druggies from across the county cleared Jeff's record, but his time spent with the bad boys along Route 23 evolved him even more in the counterculture ways of the world.

On most topics, we could never get Timmy's older brother to give us the time of day, but when it came to sex (and drugs), Jeff would talk all day. He described to Timmy and me, Ben at six is still too young to have an interest, the ins and outs of the human reproductive system. He began with the cardinal's visit to Beth, and included a rundown on everything from ovulation and fornication, and how best not to get a girl knocked up. Jeff keeps old issues of STAG magazine under his bed, so he was able to provide us illustrated pictorials for a few of his more explicit descriptions. Although he had to explain the meaning, Jeff was fond of saying, "Eatin' ain't cheatin"; having heard Ester Yoncey's outburst at Mayor Maynor this evening, I figure that a lot of what Jeff has been tellin' us about sex has been goin' on between Griffin, Ms. Yoncey and Betsy Mae Byrd. I don't remember Jeff ever using the exact word 'cocksucker' during his informal tutoring, but if I have to make an educated guess, I would say there's a good chance that particular activity, and some other sex things, are what's got Ester so riled up. Upon checking the 'C' words in the dictionary to verify my suspicions, and not uncovering anything, I feel confident that Jeff's information has been pretty accurate, even without Webster validating it for me. One thing I do know for certain, I was undiscovered at the school tonight, and I ain't sayin' nothin' to nobody!

When Momma calls me to dinner, she and Dad are already in a deep conversation on the same topic that I've heard over and over for the last three months; my Uncle Rick's legal troubles. Dad takes a moment, when I enter the kitchen, to ask me where I was when he got home, and I tell him that I ran over to Timmy's house to get construction paper for a project at school. I don't like lying to my parents, and I don't do it on a regular basis, mainly because they usually find out the truth. Tonight is an exception to that rule, and they're not likely to follow up on my story since I was home before supper.

56

Uncle Rick, Dad's older brother, is an all-around good guy that near everybody in the Armentrout clan feels has gotten in over his head as the Treasurer of the First Baptist Church in Elliston. Elliston is a moderate sized town about twenty miles from Freedom, where Rick and Aunt Jane live with my two cousins, Billy and Jeanie.

Rick, as Dad tells it, was never much of a scholar and struggled to finish High School. Before taking the job at First Baptist, Rick had been unable to complete an accounting class at Shenandoah Community College. Unfortunately, he hadn't allowed these barriers to hold him back in his desired profession. When his church was unable to find a qualified parishioner to handle the books, Rick eagerly applied for the part-time position in hopes that it would provide him the experience for a full-time bookkeeping position elsewhere. Two years later, early spring of this year, a surprise audit revealed nearly eight-thousand dollars in missing tithes and offerings that Uncle Rick couldn't explain. Local authorities were brought in, and the specifics around the investigation had hit the Bankston Post and Courier in late October. Most of the town folk that had grown up, gone to school, or know Rick socially feel that he is innocent of stealing the money, especially when they are discussing the incident with Momma and Dad. The family troubles have kept both of my parents preoccupied trying to help with Rick's legal expenses, supporting Aunt Jane and battling questions from the nosy well-to-doers in the community. Even if I had the urge to discuss what had happened at the school this evening, which I definitely don't, they have enough on their plates without me piling on something that I had no business being involved in anyway.

So, trying the best that I can to forget what I saw earlier, and rationalizing that I just might have misinterpreted what was really happening between the three adults at school, I make a half-hearted effort at finishing my homework in my room.

Completing that, I curl up on the rug in front of the old Zenith to watch a made for television movie that I've been waiting all week to see. The TV GUIDE on the magazine rack at the A&P Grocery in Bankston is prime reading material while Momma does her grocery shopping, and 'Dr Jekyll and Mr. Hyde' was featured in this week's edition, along with a hundred or so Christmas specials. As excited as I am to see the feature, sleep overtakes me as Dr Henry Jekyll is taking a drug that transforms him into a beast, Edward Hyde. Both parts are played by Jack Palance, who is as good in this movie as he is in the Westerns that Channel 2 shows after the late news on Friday nights. Shortly before Momma interrupts a dream I'm having to wake me up to send me to bed, Mr. Hyde, bearing an eerie resemblance to an unshaven Mayor Griffin Maynor, is chasing a cockney tart, which looks a lot like Ester Yoncey, through London streets that have magically transformed into a foggy replica of Schoolhouse Road in Freedom. I guess that maybe I haven't been able to push those worries of what I witnessed out of my mind after all.

CREEPY, WEIRD and MAD magazine covers are taped to the walls in my bedroom. The September '66 issue showing Adam West as Batman and Alfred E. Newman as Robin holds the most prestigious place above my headboard. NOT BRAND ECHH and THE FANTASTIC FOUR comics litter the floor around my bed, while past favorites like THOR and FLASH are stacked in every corner of the room and the shelves of my closet. A few Aurora horror models of The Wolfman, Dracula and King Kong stand guard from my bedside table, although Wolfie only has one arm since Momma knocked him over when she was vacuuming my room. I brush the magazines and my G.I. Joe off the top of my blankets, and slide under the covers too tired to remember to say my prayers. Glow-in-the-dark Dracula peeks from behind his cape on the nightstand, as I slide quickly off to sleep.

****

I had been in a dreamless sleep for what felt like only minutes, when Dad bursts into my room and begins to urgently shake me awake. As I rub the grit out of my sleep-encrusted eyes, he flips on the bedside lamp lighting the small electric clock on the bookshelf beside my chest of drawers; surprisingly, the time is 2:15 am. Feeling the strong urge to drift back to sleep, and flopping face first into my pillow, Dad yells, "BUBBA, GET UP!"

He jerks down the blankets and jars me harder this time, exclaiming a full message, but all that I recognize through my sleep-induced haze is 'FIRE'. Shocked fully awake now, I'm nearly paralyzed with fear, as I try to comprehend what Dad is trying to tell me.

A year or so ago, a fire alarm salesman associated with a local insurance company had come by our house one evening to conduct a presentation of a product that, as the salesman insisted, was the cat's pajamas in fire detection and family protection. The device resembled a flying saucer, was as big around *as a dinner plate, and weighed as much as the stones that Dad had me tote to the beagle pup's pen to keep the tin roof from blowing off of their shelter. Supposedly, you would stick four or five of these saucers on the walls throughout the house and avoid a tragedy, according to the salesman, like what struck the Fontaine family up near Windy Gap Ridge. I couldn't sleep for weeks after hearing the salesman's description of the burnt remains of the house and its occupants, both parents and four children. Per the salesman's recommendations, Dad drove us up to Windy Gap near the peak of the mountain to see for ourselves all that was left of the Fontaines, which was charred ash and a cement foundation. Yes siree, a couple of these incredible fire detection devices and the Fontaines would still be alive and kickin'. It was clear that the fire alarm salesman had done his job well because, although they were dang expensive, Momma pestered Dad until he bought six alarms and then worried him to death monthly until he tested them all.*

The saucers ain't clanging now, so I'm trying to grasp what Dad is yelling about. Even with the lamp on, I notice a dull orange glow resembling a summertime sunset sifting around the blinds and curtain near my headboard. At first, I'm afraid that there might have been a nuclear attack like on the films at school, and that the orange glow is fallout. Dad dispels those worries when he suddenly grabs both of my legs and pulls me feet first from the bed to the floor, "Get your ass up and your jeans and coat on," he exclaims, "Freedom Elementary is on fire." He lifts the shades covering my window, and a blindingly bright stream of orange and red colors fill my room. I can feel the heat from the blaze, nearly a half mile away as the crow flies, radiate through the glass, as it melts the frost that had accumulated on the window with the temperature dropping during the night. I can see Ms. Leity's lights on next door, and she is standing on her porch as fire trucks and emergency vehicles speed by her house with their sirens blaring. Momma scrambles down the hall between our bedrooms, and Dad follows closely on her heels. Quickly throwing on my jeans, flannel shirt, coat and tennis shoes that I had left on a chair in the corner of my bedroom when Momma dragged me to bed, I shoot through our living room and out the front door onto the sidewalk facing Schoolhouse Road. The temperature has dropped into the low teens while I slept, and I'm already wishing that I had grabbed gloves from the coat closet near the back door before heading outside.

A handful of townsfolk are running down Schoolhouse Road towards the fire, as two police cars with flashing red lights block access to the road just above the

Wyatt's house. The emergency vehicle's horns are blaring as they warn everyone to clear their path. The people on foot jump to the side of the road near a gully to avoid being blown over by the speeding trucks.

"C'mon, Bubba," Dad says excitedly, as he grabs my forearm and pulls me towards Ms. Leity's backyard and away from the commotion on the road. We climb the metal fence on the far side of our neighbor's house, jump a hedge and progress through a field overgrown with Virginia creeper vines and burs, retracing in reverse the steps that I had taken coming home seven hours earlier.

Slipping through the rusted barbed wire fence that we take turns holding apart for each other, and ducking under a low branch of a rotting elm, Dad points to flames that are visible above a heavy patch of trees that border the circular bus driveway beside Freedom Elementary. Sparks begin raining down on us before we clear the woods, even though we are still a good hundred yards from the playground beside the drive. The clamor of firefighters, sirens and crashing brick and timber is deafening as we get our first glimpse of the activity surrounding the school. The heat permeating from the burning building feels like it could cause blisters even at this distance from the blaze. The contrast between the icicles forming on the upper branches and leaves of the trees from the blowing water of the firemen's hoses, to the intense heat melting the hard plastic swing seats near the back of the school is creating a horrific wonderland of misty hues, haloed lights and sprite-like sparks dancing to the tones of walkie-talkie radios and police sirens.

Blockades proclaiming 'DO NOT CROSS' with bright yellow tape stretched between them have recently been set around the entire perimeter of the school. Two policemen clad in overcoats and talking on radios are responsible for allowing the emergency vehicles in and out of the circular drive. A hundred or more onlookers are crowded against the tape near Schoolhouse Road, a safe distance from the blaze, but continue to jockey for position in order to get the best vantage point from which to see. Having arrived through the field and woods at the rear of the school, Dad and me are alone and significantly closer to the action. Although still behind the barrier, we are able to hear muted conversations, directives and assessments as the firefighters perform their work.

Jack Lipsay has told us kids quite a bit about the history of the school building while setting on the bench outside of Gee's store. He took classes here a coon's age ago, and he always enjoys me updating him on the teachers and happenings around Freedom Elementary. Jack is a history buff, of sorts and can *make any topic seem like he has pulled information directly from the Smithsonian archives. I recollect a bunch of the information that he told me about the school, sadly watching the structure crumble to the ground.*

Freedom Elementary is, or was, a four-story building built around the turn of the century. Constructed primarily with fire clay brick from the long-deserted brickworks near the Shenandoah River, the school's basement houses the boiler for heating the structure, and a small office and storage room for Janitor Elwood Breffton to keep his work tools. The main level of Freedom Elementary contains the classrooms, principal's office, library, utility room, a small Nurse's office for boo-boos and fevers and other administrative areas used on a daily basis.

The third level holds old files, papers and school records that have accumulated since the beginning of time. Timmy and me sneaked up there once on a dare from Davey Grater, who had told us that the third level was haunted by a kid that had fallen from the wooden school bell loft atop the building. We had jimmied the lock on the door to get it open, and Davey served as lookout as we made our trek to fulfill the dare. While we climbed the fragile, creaking wooden steps, motes of dust lifted into the air and covered our shoes. At the top of the stairs, the slight bit of sun leaking through the dingy, cobwebbed windows highlighted old newspapers, magazines and outdated books from the library that had been piled in stacks throughout the area. There were no walls separating the third floor, and dust had accumulated like snow across the expanse. Our newly formed footprints were the only ones visible, except for one larger set near the stairs and a stack of Boy's Life magazines. There was a hint of tobacco smoke in the air, which meant that the adult prints were probably made by Elwood Breffton coming to the third level after hours where he could smoke and get out of the cold. Although the High School had a smoking area for the students and a lounge for the teachers, Freedom Elementary, per Ester Yoncey's directive, prohibited smoking inside of the school at all times. Teachers, staff and administrators needing to smoke are required to go outside and away from the view of the students.

The dare of reaching the third floor accomplished, me and Timmy had nearly run over the top of each other racing down the staircase, certain that we were being chased by the ghost created from Davey's imagination. Davey was leaning against the door when we reached the bottom of the stairs, and we nearly knocked him over as we blasted into the hall. The cool thing was that the dare gave us the chance to create a tale about the third level; one that entailed the imprint of a kid's body formed in the dust directly below the loft that housed the school bell. The girls in our class were appropriately impressed with our heroics in surviving the bell tower ghost.

And considering the bell, the top level of Freedom Elementary consists of a small attic with a thick, coarse rope hanging from its ceiling that is attached to a bell located in the loft perched on the roof. The bell has been out of commission for at least as long as I have been around. I once asked Dad about it, and he said that he had never heard the bell rung either.

By the time that Dad and me join the growing crowd at the front of the school, Freedom Elementary is totally engulfed in flame. The attic and storage floors begin crashing into the classroom level sending sparks, spears of fire and a vast plume of gray smoke into the frozen night air. The ground is being littered by blowing textbook, magazine and newspaper pages glowing with burning ash, causing the firemen to spray their hoses over the area away from the school to prevent the fire from spreading to nearby houses and the church. The recent cold front that moved through the area, dropping temperatures well below freezing, is crystallizing the spray, as it lands on the onlookers and across the already frigid pavement of Schoolhouse Road. Policemen with Bankston patches on their uniforms begin pushing the barricades and townspeople further back from the inferno. Hearing their instructions to the crowd is nearly impossible over the din of sirens, large motors running, firemen calling to one another, and the gushing water sizzling in the flames as more out of town workers and trucks arrive to battle the fire. Although the level of noise around the activity is deafening, the crowd observing from behind the barricade is standing in reverent silence, watching in shock the surreal event unfolding before us. Reverend Spicer has evangelized about what the fiery gates of Hell would offer to those that didn't follow the straight and narrow path, but his graphic descriptions from the pulpit pale in comparison to what we are witnessing.

Jimbo Byrd, obviously having returned from whatever caused him to miss the Council meeting earlier, is animatedly directing his small group of volunteers from the Freedom Fire Department. These locals are primarily assisting the police with the barricades and crowd control while the larger units and professionals from Bankston battle the blaze. Even with his subordinate role, Byrd approaches his responsibilities with a stoic intensity and an air of importance, reluctantly conceding control to the larger unit's leadership.

Mayor Griffin Maynor makes no such concessions, reluctant or otherwise. Decked out in the tailored suit with tie that he had donned at the meeting earlier this evening, but now with his pants up to his waist instead of around his ankles, Griffin is bouncing from the Bankston firefighters, to the Freedom volunteers, and then to his town constituents, all the while squawking orders and reassurances in equal measure. He swaggers to where Jimbo is conducting his Chief business, reaches up and grabs the significantly larger man by the shoulder, then points and barks expectations over the din of the sirens. Although we are too far way to hear the heated one-way conversation, I can tell from the mayor's expression that he isn't pleased that his Fire Chief has been relegated to a secondary role by the out-of-towners.

The smack of a screen door closing behind me on the opposite side of Schoolhouse Road catches my attention, and I turn to see Nance Breffton, Janitor Elwood Breffton's frail and time weathered spouse, bracing herself against the porch column of their battleship gray, wood-siding house. The flaking paint on the eaves of the porch is identical in color to the framework of the mostly brick school, and I briefly ponder if Elwood used leftover paint from Freedom Elementary on the trim of his home. Nance is staring at the blaze, as if hypnotized by the massive flickering of the fire that is turning the building into a mound of ashy cinder. As she slowly makes her way to the barricade, her fragility is accentuated by a severe slouch that gives the impression of her carrying a great weight on her shoulders. She seems oblivious of others around her, and nobody speaks to her being that they seem lost in their own thoughts, as well.

Janitor Breffton is conspicuously absent from her side and, it appears, from the entire scene. He is probably sleeping off a fifth of Tennessee mash according to the long running rumors from Jack Lipsey and everyone else that grew up with Elwood in Freedom.

Dad tugs at my elbow to pull me aside, as the police begin herding townsfolk to the side of the bus drive near an empty lot in order to create a path for a long white ambulance to enter the area inside of the barriers. It seems unlikely that any of the firefighters have been injured since the vehicle is creeping along at a snail's pace, with only its red and white lights flashing and no siren. The ambulance's brakes moan when it drifts to a stop in the school's parking lot, a safe distance from the activity and the blaze. Reassured by the lack of urgency from the ambulance workers, probably a precautionary measure or a slight case of smoke inhalation if you can believe the rumblings of the crowd, Dad makes the decision for us to begin our walk back home. I beg him to stay at least until we see if Mayor Maynor will blow a gasket arguing with the Bankston Fire Chief, but he insists that it's getting too late and too cold, and that Momma will be worried about us. I know better than to argue, 'cause I'm not yearning for a slap upside my head, and follow him up Schoolhouse Road towards home.

Minutes later, we lumber through our front yard and discover Momma sitting on the front stoop bundled in a heavy blue quilt that Grannie Bess made for her two Christmases ago. She says that she's been busy gabbing with Ms. Leity and a few other folks that passed our house going to and from the fire. Beings we don't have any fresh news that she hasn't already heard, she sends me off to bed with assurances that everything is fine and that we'll have more news when we wake up in the morning. With a hug and a kiss, I return to my bedroom, strip down to my skivvies and drift off to a restless sleep, while Momma and Dad whisper softly in their adjoining bedroom.

Orange shadows are no longer dancing along my wall, and there are no stirrings from inside the house when I wake up briefly just before daybreak. Closing my shades and curling up under the covers, I consider that now might be the perfect time to chew on the events from the last day. I make it to reflecting on arriving at school and talking to Davey, and then exhaustion overtakes me and I drop back off to a dreamless sleep.

****

The smell of fried eggs and bacon waft into my bedroom making my stomach rumble even before my feet hit the hardwood floor. Shuffling into the kitchen and hugging Momma from behind while she cooks at the stove, her favorite fuzzy, blue robe and bedroom slippers indicating as much as the sunrise that morning has arrived, I see that Dad is nose deep in the Bankston Post and Courier. Before I can ask if there's any news on the fire, Dad reaches for his coffee mug resting near the remnants of runny yellow yolk and bacon grease on his breakfast plate, and uncovers the front page of our local paper. The bold headline practically shouts:

FIRE DESTROYS LOCAL ELEMENTARY SCHOOL

A half-page photograph of Freedom Elementary engulfed in flames, taken as the top two floors were collapsing in on the lower level, accompanies the headline and article. Dad has already progressed to the funnies, so I ask if I can have the front page of the paper. I find that due to the paper's cut-off deadline, little is revealed that I didn't already know. The article reads:

Freedom – A fiery blaze that could be seen for miles engulfed and destroyed the Freedom Elementary School in the early hours of Wednesday morning. Over 70 firefighters from across the county continued to battle the flames as our newspaper went to press. Cold weather was hampering the efforts to extinguish the fire as water froze in a number of hoses causing them to burst. Secondary emergency vehicles called in from as far away as Luray were forced to navigate the icy conditions near the school resulting in a number of minor injuries to firefighters from falls.

Many in the town of slightly more than 1800 residents watched in astonishment, disbelief and sadness, as the structure where generations of their family members were educated was destroyed before their eyes.

Freedom Elementary was built in 1903 and housed grades 1–12 until 1950 when Moncross Junior High and High School opened its doors in nearby Lairdville.

During that time, the school was converted to an elementary only facility, providing two classrooms for each grade level 1–6.

Investigators from Richmond will be arriving today to determine the cause of the fire. The Post and Courier will have full coverage and updates in our Thursday edition.

Even though the newspaper article sheds little light on the cause of the fire or its aftermath, horrifying rumors, conjecture and hearsay began circulating around town by late morning. Phones are ringing off the hook, with neighbors secretly picking up on party lines to listen in on other's conversations to get the skinny on what is true, and what is embellishment. A number of folks whispered privately, to everyone that they knew, that a friend of a friend heard tell from Jimbo Byrd, with the understanding that it couldn't be repeated, that a body was found early this morning in the smoldering rubble. Speculation ran from Elwood Breffton being the victim, probably trapped in his confined Janitor's area when the boiler blew, to some little kid that a mother missed picking up from school when she thought that her estranged husband had custody for the night. All the rumors are dispelled by the Wednesday evening Channel 2 News anchorman, who wraps up the conjecture in a grisly bow with his lead story on the 6:00 newscast:

"We have a tragic story out of Freedom to report tonight.
'News 2 at 6' has learned from law enforcement officials that Freedom Elementary School Principal Ester Yoncey perished in the fire that destroyed the school in the early hours of this morning. Ms. Yoncey, lead administrator at the school for the last seventeen years..."

I'm so stunned by the confirmation of someone dying, especially since that someone is Ester Yoncey, that I am having a tough time following the rest of the story.

"...believe that Yoncey may have left the building after the Freedom Town Council meeting on Tuesday night, and returned later in the evening. According to Council members questioned by investigators, her vehicle was parked in a different area this morning from where they remember seeing the car when they arrived for the meeting..."

No shit! She came back to the school when she found Mayor Maynor's Cadillac hidden where he had parked it for his tryst with Betsy Mae. If Dad and me had crossed the field a little closer to the back of the playground last night, we would have seen her car still in the lot. Is it possible that she would have left the building for a second time, and then returned after her confrontation with the mayor? It ain't likely!

"...is believed that Yoncey was overwhelmed by smoke inhalation in her office as she completed year-end administrative duties..."

So, that's why the ambulance arrived last night, right before we headed home, without its siren blaring and crawling along like it had all the time in the world. I guess it did as far as poor Principal Yoncey is concerned.

"...appeared to have started in the boiler area of the basement.

"Freedom Mayor Griffin Maynor told News 2 that under normal circumstances, the boiler would have been turned down shortly after school ended for the day, and increased an hour or two before school started the following morning. In this case, due to the December Town Council meeting, the boiler would have been kept at daytime temperature levels until later in the evening.

"Brantley K. Dunn, the Fire Marshall from Richmond brought in to investigate the incident as he does with any fire where a death occurs, indicated that from his inspection, it doesn't appear that the boiler had been turned down at the expected time. He also told News 2 that although there was no indication of foul play, the formal investigation will continue until a direct cause is verified.

"Teachers at Freedom Elementary told our reporter that Elwood Breffton, long time custodian at the school, is responsible for all maintenance within the building. We have been unable to reach Mr. Breffton for comment.

"Mayor Maynor calls the death of Yoncey one of the darkest moments in the town's history. He said that Freedom has lost a fine woman and a great teacher. Ms. Ester Yoncey was forty-nine years old. In other news…"

My guts feel like there's a rock lodged between my throat and my stomach, but all that is coming up is bile. I run to the bathroom sink and spit, wet a washrag, and wipe my face to clear the clammy sweat from my forehead that is beginning to flow from the pores all over my body. Momma sticks her head in the bathroom door and asks if I'm OK, and I respond that I have a stomach ache and better crawl into bed. I'll pass on supper tonight.

****

Late Fall 2019

Reflection

The weeks following the Freedom Elementary fire brought monumental impact to our town, creating a sense of vulnerability and relinquishment of control that any major catastrophe will inflict upon residents of a community accustomed to a level of immunity from such occurrences. Stability and consistency had been obliterated, and there was no indication that normalcy would return soon.

But communities are resilient, and Freedom was no different.

Christmas 1967 came and went, Ester Yoncey was viewed (more accurately, her casket was viewed since she had previously been cremated in Freedom Elementary) and eulogized at the Barkley Funeral Home before being laid to rest beside her Mother and Father on Cemetery Hill, and news of the incident faded from the local paper as police reports concluded that there was no foul play. Slowly, but surely, the town had settled back into its stride of being a sleepy, rural mountain community located on the banks of the Shenandoah River.

That same level of normalization didn't hold true for me. I spent agonizing weeks churning the sequence of events over in my mind, replaying, reanalyzing and trying to rationalize what I had seen at the school. One moment I would be considering who and what to tell, the next, whether to tell anyone at all. For a nine-year-old (having had a November birthday before the holidays), even as independent as I was, that's a load to process.

Ultimately, I decided to keep what I had seen and heard close to the vest, at least for the time being. I remember spending hours rationalizing why not telling was the best alternative, and by best alternative, I meant what was most beneficial for me. The manner in which I worked my way to a final decision was pretty innovative, but not particularly surprising considering I'm a child of the South.

****

End of the Year 1967

Most Saturday mornings, Dad loads me in his faded green 1952 Chevy pickup truck with primer covering the rusted holes on the running boards, hood and body panel near the tailgate, and we head out to a little beer joint called Rodney's near the lumberyard a mile or so off of Island Bridge Road. Dad gulps Blue Ribbon beer and discusses the sorry state of affairs caused by those god darn hippies protesting the war with Rodney Whipperly and anyone else willing to listen to him. He almost always stands me on a stool in front of the Ride 'Em Rodeo pinball machine with a handful of quarters and a Coke bottle with its contents fizzing over the top from the Planter's Peanuts I have funneled into the drink. Rodney good-naturedly cusses at Dad from behind the linoleum topped bar anytime that my drink overflows onto the glass cover of the machine.

On the way to and from the bar, Dad usually takes a few nips from an Old Timers fifth that he keeps under the front seat of his truck, cranks down the driver's side window, and sings along with whatever Country ballad is blaring on WXCY 1040 on your radio dial. Although he listens to the same music every day, whether he's at work or at home, Dad can only remember a few of the words to each song, but that doesn't keep him from making them up and singing along at the top of his lungs. It is tough to understand what he is saying, anyway, with the Marlboro cigarette stuck in the corner of his mouth as the smoke wafts up into his squinted eyes (and mine).

One of his favorites is a tune by Porter Wagoner called 'The Carroll County Accident'. Porter tells the story of how a respected local businessman decides to up and run off with a town hottie that, unbeknown to the good folks of Carroll County, he has been pokin' for quite some time. As fate would have it, just as the businessman and his lover get to the county line, they have a horrific car accident that kills them both. In a major coincidence reserved only for Country songs, this fellow's son happens upon the accident before anyone else, and finds his old man's wedding ring in a rubber-banded box in the crumpled vehicle's glove compartment. Now, seeing this, he figures that his pop had been flying the coop with a hen that wasn't his momma, and takes the ring and throws it down a deep well. As the crowd of townsfolk arrive at the scene of the grisly accident, they think that the businessman was being his normal, good-guy self and driving a needy neighbor to an appointment, or home, or some other destination that didn't include a low rent rendezvous.

This might not be exactly how the song goes, but it's pretty dang close. Anyways, the moral of the story as it pertains to my dilemma is this, it wouldn't have benefited nobody to know that a beloved town resident, a staple of the community, had been screwin' around on his wife and was in the process of leavin' his family for the town tramp. Especially, when neither of them was no longer in this world.

I figure that my unfortunate discovery in Ms. Squire's fifth grade classroom is a lot like the Carol County Accident. Telling anyone about what I saw, even if they do believe me (and they probably wouldn't), would only taint Ms. Yoncey's reputation and memory. If the mayor and Betsy Mae want to have a fling, that ain't none of my business. Spilling the beans won't bring Ester back, and the newspapers and reporters all say that the fire was an accident. Case closed!

At least, that's how my nine-year-old brain rationalized the situation.

Chapter 5

Betsy Mae and the Minstrel Show

Late Fall 2019

Reflection

Long after the white actor Thomas Dartmouth 'Daddy' Rice performed minstrel routines as the fictional character 'Jim Crow', Freedom Virginia, and many other small towns across the South, continued the racist tradition of characterizing blacks as intellectually impoverished dullards too lazy to accomplish anything but the most menial tasks, while stereotyping and limiting their hobbies to dancing and eating watermelon. Most reflective of this bias were the Negro Minstrel shows; a vaudeville-themed stage production where locals would don black face and colorful baggy rags for clothes, then dance and tell demeaning jokes in a dialect typically attributed to blacks during slavery. The lack of sensitivity or, at least, the pretense of civility absent in 1968 is difficult to imagine in 2019, but only if you don't look too hard. Sins of the father aside, circumstances surrounding the Negro Minstrel Show in February of 1968 were the catalyst that propelled our town to an even deeper malaise than we had been battling through with the loss of Ester Yoncey in the school fire. Unfortunately, I was caught in the center of the maelstrom.

****

February 1968

The Negro Minstrel Show is a welcome event for everyone in town, especially considering it's coming on the heels of the holiday season where there wasn't much to feel good about. The locals lumbered through Christmas and New Year's Day before the investigation into the school fire ended with no additional findings. Ultimately, the Fire Marshall released a statement saying in so many words that, sometimes, bad things happen to good people, and that was that.

Us kids returned to school in early January to make-shift classrooms created from partitioned meeting halls in both the Freedom Baptist and God's Witness Methodist Churches. First through third grades are held in the hand graspin', fire and brimstone Sunday School rooms of the Baptist Church, while fourth through sixth grades are conducted in the fried chicken and mashed potato aroma-ed rooms of the Methodist Church.

Betsy Mae Byrd has been chairing, coordinating and planning the Black Face Ball, as Dad calls the Minstrel Show, for more than ten years. Most of the older folks in town, those over forty anyways, star in the production, while everyone else fights to get tickets to the event. At five bucks a head, the Minstrel Show is far and away the largest fund raiser for the Freedom Ladies Auxiliary. Baked goods, homemade cider and even a coupla' gallons of backroom moonshine sold secretly at the show help to more than triple the admission taken at the door and from pre-sold tickets throughout the year.

Fortunately, the detached Freedom Elementary School gym where the Minstrel Show is held had been spared in the December fire. Black soot covers a large portion of the exterior of the gym, and there was a bit of damage to the roof from fiery debris. Stu and Lump Verner funded the effort for repairs, and the volunteer firemen did the work so that the show could go on. Parking, this year, has been moved to two large open fields a few hundred yards from the building. It doesn't make much difference to my family 'cause we live close enough to walk. Others have been bitchin' and complaining since the new parking arrangements were announced. One of the fields is the area below the school playground that Dad and me crossed on the night of the fire. The monkey bars, slide and swings had to be removed so that the debris from the school could be hauled away in big dump trucks. The gym now sits alone on the old lot with only clumps of cement foundation to indicate that there ever was a Freedom Elementary School.

The somberness of the previous two months has, at least for one night, been diluted by the hoopla surrounding the Minstrel Show as hundreds of town residents begin wedging themselves through admission at the gym's double doors, and proceed onto the scuffed basketball court lined with folding metal chairs. A large portion of the audience has arrived more than an hour before the 8:00 scheduled start time to get the best seats up front near the stage. Winter

71

jackets and shawls have been placed on the back of chairs for territorial protection, and as a covert attempt to save seats for other yet to arrive family and friends, as the early-birds head to the back of the gym for first pickings of the baked goods and booze.

Grannie Bess, a fair-weather member of the Auxiliary so long as she ain't on the outs with one of the other hens, and Granddiddy Robert, bushels of yellow-gray hair flowing atop his blackened face, had arrived hours earlier with many of the other 'actors' to get in costume and practice their lines. The evening always culminates with the crowd favorite cakewalk, where each of the participants pair up and stroll across the stage, arm-in-arm, to the huge cheers, jeers, and catcalls from the well lubricated audience. Large numerals, sometimes printed backwards or upside down for effect, dangle from the participants patched and tattered suits and Sunday dresses so that the judges can determine Best in Show for the evening. The winning couple gets their choice of cakes baked by Ms. Celia Hutton, the Blue-Ribbon Award winner at the County Fair six years running. We have high hopes for Grannie and Granddiddy this year, bein' that they had taken second place the last two years. The competition is pretty darn fierce, and the rooting so strong, that a fight broke out a ways back when Jacob Rant insinuated that Barbara Lee Bain had an unfair advantage because her uncle had some black in him. Jacob later apologized to the Bain family indicating that it had been the liquor talking.

Momma, Dad and me find three seats together near the middle of the second row next to Ray 'Stump' Cheatum, and his two boys, Peanut and Gary. Ray lost an arm and his wife to the Korean War; his arm to grenade shrapnel belonging to the North Korean People's Army, and his wife to a war-time buddy that paid him a visit a few years later. While their old man works as a farmhand around town on a semi-regular basis (translated, when the urge hits and he's sober enough to drive a tractor), Peanut and Gary have the run of their dilapidated house on Schoolhouse Road. Heck, the whole town of Freedom is their oyster, for that matter.

Gary Cheatum was kicked out of Freedom Elementary near the end of his sixth-grade year and sent to a Special Education class at Bankston High. Eddie Watson, who was in Gary's class, told some of us guys that Gary had pulled his tally-whacker out in front of Bonnie Roach during recess on the playground, then asked if she wanted to go into the bushes with him. Bonnie told her momma that evening when she got home from school, and Mrs. Roach threatened to place charges if Gary wasn't expelled from school and barred from being anywhere near her daughter. Eddie said that Ester Yoncey had called Stump to come in and discuss the situation, and he arrived half-drunk and totally belligerent. After threatening to kick Mr. Roach's ass for having a daughter that would lure his boy into such behavior, and saying that it was probably Bonnie that pulled up her dress, Stump cooled down a bit when given the option of placing Gary in Special Ed., or getting the police involved where he just might end up in Reform School. Gene Roach, Bonnie's daddy, still gives Stump a wide berth anytime that they are in the same vicinity.

Peanut, though still enrolled in school, is absent from class more often than not. He was required to repeat second and fourth grade, so he's a coupla' years older than the other fifth graders in his class. Charles Cheatum acquired the nickname 'Peanut', at least as he tells it, from his since departed Momma. He only weighed about four pounds when he was born, but possessed a huge head and big bottom. Debbie Sue Cheatum is said to have remarked, as the umbilical cord was cut, "That ain't no baby. I done pushed out a peanut."

During the day, I can sometimes spot Peanut helping Elwood Breffton, as he goes about his janitorial tasks. My guess is that Elwood supplies him with cigarettes as payment for his assistance because Peanut smells like an ashtray if you sit anywhere near him at lunch (which is the one part of the school day that he never misses). Teachers used to call him out about their suspicions of him smoking at school, but they could never catch him in the act, or persuade him to rat on Janitor Breffton. I think that the teachers eventually gave up because they were afraid of how Peanut might respond if they did catch him; that, or how his old man might get involved.

Ray musta' spent the day shoveling manure before he and the boys arrived for the Minstrel Show. He smells to high heaven of shit and sweat, and his dirty bib overalls are nearly bursting at the waist from his expansive gut trying to escape the fabric. An insulated underwear top serves as his dress shirt, and his frayed jean jacket is half hanging from the back of his chair. The other half, with the pinned arm, lies in a pile on the gym floor. Since Mr. Cheatum's bottom is taking up the best of two seats, Momma sits me next to him so as to give everyone, except me, as much room as possible; at least that's the reason she gives. The empty sleeve of his shirt, where his left arm should be, keeps slapping against the side of my face every time that Ray turns to yell 'shut the Hell up' or 'settle your ass down' to either, or both, of his boys. Stump's work boots are caked with *what could be mud, but the smell drifting up from the tops of his stained white socks indicate otherwise.*

The gym is overflowing with an expectant crowd by the time that the show is scheduled to start at 8:00, and ready to bust open like an October watermelon as the anticipation reaches a fever pitch when the lights still haven't dimmed at 8:15. Once we reach the bottom of the hour, the audience high on sugar and moonshine becoming unruly, Leonard Byron, in costume, pushes through the thick, red velvet curtains in the center of the stage. From the second row where we are seated, the perspiration running from Leonard's forehead is clearly visible, and the beads of sweat are causing rivulets down his black, painted face.

The Buckwheat style wig and exaggerated dialect do little to conceal his nervousness as he tentatively grabs the microphone from its stand with a white gloved hand. Generating a smile from brightly colored red lips, Byron announces, "Hel-lo dar' y'all! I'sa wants to a-pol-o-gize for the de-lay of dis' here show. You see, Ms. Betsy Mae Byrd hasa' takin' ill, so we-sa been doin' alls we can to get this here show on da' road." The crowd appears somewhat appeased by the update, especially since it looks like the show will begin shortly. Sounds of 'shush' and 'quiet' can be heard from different sections of the gym, especially in the back where the audience is furthest away from the stage. Near silence envelopes the room, as everyone strains to hear the rest of Byron's announcement. "As you are prolly a-ware, we'ze gotta be a fixin' a batch a collards afoe' we is ready to perform, yes'um! So's if'n you fine folks'll allow us five mo' minutes, all the while enjoyin' a tune from lil' Ms. Patsy Swift, then we goin' to raise this here roof to-night!"

Momma and Dad look at each other, and Dad shrugs. Even I can tell that this ain't the way the show was supposed to start. Betsy Mae has been introducing the Negro Minstrel Show for as long as I can remember, nigh on five years. Although nobody in the audience seems to be too upset, it is clear that Mr. Byron hadn't been prepared to host this evening.

The gym lights dim as Leonard, posing as 'Kingfish', slips back through the curtains. A spotlight positioned in the rear of the building shines a bright, white circle on the center of the stage. Speakers begin to blare the tune to Nancy Sinatra's hit, 'These Boots Were Made for Walkin', from both sides of the stage. Patsy Swift, a sixth grader that had won Little Miss Freedom at the Dogwood Festival Beauty Pageant last summer, parades through the center slit in the curtain dressed in a neon yellow miniskirt, a rawhide vest and high white zippered boots.

I can't speak for the rest of the crowd, but as far as I'm concerned, the black faces backstage can keep cooking collard greens the rest of the night. Patsy, for certain, can hold my attention until the cows come home. As Grannie Bess would sometimes say when excited to see an unexpected visitor, Patsy's little song and dance 'were as welcome as the flowers in May'.

At the conclusion of Patsy's off-key, hip shaking rendition of Ms. Sinatra's song, she strolls off the stage with a wave of both hands to the monstrous cheers of the audience. I notice that the Cheatum boys, including Stump, are gazing at little Patsy with eyes popping out of their heads, and tongues lopping out of their mouths, like a wolf in a Tex Avery cartoon. Stump nudges me with his armless shoulder, and puts his grinning, nearly toothless, mouth next to my ear and mumbles, "That's a nice ass there, ain't it, boy?" I ignore the comment, and his fishy breath, and slide over a little closer to Momma.

As soon as Patsy is totally off the stage, the curtains part to a colorful hand-painted set with picket fences, hay bales and a vast cotton field backdrop. Then begins an evening of locals in black-face spouting racially focused one-liners, comically modified spirituals, and exaggerated slapstick, culminating with the popular Cake Walk competition.

With the exception of Grannie Bess and Granddiddy Robert failing to win the trophy, it was awarded to a couple that had balloons stuffed in her bra and a sock jammed in his pants, the remainder of the evening went off without a hitch. Considering the change in host, and the late start, the participants were surprisingly able to keep the fun and frivolity of the show on track without the 'under-the-weather' Betsy Mae Byrd at the helm.

****

Sunday morning after breakfast, I'm dragging my feet in gettin' ready for church, hoping that I can waste enough time to miss most of Sunday School. We didn't get back home from the Minstrel Show last night until after 11:00, but bein' tired ain't the reason for me trying to avoid old Ms. Switwater's class. Last Sunday, she was tellin' the story of Moses parting the Red Sea, and that seemed about as farfetched as the flood tale that we studied after Christmas. Then the elderly Sunday School teacher started in on the Ark, again, and got frustrated with me when I asked her how Noah captured animals from all over the world, and then got them to run up the ramp of his boat. She hemmed and hawed about it bein' God's plan, but never really answered my question. I thought it only right to give her one more shot, so I inquired as to what kept the gators and bears from eating the other animals on the ark, and Noah's family for that matter. Well, you would have thought that her blue hair was a gonna blow straight up off her head. Ms. Switwater sat me in the corner and told me to think about the questions I asked in church. So, I did, and came to the conclusion that if I couldn't get important questions like these answered, what use was Sunday School class anyways?

****

Momma is pulling me down the hall from my bedroom with one hand, while trying to snap on one of those God-awful bow ties to the over-starched collar of my white shirt with her other hand. She is about to pinch my earlobe to keep me from pulling at the neck of my shirt to loosen it up, when someone starts banging on the back porch screened door. "Shit," Momma exclaims under her breath, "we're already late for church." As the banging gets louder, Momma shouts, "Hold your horses. I'm coming!"

Flo Wyatt, Timmy's Momma from next door, is standing in curlers, nightgown, untied robe and bedroom slippers, as she shivers outside of our door waiting for someone to answer her relentless knocks. The Wyatt family has never attended church, as far as I know, and from Flo's appearance this morning, it doesn't look like they are startin' a new trend today. Flo is an overweight woman with graying black hair and a penchant for gab. She runs a hairdressing business out of the front room of her home, and does clothes alterations for the locals on the side. Never particularly warm or congenial, she nonetheless always carries the most recent gossip and town dirt that she acquires, mostly, from ladies getting their hair done in her beauty shop. Because of these contacts, she has also established a network of news pigeons that will communicate juicy information by phone at a speed that puts the Post and Courier to shame. On this Sunday morning, it appears that she couldn't even wait to get dressed before spreading the gospel of Flo. Momma ain't overly fond of gossip, which is why she don't get her hair done, or have Grannie Bess's hair done, at Flo Wyatt's.

That don't stop Flo from regularly using Momma as a sounding board for recent news.

Momma unlatches the screened door and reluctantly holds it open, saying, "Get on in the house, Flo, before you catch your death of cold. What in the dickens brings you out and about so early on a Sunday morning?"

"Bubba," Flo's gravelly voice proclaims, sounding like a lungful of mucous might get expelled at any moment, "you best go in the other room while me and your momma talk a bit." She is shifting from foot to foot with an anxiousness reflective of needing to pee, really bad.

My first concern when I see Flo so agitated, even for her, is that Timmy and me have done something bad that has been uncovered, and Flo needs to spill the beans to Momma. I figure that I need to stay within earshot in case I need to defend myself later over what she is dyin' to tell. Pretending to head back to my bedroom, I stealthily slip behind the living room door where I can't be seen, but should still be able to clearly hear what they're sayin' so long as they don't leave the kitchen.

"What in God's name is going on, Flo?" Momma states, obviously attempting to disguise her impatience, and failing. "We were just on our way to church."

"This is important, Anna. You were at the Minstrel Show last night, right?"

"Yes, the three of us went. I didn't realize that it was going to end so late. We didn't get to bed until nearly midnight."

"Then you heard Len Byron say that Betsy Mae Byrd was under the weather. Well, I hear tell that she wasn't sick at all." Flo pauses for the dramatic effect used by practiced gossipers. "As a matter of fact, Betsy Mae's not even in Freedom!"

"What on earth are you talking about, Flo?" Momma rebuts. "Leonard said she was sick. That's what caused the show to start late."

"Oh, it started late because of Betsy Mae, alright," Flo continues, even more excitedly. "Lady Louise Maynor had to take the reins late yesterdee' afternoon when Betsy Mae didn't show up for rehearsal. If not for Louise, the Negro Minstrel Show woulda' been canceled!"

I can see Momma standing next to our Frigidaire, hands on hips, waiting for Flo to get to the point of her story, by peering through the crack between the living room door and its jamb. Flo isn't visible from my position of reconnaissance, but the crackle of the linoleum flooring near the kitchen sink is a dead giveaway that she is shifting from foot to foot, baiting Momma to ask more questions.

"So, Flo, if Betsy Mae wasn't sick, where in the heck was she?" Momma's tone is the same one she uses on me when I try and circle around the truth, the whole truth and nothing but the truth. Over the conversation occurring in the kitchen, I can hear the church bell toll at Freedom Baptist signifying the end of Sunday School and the call to worship. Dad would have normally been pushing Flo out of our house, but he left an hour or so ago to take a look at a leaky faucet in the Women's restroom that Reverend Spicer has been after him to fix for weeks.

The door I'm leanin' against squeaks a bit when I crane my neck and lean forward to make sure that I don't miss any of Flo's juicy gossip, and I'm fearful that I've blown my cover.

Fortunately, if they heard the door, they're ignoring it.

Knowing that Flo wouldn't be outta' bed on a Sunday mornin' before noon if she didn't think that this was some earth-shattering news, I can almost visualize her toothy, conspiratorial grin; I've seen her use it a hundred times when gossiping with the women visiting her beauty parlor while I was playin' over at Timmy's house.

"Well, I hear tell that Betsy Mae has up and run off with some ol' boy that she met at the Moose Lodge in Bankston," Flo confides to Momma, whispering to make the information seem more secretive. "They say that she's been havin' relations with this guy for ages. Sela Marington told Inez Brown at the grocery store, C&S Market down by the Tastee Freeze in Elliston, that she heard from Louise Maynor herself that Jimbo Byrd had last talked to Betsy Mae right afore she drove to deliver brownies to the Lodge. He said that she was a takin' the baked goods to a charity sale for that little Burnette girl that's come down with the Leukemia. If you can believe what Inez Brown says, quite a few of the Bankston Moose boys are more than a little familiar with Betsy Mae's brownies, if you catch my meaning."

Momma looking stunned, and more than a little doubtful, clutches the beads of her necklace and says, "Are you sure? Betsy Mae Bennington has been a Freedom resident all of her life. She and Jimbo Byrd have been married since their senior year at Moncross High. Jim doesn't have much of a personality, and spends most of his spare time at the firehouse, but I can't imagine her just up and running off from him without some kind of prior incident."

78

"Well, it doesn't surprise me none," Flo retorts with a snort, "what with them short skirts and low-cut tops that she's been paradin' all over town in. I heard tell that Jimbo initially thought that she might be with that Nigra fella that rolls through town selling produce every now and again. Shoot, if that was the case, we all know what she'd a be wantin' him for!" Flo chuckles at the thought, possibly even thinkin' about that same fella herself, and presses on, "But, a bunch of the Lodge members saw her car at the Moose 353 yesterday morning, and Richie Ray Bryant said that she had been flirtin' with any hard-on she could find. Whoever the lover-boy is, he and Betsy Mae musta' dropped her car back by the house afore they left town, being that Jimbo found it parked in the driveway when he got back from the Fire Department yesterday afternoon. Guess she thought that he'd figure it out pretty quick if she left their car at the Lodge."

"Has Jim called the police?" Momma asks, trying to make sense of the yarn Flo is spinning. "I just can't believe that she would leave Freedom. You know her Mother is still alive and relies on Betsy Mae to take her to doctor's appointments and the grocery store. Lots of other stuff, too. I think she still helps clean Olivia Bennington's house at least once a month."

"Louise Maynor said that Jim Byrd called the cops last night," Flo explains, "but once they go sniffin' around the Lodge, asking questions and hearin' some of Betsy Mae's escapades, they're gonna tell Jim that this kinda' thing happens all the time. You just wait and see if that ain't what they'll say. If you ask me, I think that she'll find her way back home once she tires of that poor sumbitch she run off with." Flo pauses for a second, like she has forgotten some important fact in her story, then adds, "Sela said that Jimbo told her husband, Percy, you know they both work at the quarry, that he's had enough of Betsy Mae's bullshit, pardon my French, 'cause this ain't the first time that's she's gone and done the dirty on him. But I'll bet my last book of trading stamps that he'll take her back when she comes crawlin' up those porch steps with a hangover and a sore bottom."

"Flo, that's more than enough of that kinda' talk!" Momma chastises. "It's just not proper and, Bubba might be within hearing distance. So, everyone thinks that the police will drop it without much follow-up?"

"Unless somethin' else comes up," Flo answers in a matter-of-fact manner. "She won't be the first, nor last, bitch in heat to break out of the pen."

With that comment, Momma tells Flo Wyatt that we need to get to church, and gently urges her out of the back door onto the patio. Crossing the vacant lot, covered in frost, towards her house, the bedroom slippered Flo turns and yells, "Anna, let me know if you hear anything new at church!"

****

All the while that Flo Wyatt was chattering on to Momma about Betsy Mae Byrd, I was getting an increasingly bad feeling about how the story was progressing. It sure ain't any of my business if Mrs. Byrd has run off, or if Mr. Byrd gives a shit. That there ain't any firm details other than hearsay is worrisome. By the time Flo has reached her house, and Momma has yelled for me to get in the car to finally head to church, my brain is telling my churning stomach that Betsy Mae runnin' off and what I saw at the school in December are only a coincidence. Heck, it only makes sense that if she'd have a fling with the mayor, she might also be more likely to fool around with somebody else. My good sense says that adults do strange things, and what Flo told Momma don't have 'nuthin to do with what I saw after the Council meeting or the school fire.

The problem is, no matter how hard I try to make a case for coincidence, as Paul Harvey says on his 7:00 radio show, there sure does look like there could be a 'rest of the story'. Either I've accidentally fallen into a bizarre Edge of Night type scandal, or I'm riding fast on the Freedom Express, and it's bound for an off the rails collision if all the facts come to light.

It ain't particularly comforting to be one of four people that know about the affair and shouting match that took place in the sixth-grade classroom, cause one of those participants is dead, and another is missing. Man, how I wish that I had just gotten up and gone to Sunday School like Momma wanted this morning!

Chapter 6
Aftermath and Denial

Late Fall 2019

When Betsy Mae Byrd failed to find her way back to Freedom, contrary to what Flo Wyatt said the police believed would occur, that festering question of coincidence had begun to metastasize into a hundred different scenarios in my nine-year-old mind; each of which were increasingly bad, and that I felt an overwhelming sense of responsibility for. I had chided myself for hiding in the classroom over something as small as a confiscated knife, and for putting myself in a position to be privy to an altercation that I didn't have the emotional means to process. I would try to rationalize that it was simply a catastrophe that happened to take the life of an important authority figure in my life one minute, and then berate myself for not telling someone the next. The closer I would come to making the decision to tell my parents about the scene at Freedom Elementary, and Ester Yoncey's response, the harder I rebuked the thought by pondering the ramifications if I did.

The terminal winter of 1968 crawled arduously to a dreary, rain saturated spring. The uncertainty vibrating through my mind was exacerbated by the horrific assassination in Memphis of Dr Martin Luther King in April, and followed unfathomably close by the California Ambassador Hotel murder of Bobby Kennedy in June.

Both unfolded with surreal intensity on the black and white Zenith television in, what up until that time had been a bastion of safety and predictability, the Armentrout family room. The stability of nine-year-old Bubba's beliefs in authority, trust, security and public figures not ending up deceased was severely challenged, and the weight of deciding what was right and wrong regarding my dilemma didn't dissipate with time. An underlying current of ulceration wound itself around my daily activities, nonetheless, the world and I both moved forward.

During the May Day celebration at our makeshift school housed in God's Witness Methodist Church, Terri Chandler had knocked out one of my front teeth when she hurled a metal swing seat towards me, as I chased her across the playground. Momma rushed me to Dr Peter Amador, the sadist dentist from Hell that refused to provide Novocaine, ether, or any other form of numbing agent during dental procedures, to save the tooth. I recall that the purveyor of oral torture had conveyed his trademark tip on that afternoon, recommending that I 'open wide little soldier, this procedure shouldn't last past dinner'.

These words of wisdom were always accompanied by a chuckle and a wink, as if he was letting you in on his personal joke. Well, fuck him! Amador's karma eventually paid him a visit in the form of a dump truck loaded with gravel in the summer of 1975. The good doctor was crushed by the vehicle as it ran a red light, while he crossed a Bankston Street on his way to lunch. Probably took them until dinner to clean Amador off the grill of the truck.

Still, through the spring and summer, Freedom continued to ulcerate. The growing inflammation may not have been overtly visible to most Freedom residents, but a wet, oppressive sense of malaise and impending trouble permeated their mood, even if they weren't cognizant of the specific cause.

By the holiday season of 1968, Al Kaline had nearly singlehandedly crushed my beloved St Louis Cardinals in the World Series, and Apollo 8 had circled the moon. December marked the year anniversary of the school fire, and Betsy Mae Byrd continued to be unaccounted for ten months after disappearing into the ether (although, Louise Maynor swore that she had seen her double entering an elevator in an Atlanta department store, unfortunately the doors had closed before she could tell for certain). What hadn't evaporated, quite the opposite, was my near certainty that something terrible had happened in my hometown, and that I was the only person who had a reason to believe that it might be more sinister than an accident. But, fear prevailed, and I continued to rationalize the multitude of reasons to keep my mouth shut.

****

Our fourth-grade class was still relegated to a church, but had moved with the new school year in September to Freedom Baptist, our place of worship, on the East side of town. The church was a center of activity in that it was located on the lot next to the burnt school, and shared parking with the heavy equipment and trucks being used to build the new Freedom Elementary. Distractions abounded and classes were occasionally interrupted by the cacophony of construction sounds and interesting sights viewed through the church windows.

Mrs. Wanda Lamplier, my fourth-grade teacher, reigned supreme as an instructor, certainly from my perspective, and was the antithesis of Ms. Huckman from the prior year. She would allocate time each day for us to watch the construction activities, understanding that there was a subtle catharsis in us seeing the new school being raised from the ashes. Wanda Lamplier also recognized that once we'd had our fill of construction and workers, our class would be much more receptive and responsive to what she had to teach us.

Wanda had graduated from the University of Virginia in the mid-sixties, was ultra-hip to the worldly fads of the time and demonstrated that coolness factor in her personal style, and daily attire. She was viewed with contempt, and envy if truth be told, by many of her mostly older work peers that cited her short skirts and colorful vocabulary as the kindling for their ire. I overheard a conversation between the school secretary and a teacher one day while waiting in the office for Momma to pick me up for a doctor's appointment. Mrs. Hapsal's, the school secretary, comment to Jean LaRue, a sixth-grade teacher and Physical Education coach, was 'how could Wanda Lamplier provide the modeling required for these children when she looks like a Go-Go dancer on Hullabaloo'? School administrators, unhappy with her non-traditional teaching methods, attempted to coerce her with threats of termination if she didn't modify her teaching style and wardrobe. Their challenges to Wanda 'You've Come A Long Way, Baby' Lamplier went largely unheeded, and she continued to have us read and interpret simple poetry, listen to and provide our thoughts on modern and classical music, and participate in conversations about topics taken from the newspaper headlines that spurred us to question governmental decisions. We openly discussed the pros and cons of political candidates, at least on those topics we could understand and relate to (initially, those views were predominately those of our parents, but Wanda challenged us to think for ourselves), as well as the biographic background of George Wallace, Hubert Humphrey and George McGovern. Mrs. Lamplier managed to present these thought provoking challenges, and lead the associated discussions, in a way that made perfect sense to her fourth-grade population. She accomplished these feats while continuing to don her short skirts and thin, colorful blouses. By the end of September 1968, I had fallen in love and absolutely knew for a fact that when I grew up, I was going to marry Mrs. Lamplier (disposing of Mr. Lamplier never crossed my mind).

On more than one occasion, LeMaster Holmes (the one and only black male at Freedom Elementary) and Tommy Hensley (whose Daddy and Momma were first cousins) would hurl racial slurs at one another on the ball field at recess only to be pulled aside from classmates and lectured by Mrs. Lamplier on equality, inclusiveness and the destructive nature of hate and racism. Much to Tommy's parent's chagrin, he had told us, Hensley and LeMaster had become close friends with Tommy visiting the Holmes' residence for dinner one Sunday afternoon (when his parents thought that he had gone to the movies with his less pigmented friends). Such was the ability of Mrs. Wanda Lamplier to educate and create an environment for learning. Tommy and LeMaster continued to have small spats at school, but it was clear that they performed this ritual to draw the attention of our beautiful teacher. From their point of view, and most of the boys in my class, any attention from that goddess of learning was good attention.

****

Christmas came and went, as did the last Negro Minstrel Show in February (the times they were a changing, even in Freedom Virginia), and I received both with indifference as the cancer of my secret failed to diminish and, in fact, grew. By the spring of 1969, even Mrs. Lamplier's pregnancy by her asshole of a husband, Richard (a Biology teacher at Moncross High that she had married while still at UVA), didn't penetrate the malaise I had been enshrouded in, for life had continued to move forward without resolution regarding Ester Yoncey's death and Betsy Mae Byrd's disappearance. During the night, nearly every night, my dreams consisted of nefarious scenarios related to what I had witnessed that December night at Freedom Elementary. During the day, I would often be caught dumbfounded staring out the window into the spring sunshine, engulfed in my own thoughts, when asked to answer a simple question concerning Virginia history or the War of Northern Aggression. With each passing day, I became more certain that Mayor Griffin Maynor was responsible, or at least had answers, for what I was obsessed to uncover, and to what others were so oblivious. The school year ended in mid-June 1969, delayed two weeks because of heavy snow and freezing rain during the winter, as the Summer of Love began to gear up to an LSD laced frenzy. I, too, was frenetic in my resolve to find some avenue to get what I knew out into the open. Failure to act wasn't an option; my grades were declining, I often felt ill, and I was barely sleeping. The guilt of not reporting the school incident to my parents had become overwhelming. So, again, I considered my choices and weighed the consequences. The easiest option would have been to tell Mom and Dad, coming clean about why I stayed at Freedom Elementary that fateful evening, but they were continuing to deal with the delayed trial (Dad had told me that the prosecutors were considering additional charges) of Uncle Rick, and I didn't have a high degree of confidence that they would pass the information on to the authorities even if they did believe me. Another option I pondered was anonymously contacting the newspaper in writing, but decided against that route for fear that they would almost certainly consider the letter a hoax.

Ultimately, after deliberating until I'd worn a hole in my adolescent processing power, I decided that the most effective measure would be to confront the Honorable Mayor Griffin Maynor. Even with my limited experience in adult dealings, I was aware that letting Maynor know that I knew about the tryst would elicit a reaction, especially if he had more than infidelity to hide. And, if he was responsible for either, or both, the fire or the disappearance, the reaction would likely be volatile. So, in June 1969, the challenge was how to create that confrontation, validate or dispel his involvement, and, if possible, continue to remain anonymous. Quite the conundrum for young Bubba Armentrout.

Part 2
Mayor Griffin Maynor

Chapter 7

Throwing a Rock in the Dark

June 1969

Timmy Wyatt and me stand staring in astonishment at how quickly the new school is being built. Most of the facade is complete and it appears that the construction workers are nearly ready to begin the landscaping, sidewalks, and steps. Sure looks like we'll begin next year, as fifth graders, in the new building.

I am bustin' something fierce to tell someone, anyone I can trust, about my predicament and how I figure that it's related somehow to Ester Yoncey being dead and Betsy Mae Byrd disappearing. Just getting it off my chest might help me to quit worrin' about the situation every minute of the day and night.

Almost as if Timmy is reading my mind, standing next to Schoolhouse Road with his hands in the pockets of his knee patched jeans, he says, "It's hard seein' the new school almost finished without thinkin' about poor Ms. Yoncey, ain't it?"

"Yeah," I reply, a little guiltily like I had wished him to ask that question, "I still can't hardly believe it, what with me and Davey bein' in her office the very mornin' of the fire."

"You reckon' old man Breffton got drunk like some folks say and forgot to turn down the boiler that night?" Timmy inquires, freckled nose already beginning to peel from too much time in the early summer sun.

"I don't rightly know," I say tentatively, trying to find an opportunity to leak just a hint of what I've been a holdin' inside of me, wanting to see how Timmy would react, "but there is a LOT more to the story than everyone is talkin' about!"

Scratching his reddening neck, and shaking his head from side to side, Timmy seems caught off-guard by my comment, "What cha' mean, Bubba? The

PoPos and the Fire Inspector dug around in ashy crap for days and didn't find anything to speak of."

I hesitate a moment, then think 'what the Hell, things ain't gonna get any worse'. "Timmy, you're my best pal, right? We've looked out for each other since we were babies, and I trust you; trust you with my life. But, if I tell you somethin' that I saw, somethin' God awful, you got to blood oath promise me that you won't tell a soul... NOBODY!" I'm shaking from head to toe, feeling the swell of emotions burst from my eyes like a punctured water balloon. In all the years that we've known one another, I can't remember Timmy ever seeing me cry, but today ain't a normal day.

"Shit, Bubba," Timmy replies with both a hurt expression that I would question his loyalty, and sincere concern for what was clearly causing me emotional pain, "I ain't never said nuthin' to nobody about the stuff we've done. Member when I told your momma that it was me who broke her lamp when we were throwin' the ball in your living room? You know for a fact that you can trust me."

"Timmy, this is bigger than that, bigger than anything that we ever done. Do you swear on your grandma's grave?"

"Sure, as shittin', and on my grandpa's, too. I swear!"

The story pours out of me like rusty water from a busted well pump. Every minute detail, from the Swiss Army knife to Flo's early Sunday mornin' visit to our house the day after Betsy Mae Byrd disappeared, gushes without hesitation or a breath between sentences. Somewhere in my reliving and relating those chain of events, Timmy Wyatt sits down on a flat rock near the brick wall that borders the school, and his jaw plops open wide enough for a family of June bugs to reside in. To his credit, he doesn't utter a peep and is all ears, as I tell him how I have thought of that night nearly every minute of every day, how I haven't been able to sleep without having nightmares, and about how strongly I feel that I just gotta find a way to make this terrible situation right. When I finally finish and take a deep breath to steady my nerves, sweat and tears running down the side of my face and pooling on the collar of my white T-shirt, I feel like I've run a day's worth of quarter-mile laps on the school track. Worse than when we are forced to complete the President's Physical Fitness test each year, where about half the kids in class puke before they finish the run.

I look at Timmy, and he is staring at the ground, kicking pebbles across a dirt path where cement will be poured to form the main sidewalk. When he *doesn't respond immediately, I start to get a bad feelin' in the pit of my stomach that Timmy doesn't, or won't allow himself to, believe me. Before I have a chance to tell him to forget it, to pretend that I never said nothin', he looks up from having reflected on what I had to say, and sympathetically professes, "God Almighty, Bubba. Why in the Hell ain't you told somebody about this before now? I don't know how you've kept this in."*

"Think about it, Timmy. We're talkin' about the mayor here; the God-dern mayor! Plus, I don't know nuthin' for sure 'cept he'd been screwing Ester Yoncey, and gettin' his tally whacker sucked by Betsy Mae Byrd. How about that for a helluva' lead in when I go to tell somebody about why I think that Griffin Maynor is behind the fire and Betsy Mae's disappearance. Ain't nobody gonna believe me when it's the mayor's word against mine."

Timmy remains silent, apparently in deep thought, pulling the tops off of dandelions that he has gathered from around the rock where he is sitting. Finally, jaw set with determination, he looks me in the eyes and states resolutely, "Alright, Bubba. So what are we gonna do now?"

Relief, hope and a brother-like love all converge in my chest, as I feel a large portion of the weight of the world being lifted from my shoulders with that one word, 'we'. I want to run over and hug him, but I'm afraid that he might think that I'm ready for the mental hospital at Eastern State. Not only does Timmy believe my every word, but is willing to put his neck on the chopping block alongside mine to help me do what I feel needs doing. Until this moment, I ain't felt like Bubba Armentrout in a coon's age. After my best friend's simple response, I know that I have an ally to fight beside me in the battle to come.

"Well, I've got an idea," I start slowly, testing to see if Timmy might be having second thoughts. "You ever hear the saying 'throw a rock in the dark, hit a dog and he'll bark'?"

"I ain't much on harmin' defenseless animals, Bubba. And neither are you," Timmy replies with uncertainty. "So, how's that goin' to help us with the mayor, anyways?"

"People who say that don't mean it literally," I explain.

"What it means is this. Say, you think that somebody has done somethin', especially somethin' really bad, but you ain't sure. Well, then it's up to you to start askin' a bunch of questions about this really bad thing that happened. Usually, the guilty party will be the person to speak up so as to tell you why what you believe ain't so. Get it? You are throwin' a rock, a question, in the dark,

since you don't know the answer for sure and certain. If you hit a dog, the guilty person, then he'll most likely bark...you know, speak up so as to make sure that you think it wasn't him that done the deed."

"I think I'm startin' to understand!" Timmy states with a wide grin. "It's like that time that Beth ran outta' Kotex 'cause you and me had used her last rag to wipe down our bikes when we couldn't find a cleaning cloth in the garage. Beth yelled down from the bathroom window in a panic wantin' to know who stole her rags, and you and me both screamed back together that it wasn't us. I reckon' that she did hit two dirty dogs with a rock, and boy did we yelp!"

"You got it," I chuckle, remembering how aggravated Beth had been. "That's how we're gonna tell if Mayor Maynor is involved in this, or if everything is just a nasty coincidence. So, here's the plan."

****

A few hours later, while Timmy's half-brother, Jeff Winegard, is out peddling dope or crawled up naked on a lunch table somewhere, me and Timmy are riffling through the raunchiest of his dirty magazines. Pages and pages of twisted bodies in pretzel-like contortions, men and women, men and multiple women and women on women flash through our fingers as we work to choose three or four magazines to suit our purposes. We really only need two, but figure that Jeff won't miss a couple more with the hundreds that he has stored in his room, and you never know when they might come in handy. With that task accomplished, the magazines stuffed down the back of our jeans in case Flo confronts us as we leave Timmy's house, we hop on our bikes (mine is an AMF Roadmaster, and Timmy's is a Columbia Thunderbolt with a banana seat that we salvaged from the dump), and head straight for Elmer Smiley's trailer on the outskirts of town.

Elmer, who looks to be forty even though he's only in his late twenties, lives alone in the rented mobile home near the Shenandoah River. He isn't a native of our area, having moved to Freedom from somewhere further South a few years back. He keeps his long hair pulled back neatly in a ponytail, wears tank top shirts with peace signs on the front and nearly always reeks of what most likely is pot. Either that, or he and Jeff Winegard use the same smoky aftershave. Smiley is widely known as the town supplier of illegal firecrackers, among other contraband, that he purchases on regular pilgrimages to South Carolina. One of Jeff's friends, who is a regular smoking buddy of Elmer, told Timmy's brother *that Elmer has a fondness, no make that obsession, with pornography. An obsession that, as Jeff and Elmer's mutual friend described, led to Elmer being caught in the restroom of a Bankston drugstore masturbating to the pictures in a magazine that he had stealthily stolen from the stand at the back of the store. Since Timmy and me don't have money to buy fireworks, we figure that a small sample of Jeff's vast collection of rags might warrant a swap for a couple of cherry bombs that Elmer has been verbally promoting around town for the last month.*

As expected, Elmer didn't flinch one bit in accepting the trade. He also couldn't have been more receptive to my additional proposal of providing another skin magazine in a week or so, after we are certain that he won't squeal if asked, say, about selling a few of his prized cherry bombs to minors.

Achieving our desired goal at Elmer Smiley's, him waving and flashing a peace sign as we ride off, we bike to my house to complete the preparations necessary to 'throw our rock'.

****

Me and my buddy spend the rest of the afternoon in the basement of my house, a furnished and paneled set of rooms that serve as a recreation and family room in one section (complete with a ping-pong table and barely functional old television), and my hideaway behind a maze of pipes, the water heater and furnace in the other. My remote area has the added benefit of a concealed door leading to an outside stairwell; intended to be an external access to our sump pump during heavy rains, it also serves as an unobservable path to Dad's storage shed near the rear of our backyard. We spend a little time eating peanut butter sandwiches and watching a 77 Sunset Strip rerun, the one where Kookie is nabbing a gang of car thieves and running a comb through his Brylcreemed pompadour, before scrounging through Momma's old Southern Living magazines and National Enquirer tabloids that she stores in the shed.

After toting our haul to my hideaway, we begin cutting, piecing and pasting single letters from the magazine script to a single sheet of construction paper. Our hope is that this part of the plan will either help validate, or dispel, the mayor's involvement in the demise of Principal Yoncey and Betsy Mae Byrd's disappearance. With the last letter in place, Elmer's Glue and red construction paper sticking to my fingertips, I hold up the masterpiece for Timmy to see:

*I saw w_hat Y_ou **Did** AT THe sCHoOL!*

A picture from Stag Magazine simulating the act that I saw Betsy Mae performing on the mayor is pasted below the message; then another line of script:

YOU GOT rId OF esTER
YoNcEY THen BEtSY _MAE
BYrD

Seeing the results, Timmy beams a toothy grin, and quips, "Well, it ain't perfect, but I believe it's goin' to be good enough for us to get that ol' coon dog Maynor to bark!"

Carefully folding the construction paper and gently stuffing it in my back pocket, I respond, "Come on back to the house around 9:00. We'll wait 'til it's good and dark to head out. If we set the trap about the time the mayor and Lady Louise go to bed, there won't be much traffic, if any, on Route 23. Tell your ma that you're spendin' the night over here with me."

"Sure, as shootin', Kemo Sabe!" Timmy replies mischievously, and slaps me on the back. He waves over the top of his Sargent Carter style crew cut as he heads for the steps in the stairwell.

****

Chestnut Hall's front porch light is casting dancing shadows across the wind-blown hedges, as I wait in the dilapidated woodshed for Timmy to return from his dangerous part of the mission. From my vantage point in the shed on the edge of an overgrown field on the opposite side of Route 23 from the mayor's house, peeking between termite infested and long rotted boards, I can see the outline of Griffin Maynor's upper torso reflected in the pulled shades as he sits performing some task at a desk in what is probably a downstairs study. A more muted light is shining through an upper story window with shades drawn, possibly Louise Maynor preparing for bed.

Over the last few minutes, I've anxiously watched Timmy carefully place one of the cherry bombs into the Maynor's mailbox that is affixed above a banister post located at the bottom of the steps leading up to Chestnut Hall's massive front porch. While nearly every other home in Freedom has boxes by the roadside that can easily be reached from the courier's vehicle, the mayor demands walk-up service for his and Lady Louise's convenience. Les Ray Combs, the town mail carrier, told Dad that the mayor berated him one rainy afternoon because his mail, newspaper and himself were soaked from the walk to the mailbox at the road and then back to his house. Les Ray said that he didn't want to have to continue to put up with the mayor's 'horse shit', so he told Griffin that he could shove the mailbox up his god-damned ass for all Les Ray could care. The mail carrier nearly lost his job over the altercation but, ultimately, Maynor got his mailbox next to his house.

I nearly piss my pants when the mayor's shadow slides back from his desk, as Timmy wraps the modified fuse of the cherry bomb down the length of the post. Earlier today, we had nabbed a couple of feet of twine from Dad's workshop, and squirted the rope with fluid that he uses to fill his Zippo cigarette lighter. Attaching the twine to the firecracker fuse will, we hope, give my fleet footed buddy enough time to get to the woodshed before the explosion occurs. Seeing the mayor's movement, I consider yelling for Timmy to abort the mission, but change my mind when I see Griffin return to the desk with a drink, maybe a late-night toddy, in hand. Now, Timmy is using masking tape to stick our folded note about halfway up the banister post, well below the metal box but still where it won't be missed in the commotion I expect to happen shortly.

Only two cars have passed down Route 23 in the time that it has taken for Timmy to set the stage for the main performance, and the road is totally deserted as my Timex glow hand greenly reflects 12:02 am. My best buddy pulls a wooden match box from the breast pocket of his black windbreaker jacket, and holds the fuse in one hand as he takes a match from the box with his other. I watch with nervous anticipation, then worry and finally fear when the stiffening breeze blows out match after match every time that Timmy tries to ignite one on the side of the box. Glancing to the window, my heart jumps to my throat when a second figure joins the mayor and stands beside him at his desk. The figure, who must be Louise, grabs the toddy glass from Griffin's hand and turns to walk away. He quickly stands, jerks her arm and the glass falls to the floor. The mayor appears to be angry, waving his arms and then pointing a finger in Louise's direction. She turns her back on him, and Griffin disappears from in front of the window. Louise bends to retrieve the glass from the floor, and then follows after her husband.

Too much unexpected activity is starting to happen, none of it good, and the likelihood of getting caught is increasing by the second. Making the decision that this idea isn't near as good as I thought it was, I begin to crawl out of the dilapidated woodshed in hopes of getting Timmy's attention before the Maynor's argument peters out and my friend is caught on their front lawn with an empty box of matches and a cherry bomb fuse covered in lighter fluid. Just as I clear the lot and make the edge of the road, I see a flash, the wooden match flaring against the fuse, and the fire starts a rapid progression up the twine towards the mailbox.

I have seen Timmy run like a Wild Kingdom gazelle during pickup football games on the school playground, but tonight he's covering the Chestnut Hall grounds as if he has one of Elmer's lighted firecrackers up his butt. His feet are pounding the acre of front lawn like pistons, he scoots through the grape-vined lattice near the cherub-pissing fountain, jumps the lighted yard jockey beside the sidewalk and hardly touches the road as he shoots across Route 23 without taking a glance for oncoming traffic. The flicker of fire on the twine has only moved halfway up the post when Timmy slides in the woodshed door moments after me, and breathlessly pants, "Do you think anybody seen me?"

"Not that I could tell," I say with satisfaction. "It looked like they were having an argument, maybe over Griffin drinking, and I figured that I better come and get you when the matches wouldn't light. You done good; that things gonna go off any second."

The closest buildings to Chestnut Hall are businesses; most prominently, Cline's Barbershop and Gee's Grocery, all a far piece down Route 23 and long closed for the day. The old farmhouse next to the woodshed where we are waiting has been vacant since Eisenhower was President. Its tin roof has collapsed into the kitchen on the backside, and overgrown weeds are pushing through the rusted screen of the porch in the front. The lot between the farmhouse and woodshed is covered in rubble, broken glass, crushed beer cans and a few used condoms. I have heard that the mayor has been trying to purchase the property for years to have it bulldozed, but the deed is tied up in court over a challenge to the will that Leighton Sheets left when he died in the late '50s. His three boys have been fightin' over the land ever since.

The nearest occupied homes are almost a quarter mile away on Benson Run, or the Byrd house across Mill Creek from the Grocery. With no townsfolk out and about at this hour to see our fireworks display, and still no car lights in sight, the worst that our little commotion might cause the citizens of Freedom is for them to be woke up from a restful sleep thinking that they might have heard a car backfire. Thankfully, we ain't close enough to our house to wake Momma and Dad. Once they checked in on us about 10:00 in my hideaway room at the house, they headed to bed, and we shot out the stairwell door headed for Chestnut Hall.

So far, it seems like my plan is playing itself out pretty doggone good.

Then, moments before the blaze reaches the lip of the slightly opened mailbox, the massive oak front door of Chestnut Hall opens and Mayor Griffin Maynor steps out on the front porch clad only in his skivvies and nightshirt. Unaware of the glowing fuse, he strikes a match to light the tip of a Churchill cigar.

From somewhere within Chestnut Hall, I hear Franklin, the Maynor's dachshund, bark and Louise opens the back door to let him out for his nightly constitutional.

Worrying that the mayor is going to notice the lighted fuse entering the mailbox, a small popping sound, like static electricity, begins and grows louder as the fuse ignites the powder in the cherry bomb. Griffin is turning towards the noise when, in the next instant, the explosion commences.

The pristine mailbox rises like a NASA rocket, fire bellowing from the now open flap and propelling the metal box from the banister post at the foot of the porch steps. Smoke and sparks trail from the fiery projectile until it reaches the height of the second story of Chestnut Hall, and then combusts into flying metal shards. The largest dented and smoking portion of the mailbox, including the bent red flag, lands in the fountain next to the pissing cherub causing a plume of evaporating steam to waft above the naked figure.

The mayor, obviously scared shitless, covers his head with his arms and drops to the porch floor. Crawling to the edge of the porch and peering over at the smoldering post that had previously held his mailbox, he appears to realize what has occurred and juts his head from side to side looking to spot the culprit. Seeing no one, Griffin stands and rushes down the flight of stairs, his bare feet nearly tripping over themselves as he takes two steps at a time. My letter, masking tape holding it firmly to the post, flickers in the slight wind as the mayor cautiously touches the wood to ensure that no lingering fire is about to consume the banister. The emotion of the moment finally overtakes him, and he screams, "Those goddamn vagrant kids," then his eyes discover the note dangling near the middle of the blackened post. He irritably grabs the letter, unfolds it haphazardly, reads it and then freezes dead still, as frozen in place as the fountain's pissing figurine.

Louise Maynor, having heard the blast from the rear of the house, turns on the porch lights, and bursts through the front door, Franklin in her arms, crying, "Griffin, what is it? Are you alright? What was that awful noise?"

Griffin, his back to Louise, discretely and with as little movement as possible stuffs the letter down the front of his boxer shorts and replies with forced calmness, "Louise, get the hell in the house." When she fails to react, Griffin raises his voice slightly, and growls, "NOW!"

"But Griffin," Louise exclaims, "shouldn't we call the police?"

"I said now, goddamn it," the mayor reiterates, his tone turning abrupt and loud. "And, NO! Don't you say a fucking word about this to anybody!"

Louise Maynor moves reluctantly back through the ornate front door as the mayor turns and rushes up the steps, dodging shrapnel from the obliterated mailbox lying across his path.

Stepping on a jagged piece of metal near the front of the porch, Griffin yelps and crouch walks with his hands nearly dragging the ground, limping to follow her inside. The front door slams shut, and then an odd thing happens. Every light in Chestnut Hall, front porch first, then the other rooms in quick succession, go dark. It surely appears that Mayor Griffin Maynor isn't taking any chances that a neighbor or passer-by might have questions about the commotion.

In the woodshed, the humid night is as still as the early summer breeze and the chirping crickets will allow. The darkness of the witching hour is broken only by the faint glimmer of moonlight wafting through the rotting boards of the shed. I turn to Timmy, grin and gleefully exclaim, "Well, how's that for getting that ol' mongrel to bark?"

Chapter 8

Tasting My Words

June 1969

The heat and humidity riding every molecule of the stagnant air inside the Freedom Baptist Church helps emphasize the sermon that Reverend Ross Spicer, in deepest baritone, is delivering to his parishioners on this summer Sunday morning. Sweat is pooling in the armpits and around the collars of the congregation as Spicer adamantly describes the torturous Hell that potentially awaits our church full of sinners on the flip side of heaven. He has progressed through three handkerchiefs during his, up to this point, thirty-minute sermon, dabbing at his receding hairline and under his prominent jowl. The reverend shows no signs of slowing down as he paces from one side of the transept to the other, pointing directly at those who he thinks are at the greatest risk. I have been a devout Christian soldier, not missing one of Ms. Switwater's boring Sunday school classes, since the morning that Flo Wyatt stopped by our house to deliver the news about Betsy Mae Byrd's disappearance. This Sunday is no different. Prior to marching directly to the sanctuary from the young people's bible study room to join Momma and Dad for the service, I had managed to fidget my way through uninspiring tales of Shadrak, Meshak and Abendigo without so much as asking a question, or getting a nasty glare from the old biddy at the front of the room. Shucks, Grannie Bess has recently bought three new hamsters to replace Bobby Burgess and Sandi Griffiths, named for her favorite dancers on the Lawrence Welk show, after they died a week after each other a month or so ago. My level of commitment to my Sunday school teachings is so high that I'm thinkin' about askin' Grannie Bess to name her new rats after the three Jews thrown into the fiery furnace that we learned about this morning.

Well, to be totally honest, like the Good Book wants us to be, a big part of the reason that I was able to sit through the biblical filibusters in Sunday school, and now during Reverend Spicer's droning sermon, is that I have discovered how simple it is to stuff my transistor radio in the back pocket of my heavily pressed khakis and run the flesh-colored ear bud cord up the back of my shirt to my ear without anyone being the wiser. This trick has worked like a charm at Freedom Elementary when I chanced to listen to World Series games on early October afternoons. The repercussions of getting caught at church don't seem much greater than being found out at school; heck, I've gotten pretty dang good at hiding the ear bud with my hand by resting my head on my palm.

Today, I was diggin' 'Peter, Paul and Mary' and 'Jefferson Airplane' while Ms. Switwater rambled through the lesson, and she had dismissed the class to 'Elvis' lamenting about the 'Heartbreak Hotel'. The Washington Senators, the major league baseball team that WROK 'The Rock of the South' carries every weekend is playing a day/night doubleheader this afternoon, and I'll be able to catch the first few innings during communion if the service continues to run on as long as it usually does when the Reverend gets rollin' before serving the wafers and grape juice.

On this Sunday morning, Freedom Baptist is packed to capacity with all the pews full, and metal chairs lined down the aisle and in the back of the sanctuary. Attendance is always heaviest on the third Sabbath of each month, filled with gray hairs and chrome walkers in the event that THIS communion would be the last before their crotchety old souls met up face-to-face with Saint Peter at the Pearly Gates. Interestingly, there are two notable exclusions from the regular group of churchgoers, especially on communion Sunday when everybody notices who is missing. The Honorable Mayor Griffin Maynor and Louise, always stalwarts on the front row of Amen corner, have been replaced this morning by the late arriving Seton sisters, flowery yellow hats so large that the next four rows behind them have to lean sideways in their seats to view the pulpit.

Before Timmy went home early this morning, we talked about last night and the mayor's reaction to my note. I was anxious to see how the mayor and Louise behaved at church today, and am disappointed that they didn't make the service. The two of them missing church for the first time that I can ever remember, except for illness or vacation, is just another indication that there is a lot that the mayor is trying to hide.

Reverend Spicer is nearing the end of his message titled, according to the bulletin, 'No Bad Deed Goes Unpunished', spouting off about coveting thy neighbor's ass, when both Maynors creep softly through the swinging doors of the vestibule, and stand as inconspicuously as possible next to the occupied last row of folding chairs. Most of the congregation pretend not to notice, but Harold Haynes stands and asks Louise to take his seat at the end of the back pew.

I chance a quick, nonchalant glance to the back of the church and discover two weary individuals whose appearance is in sharp contrast to the self-confident, omnipotent, arrogant and overbearing demeanor normally associated with the Maynors.

Griffin looks worn and weathered like an old shoe laying beside the road, bounced from tire to tire of oncoming traffic after falling from a truck bed on its way to the dump. Louise is flush and distant, as if only her wrinkled shell has made the trip to church while the emotional workings were left back at Chestnut Hall. Both appear sleep deprived, verifying that the previous night's adventure probably hadn't ended at midnight for the Maynors.

While I replay the mayor's response to reading the letter over in my mind, Reverend Ross Spicer completes his lengthy Hell and Brimstone diatribe and announces for the congregation to, "Please stand as we sing in holy ad-or-a-tion 'How Great Thou Art'." As we stand to sing, everyone perusing the wall placard to get the hymnal page number, I decide to turn the volume wheel to full throttle on my transistor radio. More as a remedy to get the mayor out of my head than any real dislike for George Beverly Shea or the traditional communal hymn, my thoughts wander to the popular song by the Cyrkles 'Red Rubber Ball' blasting in my radio's ear buds. The music drowns out the congregation's off-key notes and lessens my anxiety regarding Griffin Maynor. When the hymn winds down, and everyone is repositioning themselves on the pew, I can see Reverend Ross mouthing for us to, "Bow our heads in prayer for the blessings we are about to receive."

Even though I can't hear him over the tune blaring through my Regency TR-1 with the black leather case, I have sat through the same prayer a hundred times in preparation for communion. "Great father," Spicer begins, adding a pause for dramatic effect, "forgive us sinners for the evil deeds that we have perpetrated against your word. We will one day lift our heads in joy, knowing that the sadness that we have caused you in this life, the tears begotten by gluttony, perverseness and greed..."

Dad is setting next to me on one side with his head bobbing ever so slightly, as he begins to nod off. Momma, on my opposite side notices and reaches across my back to nudge him back to wakefulness. Just as she is about to poke him on the shoulder, her wedding ring catches the cord to my ear bud and pulls it free from the input on my transistor radio. Before I even realize what has happened, the reverent silence within Freedom Baptist is totally violated by Ray Charles crooning at seventy decibels, "Oh, it's cryin' time again, you're gonna leave me."

I'm frantically slapping my pants pocket trying to find the volume, the minister's jaw drops in disbelief, and every bifocal-ed eye in the congregation, including Fess Shifflet who is three quarters comatose and wouldn't know that his throat was on fire while you pissed in his mouth, stare directly at me in unabashed contempt.

Standing and pulling the radio from my pocket, the transistor slides from my sweat covered hand and bounces under the pew in front of us. Dad, no longer showing signs of drowsiness, roughly grabs me by the shirt collar and drags me down the aisle towards the back of the church. Momma searches frantically for the radio under the pew, while Ray's message for the congregation continues, "Well, well, well, it won't be long before it's cryin' time." A couple of hundred eyes watch as I pass their pews, my legs intermittently running and then dragging with Dad lifting me off of the maroon carpet runner by the nape of my neck.

My gaze unintentionally locks on Mayor Maynor's surly stare, and that one look supersedes the panic and embarrassment I'm experiencing in knowing the hot water that I've thrown myself into with my parents. Where all of the other parishioners hold me in contempt and disgust, the mayor's eyes indicate a calculating quality, cunningly assessing opportunity, as he sizes me up.

Pulling me from the sanctuary and down a short flight of stairs that lead to a hallway of Sunday School rooms, I hear Ray Charles finally go mute, and Ross Spicer apologize then continue with the communion ceremony. Dad nearly tears the loop off of his dress pants as he jerks out his belt and folds it in half for maximum control. He leads me into an empty children's classroom, paper cut-outs of Jesus herding a flock of sheep crayon colored earlier this morning are taped to nearly every square inch of the cinder block walls. I look at the tile floor, knowing what's coming and focus on Dad's heavily spit and polished dress boots; Spider Killers, he proudly labels the footwear, because of their pointy toes that can adeptly squash any arachnid crawling in the corner of a room.

Dad still hasn't said a word as he begins to heartily flail the back of my legs and ass with the thick, brown belt. Tears roll down my face, and my hind end burns like fire, but I know better than to wail excuses. After five or six hard lashes, and having reached satisfaction that he has made his intended impression, both on my ass and my psyche, he slides the belt back through the loops in his pants. With frustration and disappointment more than anger, he finally speaks, "Bubba, you know better than pulling that kind of stunt at church. Boy, you're ten...almost eleven years old. Your momma is goin' to be fit to be tied." One of the great things about my dad is that when he gets worked up, which is pretty dang often, he calms down just as fast. After the quick, effective punishment, he is ready to help figure out a way to minimize the repercussions, especially with Momma.

"I'm sorry, Pa," I respond through short intakes of breath, fighting to hold back more waterworks, "the last thing that I would want to do would be to embarrass you and Momma. I don't know what I was thinkin'."

A slight smile lifts the corners of Dad's mouth that he doesn't try to conceal. "Spicer's sermons would make anybody that wasn't half asleep pray for intervention before they were to die of boredom. Hell, it's the first time I've seen Fess Shifflet act like more than a tomato plant in years." Dad starts walking towards the open door of the room, then turns and adds, "You best stay put 'til after the service so as the good reverend don't come out of the pulpit and kick your bony ass, too. I figure that he's pretty pissed, and rightfully so. I don't want to have to tangle with him and your momma. When we get home, you can spend the afternoon cleaning the beagle pen. It's been needin' it a plenty for some time. Plus, it will keep you out of the house and away from your momma."

"Yes, sir," I respond gratefully, knowing that an afternoon shoveling dog logs would be an end to my punishment, at least until Momma got in her two cents worth.

****

Dad has been gone for a couple of minutes, and I've plopped myself down on one of the way too small colorful tyke chairs to stare out of the Sunday School classroom window and lament my transgressions. This room served as the other fourth grade class during the school year, while the new school was being built, but the desk and chairs have been returned to tyke size now that the elementary school year is complete.

Movement behind me pulls me from my thoughts about last year, and I turn expecting to see Dad telling me it's time to head home. Lord, I hope that's the reason and not that he's reconsidered my punishment after getting an earful from Momma.

Instead, it's a much shorter figure blocking the doorway, captured in the glare from the window of the room across the hall. At first, I can't make out the person's identity, but as he takes a step further into the Sunday school room, Mayor Griffin Maynor's profile becomes clear. All of my survival instincts instruct me to bolt for the door but, thankfully, that initial response was quickly replaced by an understanding of what that action would probably mean to Maynor.

The mayor, looking much spryer and imposing than he had when he entered the church with Lady Louise earlier, waits a few moments, probably considering how best to proceed, then says in his gravelly drawl, "You're Arle Armentrout's boy."

Although a statement rather than a question, I force back the panic welling in my chest and respond, "Yes, sir. Robert, after my granddiddy, but everybody calls me Bubba."

"Well, Bubba. That was quite the scene that you made."

Goosebumps run up and down my spine with the fear that he might be referring to last night instead of this morning in church, until he adds, "I trust that your father wore your backside out?"

With a sigh of relief, I exclaim, "Yes, sir. He sure did. It will be a cold day in Hades before I do anything like that again."

"Good, good." He feigns satisfaction and shakes his head in acknowledgment. "Children today are finding far too many ways to make themselves a nuisance by disrupting the lives of God-fearing folks, and most fail to receive adequate punishment for their deeds." I sense that there is an underlying meaning in his words that go deeper than the incident at the church.

"I have an issue, Bubba," he continues sternly, glancing back into the hall to ensure that no one is within listening distance, "that you just might be able to assist me with."

All of my internal organs decide to take up residence in my throat as I croak, "What kind of issue, Mayor Maynor?"

"A despicable issue, Bubba. Someone," he pauses, slowly considering his next words, "a very BAD someone, came by my home last night, the place where I make VERY important decisions regarding our beautiful town, and performed a horribly destructive act involving firecrackers." Maynor takes two large

strides forward, covering half the distance between the door and my chair by the window.

It is all that I can do not to make a break for the hallway, realizing that I'll probably need to bowl over the mayor to get there, when I remember the dog and rock tactic. Man, I bet that the old bastard is using the same strategy now for his own purposes.

So instead of running, I provide a questioning look, and intentionally make my voice as calm as possible, "Firecrackers, sir?"

He watches me intently for a second, then continues, "Yes, firecrackers. I know that many of you little shits in town enjoy setting off those dangerous, and I might add…illegal, tools of the devil, but I won't stand for this intrusion of my privacy and destruction of my property. Do YOU know anyone, Bubba," he says my name like it has a nasty taste, as it passes over his lips, "who might be in possession of those illicit monstrosities?"

My first inclination is to scream, "It wasn't me!" but instead pretend that I am in deep thought, then casually reply, "Me and my buddies was doin' some river fishin' last Fourth of July down near where Tryon Road forks at the dam. Vince Spenser, Senior and some of his cronies from work was drinkin' beer and shootin' off bottle rockets on the edge of his property. That's the only time that I can remember anybody setting off fireworks 'cept the Freedom Fire Department's yearly show, Fourth of July, at Moncross High." I'm gaining confidence and decide to poke the bear just a little, "You might want to ask Mr. Jim Byrd if there's any missing from what they've bought to set off in a few weeks."

The mayor's left eye has a perceptible twitch when I mention Byrd's name, as if he started to grimace and caught himself. I let silence rule the moment, but want to help alleviate any suspicions that the mayor might have about me, so eventually I add, "I asked Pa if we could buy some from Mr. Spenser the next time that we see him at Gee's Grocery or Cline's Barbershop, but he said no because they are illegal. Dad said that he knew kids when he was young that blew their fingers clean off messin' with 'em." I hold up both of my hands and wiggle all ten fingers for effect.

Although difficult to tell for certain from his stoic reaction, Mayor Maynor seems reasonably satisfied with my response and says, "Your father made a wise decision. Every parent should be so practical and persuasive." He purses his lips, contemplating for a minute, then confides, "This is a very sensitive issue for me, Bubba. If I am to catch the perpetrator of this heinous act, and I will, then I need for our little conversation to remain SOLELY between YOU and ME." Stepping towards me and placing his hands on each of my shoulders, squeezing ever so slightly, he whispers ominously, "Can I trust that you can do that, Bubba? We wouldn't want this incident to get ugly, now would we?"

"I'm as trustworthy as the day is long, mayor," I say with all of the conviction and believability that I can muster. "I hope that whoever caused your troubles gets the same strappin' that my Pa just laid on me."

"Oh, I'll see that they get that and more, Bubba. Much, much more." I can nearly smell the threats left hanging in the air, like sulfur from a bathroom match, as the mayor quietly exits the classroom.

Exhausted from my conversation with Griffin Maynor, having needed to taste each word carefully before it came out of my mouth, I am more certain than ever of two things; that the mayor is responsible for what happened to Ester Yoncey and Betsy Mae, and if I'm not careful as heck, he is more than capable of adding me to that list. Sometimes when you hit an ol' dog with a rock, you can make him pretty damn vicious.

Chapter 9

Traffic Stop

Late August 1969

I have laid low and stayed off of Mayor Griffin Maynor's radar since the church incident, so I'm no closer to having him fingered today for the shit he did than I was back in June. I'd seen him around town a coupla' times since he had confronted me, once in the Moncross High parking lot having his Caddy washed and waxed by the basketball team who were tryin' to raise money for a fall trip to an eastern shore tournament, and again at the monthly lawn party on the Baptist Church grounds, meeting and greeting his taxpaying constituents. I don't think that he saw me neither time. At church, I been volunteering to fold chairs in the adult Sunday classes before church service, and hustling out to talk with other kids or staying close to Momma and Dad afterwards. For whatever reason, he ain't paid me no mind. So, for the most part, I've made dang sure not to draw Griffin's ire, or attention, by showin' up in the vicinity of anywhere that he was likely to be. It ain't like we run in the same circles, anyway.

It's not that I'm any less infatuated with getting the truth out, or that the events of nearly two years ago are weighing any lighter on my mind. The main reason that I have avoided the old codger like a bad case of the scabies is that with age comes wisdom, as Jack Lipsay is apt to say, and after our conversation at the church, I have no doubts that Maynor will kill me if he finds out that I'm the anonymous letter writer and mail box destroyer. After much consideration, I've decided that I'll just need to bide my time until I can come up with a sure-fire plan, or the perfect opportunity comes my way to out the rotten bastard. An alive and kickin' Bubba is a whole lot more likely to leash that mangy mongrel than a dead as doornails Bubba.

Today is the last Saturday before Labor Day, and summer freedom ends next week with the beginning of school on Tuesday. Timmy Wyatt and me have been cooped up for the better part of the last two weeks as the weather in Freedom has gone through a spell where we've had rain nearly every day. Tonight, is our first chance in a while to camp out in his backyard, and to enjoy a little diversion from the angst and worryin' that I've been experiencing. As Grannie Bess says, some fun will be good for my soul.

I spent most of the morning with my buddy exploring the old cinder block chicken house behind the Wyatt's home. It's been almost a year since we've looked for hidden treasures in the nooks and crannies of the neglected building. The hens from the chicken house have either flown the coop, or been eaten for Sunday dinner long ago because the crumbling construction is now only used for storing all of the Wyatt family castaway junk too old to use and too good to trash. While creeping past tangled mesh wire cages and metal feeders, we pretend to search ancient caves for hidden gold or, possibly, the lost tribal civilizations that once lived here. Torn rags tied to a broken broomstick, ablaze with gasoline siphoned from Bob Wyatt's lawn mower, light our way. Long forgotten magazines littering the cracked concrete floor became manuscripts and maps pointing the way to the X marking buried treasure, and discarded clothes in moldy, cardboard boxes were perfect disguises to infiltrate enemy camps. A broken radio with its cord chewed off by a rat, and the shell of an ancient black and white television tossed in a corner, coated in crusty petrified chicken shit, became our electronic equipment to decode the ultra-secret messages from our make-believe commander.

During the afternoon, after we prepare a hearty lunch of tomato and mayonnaise sandwiches accompanied by Cap'n Crunch cereal lathered in Karo syrup (Flo Wyatt wouldn't have thawed a frozen pizza for the Pope), we had toted a metal ladder borrowed from my dad's workshop and propped it against the side of the chicken house not visible from Flo's beauty shop. After checking to make sure that the rungs were securely clasped (a lesson that Dad taught me when I helped him put on a new roof on Grandma and Granddiddy's house), we crawled onto the scalding tin roof, and jumped from the single-story cinder block building into a pile of rotting potatoes pulled from Bob Wyatt's prized garden. There was a higher than normal potato pile because the constant rain had made harvesting the vegetables at the appropriate time nearly impossible.

A little after dark, we had gathered up a batch of hard, green apples that had fallen from the tree in Timmy's front yard, and toted them in a large burlap sack to a strategic area of his backyard. We proceeded to pull the apples from the *bag, and stack them in ammo piles next to the picket fence separating the Wyatt homestead from the widow woman's house next door, Mrs. Golden Jennings. Golden, and her late husband, Picard, who had been bayoneted to death like a shish kebob in World War I, hadn't had any children of their own, and she made it perfectly clear, every chance that she got, that aging hadn't helped her embrace the idea of having tykes within shouting distance of her house. Golden is reaching the dead end of life's highway, and she definitely wants to burst through that guardrail and over the edge of the cliff without any damn kids annoying her on the short trip.*

Each Halloween, Golden turns off all of the lights in her house and positions herself on the porch with a pellet gun by her side. Any brat approaching for candy or mischief is greeted by a spray of metal that helps to ensure that the 'Lil Bastards' won't trespass on her land in the future.

One Christmas, Momma prepared a plate of leftovers to take to Golden as a Christian gesture, and asked me to tag along. Before we could reach her front door, Golden came out on her porch and yelled, "Can't you see the No Trespass sign on my fence. Are you blind?" Momma had calmly stated that we had leftovers from Christmas dinner, and thought that she might enjoy the meal.

Golden informed us that 'she was perfectly capable of fixin' her own damn dinner', and slammed the door in our faces before Momma could say another word. Bitter old bitch!

Tonight, me and Timmy had set up camp behind the wooden picket fence on the Wyatt lot, apple ammo in place on each side of us, with a perfect view of Golden Jenning's house. Our canteens were filled with Grape Kool-Aid, and we had enough deviled ham and crackers to gag a maggot off a gut wagon. We waited for the half-blind woman to retire to her upstairs bedroom for the evening, and we knew that she had when a bedside light flicked on beside the shadeless, screened window. Providing Golden a couple of minutes to get ready for bed and settle in all comfortable, when the light in the room was turned off, we bombarded her tin roof with nature's grenades. After each round of apple tosses, the bang as they bounced on the roof and then the roll as the apples made their way to the gutter, Golden's bedside light would pop on and she would scream obscenities in our direction through the screened window. We figured that she'd had enough when, after an emphysema-sized coughing spell, she had stood silently at her window watching for movement from down below. Sensing that we might have pushed her just a bit too far, and fearful that she might call the Bankston police if we kept it up, we crawled to Timmy's back porch military style, crabbing on our stomachs and slipped quietly into his house with Golden Jennings still perched at her window scanning the yard for the source of her irritation.

****

Bob and Flo Wyatt are gone for the evening, deciding to drop in on a dance at the Moose Lodge in Bankston, leaving the two of us, and Ben, in the care of Timmy's older sister, Beth. Ben is already napping on the couch in front of the television where he has been watching Detective Steve McGarrett solve a case involving a bikinied babe on Hawaii Five-O. I think that it's a rerun, but can't tell for sure since nearly every episode includes half-naked girls; not that I'm complaining. Beth is preoccupied with gabbing on the phone with one of her girlfriends about some new flame that she has the hotty-twatty for, and is paying zero attention to us. Her record player is blasting 'Hang on Sloopy' and her bedroom door closes when me and Timmy come in from our apple throwing escapade to grab a couple of blankets for camping out.

We've decided on camping in the bed of Bob Wyatt's '56 Chevy pick-up truck that he uses for his construction business, when my buddy validates that idle hands are the Devil's workshop. We have been challenging each other to see who can produce the loudest and longest deviled ham fart by placing our asses over the camper holes in the truck bed, when Timmy muses, "You 'member last Halloween when we took one of Ma's dress alteration mannequins and tossed it in the road to see if we could scare a driver?"

"Yeah," I chuckle, "those Moncross High guys would have killed us if they had found us up in your apple tree."

"Naw," Timmy responds, a wide grin covering his entire face as he shakes his head, "we were just funnin'. What say we give it another shot tonight? Ma and Pa won't be home for hours, and you said that your parents are over at your Uncle Rick's for the evening." Then, as if reading my mind that I'm frettin' about his big sister tattling on us when Timmy's parents get home, he continues, "We surely don't need to worry 'bout Beth. She's so damn busy talkin' 'bout gettin' laid that she doesn't even know or care that we're here."

"I don't know, Timmy," I say hesitantly. "What if ol' Mrs. Jennings has called the Bankston 'po-pos' to come and see who's been throwin' apples on her roof?"

Timmy exhales, exasperated, like I have asked the dumbest question known to man. "Pa said that she calls them about crazy shit that she sees and hears all the time. They quit comin' after the time she swore to them that her dead husband's picture on the mantle over the fireplace was tellin' her that the cows had broke through the fence and were out on the highway."

"Mrs. Jennings ain't had livestock since we've lived here," I question, trying to determine if Timmy is bullshitting me.

"Exactly," says Timmy laughing. "Not to mention WHO told her that they had knocked down the fence! The 'po-pos' sure as shit ain't gonna come all the way out here from Bankston over a couple of apples that MIGHT have fallen on her roof. That is, unless Picard Jennings calls 'em from the mantle." We both break out in unrestrained belly laughs, before he adds, "Anyways, the police are the ones that told Pa about her acting all crazy, and asked if Ma and Pa would keep an eye on her. Pa told 'em that she ain't one that likes others in her business."

What Timmy is saying makes some sense, I guess, so I finally agree. "I reckon' it might be fun, so long as we're careful not to get caught."

"Sure, sure," Timmy responds, immediately jumping over the side panels of his dad's truck, and heads for the house. "Don't you worry 'bout a thing, Bubba."

****

A short time later, Timmy has gotten one of Flo's alteration mannequins that she uses to 'take up' or 'let out' the local's clothes in her side business. The white, Styrofoam body is covered in a gray wool sweater and plaid skirt that he retrieved from a cardboard box that we saw earlier today in the chicken house. A blond wig from a Halloween costume, probably Marilyn Monroe, sits cockeyed on the mannequin's lopsided head. I have tied a pair of knee-high women's boots that I scavenged from the clothes Momma is collecting for Goodwill to cover the metal base and provide Marilyn legs not included with the stand. Timmy adds the final touch by pouring nearly an entire bottle of Heinz ketchup over the Styrofoam form from wig to boots, and then attaches one end of a roll of twine

111

to the base of the mannequin. Taking Marilyn to the apple tree near the brick fence bordering Route 23, he unrolls the twine and tosses the loose end over the first branch of the tree.

"Go ahead and climb the tree, Bubba. I'll take Marilyn to the road. Grab the twine as you go up."

"Are you sure this is a good idea, Timmy?" I say nervously, but he has already cleared the Wyatt driveway and the cut-off to Schoolhouse Road, and is placing the mannequin on the double yellow line of Route 23.

Timmy is back in a flash, grabbing the first branch and swinging himself up to get footing for the climb. I'm on a thick limb near the middle of the tree that provides good cover and, most importantly, a perfect view of the road in front of the Wyatt's house and a quarter-mile stretch of Route 23 in both directions. Timmy can sense my concern, as he slides in beside me on the thick branch, and I hand him the twine, "Sit tight and relax, Bubba. After the driver plows over our bloody babe, I'll pull her up here with us before they even get turned around to see what they hit. No problem! We'll get some chuckles while they search the road, but when they can't find Marilyn, they'll be on their merry way. Ain't nuthin' bad that can happen."

Sensing my continued reservations, he adds emphatically, "Look, the only reason that the carload of Moncross football players nearly caught us last Halloween was 'cause the damn string broke and left the dummy hanging on our fence in front of the house."

He holds up the twine to my eyes so that I can see it in the dark, "See, I doubled the twine up this time!"

Suddenly, the faint glare of headlights slice through the night coming from the direction of the Ruritan Club Hall a short piece down Route 23. My heart is pounding with uncertainty that transforms into dread, as the vehicle passes near the all-night florescent lights over the pumps outside of Holt's Gas Station.

I grasp the branch above me to keep from falling out of the apple tree, light-headed and dizzy with fear. The car, flashing by the pumps at what looks like the speed of sound, heading directly for our ketchup covered Marilyn, is a white Cadillac. A FAMILIAR WHITE CADILLAC!

Feeling nauseated like after a gut punch to the stomach, realizing what is about to play out before my very eyes, I scream, "HOLY SHIT, PULL THE TWINE!"

Timmy jumps from my sudden outburst and bumps his head on the tree limb above us, but continues to hold the twine slack while gazing at me dumbfounded. "OUCH, Bubba. What's the matter..." he begins, but I have already jerked the twine from his hand and yanked as hard as I can, yelling, "IT'S MAYOR MAYNOR'S CADILLAC! MRS JENNINGS MUSTA' CALLED HIM WHEN THE POLICE WOULDN'T COME!"

The mannequin hops in the center of the road like a goosed jackrabbit with my initial tug, and then rolls head over base as I haphazardly pull it through the culvert beside the highway and over the brick fence beside the Wyatt driveway. Time is moving like the Twilight Zone clock as Marilyn clunks to the base of the apple tree, her wig lying in the middle of Schoolhouse Road, and her boots standing askew halfway between the driveway and the tree. Unfortunately for us, my reaction time was a little too slow. The Cadillac's driver had obviously seen the mannequin jump off of the pavement in the car's headlights, because the vehicle is now slowing to a stop near the Wyatt's driveway entrance. A streak of disrupted gravel shows the path that Marilyn took on her way to the apple tree.

"RUN, TIMMY!" I yell frantically, shimmying down the tree trunk as if it's a fireman's pole. When Timmy, paralyzed with fear, fails to follow, I grab him by the leg and pull him after me. With the friction increasing from my slide down the bark, I lose my grip on his sweaty leg near the lowest branch, and fall with a heavy thud to the ground. Landing on my back with a gnarly protruding tree root tearing my shirt and poking into my ribs, a second later, Timmy's falling torso lands on top of mine breaking his fall but knocking every breath of air out of me. I heave, chest pumping up and down, gasping to suck oxygen into my deflated lungs, but they remain as flat as a dry rotted bike tire. Certain that I've broken my back and will be paralyzed for life, it takes every ounce of effort that I can muster to whip my head back and forth, trying to locate the mayor.

Maynor's Caddy remains running with its headlights casting a wide glow over the yard between his car and our sprawled bodies.

Although I can't pinpoint exactly where Griffin is because of the glare, I can see that he has left his driver side door open when he exited the vehicle.

Timmy, in a failed attempt to crawl off of me on all fours, knees me in the crotch sending the bile from the tomato and mayonnaise sandwich that I ate earlier today into my already burning throat. Pushing my buddy off of me, cramping from the needles in my nuts while still gasping to draw air, I'm somehow able to get to my knees, and then finally into a crouched stance. I reach

113

down, grab Timmy's T-shirt and lift him from the ground. The best that I can manage is to croak urgently, "Run for the field." I can only hope that he can understand my breathless words or, at least, read my lips.

Evidently, I got the message across because Timmy shoots into the night like a bullet, the bottoms of his Converse tennis shoes nearly flapping his ass as he crosses his yard into the field beyond the chicken house. This time of year, the grass and bramble are so thick that he should be able to find a safe hiding spot. I follow as best I can, more lunging than running, continuing to struggle to inflate the burning, compressed balloons in my chest.

Suddenly, just as I'm beginning to taste the freedom of the warm night, picking up speed in my pumping legs and gulping air that's finally fueling my regeneration, a bony leg juts out from behind a Hydrangeas bush when I'm about to pass. My feet fly out from under me as I connect with the appendage, and I slide face first across the pebbles surrounding the plant and the dew-covered grass. Spitting out blades of grass and dust, nose bloodied, and a raw patch of friction burn on my chin, I feel the hard leather sole of a shoe land in the small of my back, pinning me to the ground. Well, now I know where the mayor is; he must have chased Timmy, and when he couldn't catch him, waited in hiding for me to pass.

"So, Mr. Armentrout," Griffin Maynor says condescendingly, a smug expression covering his leathery face, "we meet again. After our last conversation, I had high hopes that you might be the rare exception to lessons learned. Now, it appears that it is going to require the local authorities to deter this deviant behavior of yours."

As frightfully scared as I am of the mayor, and of the prospects of facing the Bankston police, those outcomes take a back seat to my absolute certainty that if the mayor involves the authorities, no one will ever believe me, proof or no proof, about Maynor's crimes. After all, they'd think that I was using my tale to get back at him, and slip myself off of the hook. Plus, with the beatin' I'll get at home, I won't need a desk to sit on at school for a week.

"Cat got your tongue, boy?" the mayor continues, pulling me by my shirt to my feet. "Throwing apples on an elderly woman's roof, scaring her nearly to death. Then, potentially causing a severe accident on our town road with obviously no regard for human life. I suspect that those actions are quite sufficient enough for the Bankston police to prescribe significant time in reform *school, if not formal charges for you and your friend. It will be my pleasure to provide that recommendation."*

Holy shit, I hadn't even considered that throwin' a few apples and participating in a little prank could get you sentenced to reform school! With no time to think, the situation already way out of hand, I know that I need to act fast and come big. Staring directly into the mayor's steely gray eyes, snarling like a rabid dog, I declare with as much piss and vinegar as I can muster, "I KNOW what YOU did at the school, you SON-OF-A-BITCH! I saw the whole thing, YOU and MRS BYRD, and YOUR argument with PRINCIPAL YONCEY! I hope you fry in Hell for offin' Betsy Mae. GO AHEAD AND CALL THE POLICE, ASSHOLE! GO RIGHT AHEAD!"

Obviously stunned by my unexpected outburst, and my rebellious response to his threats, Mayor Maynor releases his grasp on my collar and drops his hands to his sides. Griffin's body goes as limp as a newly wet washrag, and he stares silently in my direction, almost as if he is looking through me instead of at me. The pause provides me the time I need to turn on my heels and haul ass for the field. With a quick glance back over my shoulder as I pass the chicken house, suspecting that the mayor will be lunging for my backside, I'm surprised to see that he has dropped to his knees in the dewy, late August grass. I can't tell what's goin' through his mind, but I ain't slowin' down to ask him. One thing that I am certain of as I disappear into the night, I gotta find a way to prove the mayor's terrible deeds, otherwise, I'll need to be spendin' all of my time figurin' out how to stay alive.

Chapter 10
Close Call

Early September 1969

Seeing Davey Grater back at school on Tuesday after Labor Day helped jump my spirits out of the fog that they've been sloppin' around in since the Saturday night altercation with the mayor. In addition to all of the other mumbo-jumbo that had happened last year, the good stuff like having Mrs. Lamplier as a teacher, and the bad in trying to handle the Mayor Maynor situation, Davey's parents' bait and tackle shop had gone out of business right before the fourth-grade school year began. Ever since the pharmaceutical plant upriver started producing a medicine for high blood pressure in the early '60s, and funneled the waste from the drug into the Shenandoah River, the fish population, especially bass and crappie, have nearly gone to hell in a hand basket. Davey's pop, never having much gumption to begin with, had moved the family up to Cloverdale in neighboring Nelson County for a new job. Seems like I remember it being a counter salesman at a gun shop, or somethin' similar to that. Anyways, Dad says that Ralph Grater is gonna struggle with that job 'cause he was used to being able to go fishing in the afternoon most days when he owned his own business. There ain't much free time when you're workin' for somebody else.

After a year away from his friends, and Davey struggling mightily at his new school, his parents have sent him back to stay with his Grandma Grater so he can attend class this year at the new Freedom Elementary.

What with all of the crazy shit goin' on in Freedom, Davey's tales about his teacher in Cloverdale, and her girlfriend with a crew cut, jeans and string tie that came to pick her up after school each day, are a welcome relief.

The new Freedom Elementary School is also a breath of fresh air. From the brightly painted and colorful hallways, and the spotless linoleum tiles, to the shiny stainless steel freezers and cooking equipment in the lunchroom, the school

116

has the same feel as an early April mornin' when the first blades of bright green spring grass peek through the thawed Virginia dirt; kinda' helps you forget the trials and tribulations of the previous winter. None of the classes will be able to go outside for recess until the construction workers pour the cement for the sidewalks into the wooden frames that have stood empty waiting for the wet, red mud to dry enough to receive the mortar. Mayor Maynor has postponed the dedication of the new school from the end of August until this coming Sunday afternoon in hopes that the delays caused by the late summer monsoon-like weather is over, and all of the construction and landscaping is completed. Peering through the spotless windows of Mrs. Kent's fifth grade classroom at the playground and the muddy, wooden framed areas leading towards it, my guess is that the delayed dedication will probably still take place before the workers are entirely done.

Even stuck inside the classroom working jigsaw puzzles of the United States, or in the gym playing kickball against Timmy Wyatt's fifth grade class hasn't taken away from the positive vibes that the new building is producing in helping to bury the rotten apple that the burnt school had become. If Reverend Spicer was to describe the new Freedom Elementary, he would probably call it an educational Eden. And the congregation replies Amen. Unfortunately for me, an old serpent named Mayor Griffin Maynor still lurks prominently in this field of bliss.

And speaking of the snake, I haven't seen hide nor hair of Griffin since I hauled ass into the field on Saturday night. After finally catching up to Timmy, who had been hiding in a honeysuckle tangle that hissed at me as I shot by, I stopped just long enough to tell him what had happened with the mayor, and we quickly decided that the best idea was to head to our own homes and wait to see what happened next, if anything. I had paced back and forth down the hallway in front of my bedroom, and then laid awake in bed, alone in the house, covers pulled up over my head and nervous as a whore in church, waiting for the doorbell to ring with either the mayor or the Bankston Police standing on the other side of the door. My anxiety continued to grow when neither happened; at least a confrontation with the police on Saturday night, as bad as that would have been, would have ended the nightmare. When no one showed, it not only prolonged my agony, but justified my fear that I just might be next on Mayor Griffin Maynor's hit list. In my head, I can almost see Dick Clark pulling the slat from the NUMBER 1 position on the round American Bandstand Top 10 board, and Bubba Armentrout coming in at the choice spot to be the most likely to meet and greet the late Ester Yoncey; if I could make the grade of achieving eternal bliss like her.

On Sunday morning, figuring that I was well on my way to Hell anyway, conveniently forgetting my fervent promise to Jesus to never miss another day of church for all of the transgressions that I had recently accumulated, I faked a fever by running the thermometer under hot water in the bathroom sink right before Momma came in to shake me awake for Sunday school. The last thing that I wanted to do was run into the mayor at church, and this was the only way that I could figure to avoid that potential confrontation. I dang near burst the thermometer before I realized that it had risen above 107 degrees, and needed to let the mercury cool down before producing it as evidence of me taking ill. Momma and Dad had gotten home well after midnight from Uncle Rick's place, so she didn't question me too much when I told her that I came home early from Timmy's after puking my guts up on the Wyatt living room floor in the middle of a game of checkers. Shoot, what was one more little white lie?

I had anxiously waited the next coupla' hours for them to come home from church, almost hoping that the mayor had blown the whistle to them on what had happened the night before. I really did feel sick by the time that Momma came into my room and checked my forehead for a fever before saying, "You look flush, Bubba, but it seems like your fever has broken." After a kiss on my cheek, she headed to the kitchen to prepare our sit-down Sunday dinner.

Monday morning, Labor Day, Momma fixed a picnic lunch for our family and we headed out to the community park in Sweeton, another thirty miles north of Bankston, to swelter in the last hot rays of summer, and watch the Statler Brothers in concert with three-thousand other sweating 'Flowers on the Wall' fans. While I moped around the grassy area of the park where we had eaten our lunch, Momma and Dad thinking that I was still under the ill effects of the flu that had overtaken me on Saturday night, left me alone to wallow in my thoughts on what in the Hell to do next regarding the mayor. Minutes before the concert was to begin in the evening, I made the decision to bare all that I know about Griffin Maynor to Dad, and then hope for the best. Whether or not he would believe me, at least he would know where to start lookin' if I vanished, or worse yet, if they found me pushin' up daises.

Dad was standing by the tailgate of his '52 Chevy pickup, loading the last remnants of our picnic into the truck's bed, when I reluctantly walked over to

118

him and asked, "Pa, you 'member when you told me that I needed to let you know if I ever felt like I had anything on my mind that I couldn't handle by myself?"

He crawled up into the bed of the truck and pushed the basket filled with dirty cloth napkins and utensils to the back near the cab, then turned to me and responded, "I do. You got somethin' that you're chewin' on, Bubba, that we need to talk about?"

Looking up at him, the wear of working outdoors and the tribulations of our family issues unable to hide the physical strength and character he possesses, I stuck my hands in the pockets of my jeans, shifted uncomfortably from side to side and tried to find the words that I had been practicing over and over in my head all afternoon. Resolved to get it out in the open, I stuttered, "I know somethin'...saw somethin' that's really weighin' heavy on...". At that critical moment, Aunt Jane Armentrout, Rick's wife and Dad's sister-in-law, arms flailing like a windmill in a tornado, ran across the open area where we had been picnicking, yelling "Arle! Arle! I been a lookin' for you all afternoon!"

Dad spun around towards her wailing voice, then quickly hopped down from the bed of the Chevy and grabbed her in a bear hug. Aunt Jane, looking terror stricken, tears dripping from her chin, stared into Dad's eyes and moaned in despair, "They've come and arrested Rick! I told 'em he didn't take any money, but they wouldn't listen. They handcuffed him and took him away!"

"Just calm down, Jane," Dad said, deep concern seeping through his attempt at a composed demeanor. "Tell me EXACTLY what happened."

"I told you! They TOOK him...AWAY!" Aunt Jane screamed, nearly incoherently. "The Sheriff said that they found more evidence, and that they're afraid that he might try and run off afore the trial."

"It's gonna be alright. Where did they take him?" Dad prodded for an answer.

"To the Bankston City Jail," Jane whimpered, her energy being drained by emotion. "The law said that the charge is being increased from misappropriation of funds to embezzlement. Then a Deputy read him his rights, and threw Rick in the back of a squad car."

"OK, that's what I needed to know. Everything is gonna be OK," Dad repeated, almost as if trying to convince himself as much as Aunt Jane. It's nearly a transformation that I could see happening before my eyes, as the weight of this responsibility for his brother was causing deeper crevices in the wrinkles around Pa's sunburned eyes. "Let's go and see if we can get this straightened out."

Turning his head in my direction, while still grasping Jane in a vice-like grip, he said, "Bubba, go find your momma, and then y'all head home in the truck. She was tryin' to find a place to wash out the potato salad bowl the last time that I saw her. Tell her that I have gone to the Bankston Police Station with Aunt Jane, and that I'll call her as soon as I know somethin'." With that directive, he turned Jane towards the parking lot to find her car, more carrying his sister-in-law through the crowd settling in for the concert than leading her.

After searching the park for what seemed like an eternity, I found Momma coming back from the public restrooms where she has been cleaning baked beans and potato salad from her good cookware. Although she tried to minimize the Uncle Rick predicament for my benefit, I could see in her expression that she was deeply troubled with the news, even though it wasn't totally unexpected. We headed home in near silence, Momma stripping the gears of the manual transmission in the old truck with every shift, worrying about Dad and Rick, with me self-absorbed in trying to figure out how to handle the Mayor Maynor deal all by myself.

****

That's pretty much how this week has gone. Today, Friday, I'm getting ready for school, finishing off my first week of fifth grade, with all of my troubles still dragging along behind me like dingle-berries on a dog's butt. At least tomorrow is Saturday and, hopefully, I'll have some time over the weekend to sort through things. Momma and Dad have spent most of the week in Bankston, or at Aunt Jane's, so Grannie Bess has been stayin' at our house tryin' to keep life as normal as possible; which in my case, ain't normal at all. With everything that Dad has on him right now, it probably ain't right to throw the mayor shit his way, too. Heck, I ain't heard for sure if him and Momma are coming home tonight, anyways.

Grannie Bess has prepared a full course breakfast of eggs, fried ham, biscuits and sausage gravy for me this morning; pretty much the same as every other day this week. And, like those other mornings, I disinterestedly flop the greasy food around my overflowing plate with my fork, eating nearly nothing and thinking only about my potential demise at the hands of Mayor Maynor.

"Bubba, you're not eating enough to keep a fly alive." Grannie Bess says, faking a stern look. "Listen, your Uncle Rick is going to be just fine. Don't you

120

worry so dadgum much about things that you don't have any control over. Now, you best get that mop of yours combed and shove off for school. I don't want to be getting any calls from Principal Nutley!" Grannie Bess is well aware that Freedom Elementary School's new principal is named Nockley, but she also knows that she can always get a chuckle out of me when she mispronounces his last name.

Playing along, I respond by grinning genuinely and saying, "Yeah, well why don't you just say it's the wrong number if the 'Nut' calls."

She smiles warmly in a way only a grandma can, an aura of goodness surrounding her, and hugs me to her ample breasts.

Before I can escape to the door, she begins wiping what little sausage gravy that I did manage to get to my face off of my chin with a clean, checkered napkin.

Grandma Bess and Granddiddy Robert only had one child that lived, my momma, Anna. Two other baby boys were stillborn sometime in the early '30s. Probably because of the early deaths of her two male babies, Grannie Bess overcompensates and overprotects me. At times, it can be overwhelming. Where Momma and Dad set rules and punishment if I get caught colorin' outside the book, Grannie Bess assumes full responsibility for keeping me colorin' within the lines. I'm lucky to have folks that care about me, and I've even thought about talking to her about the mayor. Ain't no doubt that it'd be tough discussin' the sex parts with her. She'd probably have a heart attack, and then that would be on my conscience too.

****

With my schoolbag strapped on, and cowlick pressed firmly in place with Grannie Bess spit, I hop on my bike like I have every day that the weather would allow over the past five years, and peddle down Schoolhouse Road on the short trek to school. During the summer, me and Timmy rode our bikes up to the dump on the back edge of town, out past Howard Moomaw's place where we sometimes go in the winter to buy firewood, and pulled two discarded Soap Box Derby cars from the stinking mounds of trash.

We had found those treasures between a rusted-out Frigidaire freezer with its door removed and a dozen broken Bell jars that had leaked somethin' vaguely resembling motor oil. The Derby cars were well beyond a repairable condition, but the steering wheels, covered with racing emblems of checkered flags, were

121

still in pretty good shape. We had pulled the steering wheels from the cars and bolted them to the shafts of our bikes where the handlebars had been. Relearning to steer a bike with a wheel instead of handlebars had taken some time, a learning experience filled with crashes and skinned knees, but we eventually got the hang of it. And, you know what? The modified steering on the bikes are a pretty cool compliment to the squirrel tails flapping in the breeze from the back reflectors, and the ACE playing cards clicking on the spokes. Most of our classmates loved our bikes when they seen them, but a few made fun of the wheels. Timmy and me have chalked that up to jealously, especially when a couple of the ones that had laughed asked us how much that we would take for the unique modifications.

The air, still warm and humid for September, presses against my face, the cowlick so carefully slicked down by Grannie Bess popping up on the back of my head, as I speed down the road to school. Reaching the crest of the hill above the Cheatum brother's house, and continuing to pick up speed on the downward slope, I see movement behind the woodpile near the edge of Stump Cheatum's gravel driveway. I'm flying like the wind when Peanut Cheatum pops into view behind the sloppily stacked logs at the base of the hill. It takes me a few seconds, and that is a few seconds too long, to recognize what he is pushin' towards the asphalt as my Roadmaster achieves hyper-speed. Peanut is rolling an old spare tire towards the middle of Schoolhouse Road, a goofy smile of anticipation on his ruddy face, and directly into the path of my oncoming bike. It is way too late for me to stomp on my brake pedals to avoid a collision with the tire by the time that I realize his intentions. The huge, old tire wobbly rolls into the center of the road, the timing perfect to catch the front wheel of my bike on the metal rim of the truck tire. The Roadmaster comes to an abrupt stop, flipping me headfirst over the bike's steering wheel. The wobbling truck tire falls limply over on top of my body, as I skid ass first, legs straight up in the air, to a grinding halt on the rough pavement.

At the exact moment that my bike peddle scrapes the road, and the Roadmaster rotates one full turn on its side, a green flash, sun reflecting brightly off chrome, shoots out of the vacant lot directly across from the Cheatum house, missing my head by less than three feet. Laying flat on my back, I watch the vehicle speed away with tires squealing, a Green Chevy Impala with no rear license plate to identify it.

Too scared to move, I realize with horror that if not for Peanut's mean-spirited practical joke, the Impala would have crushed me under its heavy carriage a few yards from where my bike fell.

Finally gathering my wits, and standing, I move to the side of the road where the Impala had been hidden to try and comprehend what just happened. Sore as hell, I look down and see scrapes covering my arms and legs, and reach up and feel a small bump on my head. My lip is busted and a little blood trickles out on the back of my hand when I wipe it across my mouth. Other than those issues, it seems that I still have all of my parts and none seem broken. Replaying the last minute over in my head, the action moving in slow motion, I'm struggling to recount the quick series of events. Peanut, who prior to seeing the car burst from cover, had been jumping around exuberantly like Ernest T. Bass after successfully throwing a rock through a window. Now, mischievousness replaced by concern, he runs to me on the far side of Schoolhouse Road and exclaims breathlessly, "Holy Shit, Bubba! I was only funnin'!"

I start to ball my fists, stunned and angry from the spill, and take a determined step towards the juvenile delinquent. Ready to try and knock his damn head off, Peanut takes a defensive step backwards and holds his hands up in surrender. His reaction is even scarier than having to fight him because the way he responds ain't ever been in the Cheatum playbook. Always looking for trouble, and willing to fight dirty, Peanut seems as shocked as I am by the Impala driver's intent,

"Goddamn, whoever was in that fuckin' car musta been layin' low since I came outta the house a few minutes ago. Shit, if I didn't know better, I would swear that they was a tryin' to run over your ass!"

Seeing his unexpected response, I drop my fists and take another look down the road to make sure that the car isn't coming back to finish the job. Apparently, the driver had been as oblivious to Cheatum's hiding place behind the woodpile as Peanut was to his location in the overgrown, tree filled lot across the street. I walk over and check my bike for damage, and unbelievably seeing nothing but broken tire guard chrome, a few bent spokes, and some added scrapes on the metal frame, I say with slight relief, "Peanut, you son-of-a-bitch, I don't know whether to hug you, or try to take your damn head off." With a shrug of my shoulders, my nerves jumping like a wet cat on a power line, I crawl back on my bike and test it for stability.

123

"Yeah, I ain't fightin' you today. Don't mean I won't, but I damn near shit myself when I seen the car headed towards ya'."

"Have you seen that Green Impala before?" I question him, hoping that maybe the driver ran in his daddy's circle of friends.

"No, there ain't one like it in town far as I know. It wasn't there last night late 'cause I was over there lookin' for night crawlers. You notice that there wasn't no license plate?"

"Yeah, I did. Listen, I gotta get to school. I still think you're an asshole, but that ain't gonna change. Can you and your brother ask around and see if anybody knows anything about that car?" I ask, certain that if one of the Cheatum's buddies know the owner, they sure as hell won't tell.

"I'll ask around," he responds, turning towards his house before remembering the truck tire in the road. He spits a glob of phlegm in the gravel, lifts the tire and rolls it behind the woodpile, then heads in the direction of the torn screen door nearly hidden by his cluttered with junk porch.

I point the Roadmaster towards school, and peddle slowly to test its stability and my balance.

My inclinations have been right; the damn mayor has been watching me. He had obviously known that I would be riding my bike to school, just like every other good weather day, and evidently felt that this was his best opportunity to tie up the last of his nasty loose ends. If nothin' else, it's totally clear now that Griffin Maynor ain't gonna rest easy until Bubba Armentrout is totally erased from the picture.

Chapter 11
Lawn Party

Late Fall 2019

Reflection

Timmy Wyatt and I had spent that following Saturday morning looking for the pea green Impala with the shiny, white and chrome top. It wasn't so much that we were dead set on finding the driver, I was certain that it was Griffin Maynor or someone he had hired, but the activity was an exercise that had given young Bubba Armentrout a sense of purpose when the entirety of my world seemed wildly askew. In retrospect, the only positive to the deadly situation that I had found myself thrust into was that, as a child, there were no analogous experiences that I could relate to the magnitude of this one. In essence, I realized that I had fallen in shit, but was too stupid to understand that this brand of feces was cesspool deep and had the qualities of quicksand. Fortunately, with youth comes hope, and the naivety that I possessed in regard to this dilemma, also allowed me to believe that any problem, even one with the potential for the direst of consequences, could somehow be resolved. Crazily, the encounter with the Impala had only strengthened that resolve.

****

September 1969

"Bubba, can we take a break?" Timmy exhales, exhausted from peddling from one end of Freedom's town limits to the other. He leans his bike against a fence post, carefully slides under the electrified barbed wire installed to keep cows off of route 23, and turns his back to take a piss in the field owned by Joe Elby Dixon.

The closest we have come to finding a car similar to the one that had intended to use me as a speed bump yesterday is when we passed Johnson Greeley's tomato stand, down the road a piece from the Post Office, where Ms. Julia Eaton's green Ford Galaxy 500 was setting after picking up a two penny nail in its front tire. Old man Greeley was hitched over at the waist with the arthritis in his back, trying without success to lift the car up with a metal jack that Ms. Julia had produced from the Ford's trunk. When we first arrived, Johnson started tellin' us the troubles he was havin' with the jack, but we couldn't understand a word he was sayin' 'cause his voice comes from a gizmo lodged in a hole in his neck. I saw him at Holt's Gas Station one Saturday a few years back, and he told the guys around the wood stove in the station's office that his doctor had informed him that he was goin' to get a throat ailment if he didn't stop smoking unfiltered cigarettes. I ain't seen him in a while, but it looks like his doctor was spot on.

Anyways, Timmy and me changed Ms. Julia's tire, and she rewarded us with a quarter each for the effort. I was tellin' Timmy about the Good Samaritan story in the bible, and how good deeds get repaid many times over. I don't know that he is totally bought in to the concept, but we sure did have fun spending our money at Gee's Grocery. Between the two of us, we bought a couple of Grape Nehi sodas, a Three Musketeer bar, and a handful of Mary Jane taffy that is still stuck to the fillings in my teeth an hour after cramming four in my mouth at the same time. Now I'm prayin' that the filling doesn't pop out 'cause I damn sure don't wanna' pay a visit to that asshole dentist, Dr Peter Amador.

Outside of helping Ms. Julia, the only other thing that we've accomplished all morning is marveling at the stream of urine that 'Scooter', Mac Shipp's flea bitten and half blind Basset, deposited on the dying shrubs circling Cemetery Hill. Well, that, and stopping for a minute to listen to Johnny Miller and his bluegrass band, 'The Virginia Pickers', practice riffs in his detached garage; and following Mason Senman, a local hobo with greasy hair to his waist and a scraggly beard that he doesn't ever trim. Mason trolls around Freedom most days on a three wheeled bike with a 'Jesus Loves You' handwritten cardboard sign propped up in the basket attached to the bike's handlebars. He passes out mimeographed pamphlets proclaiming the Ten Commandments, that he dug out of the trash bin behind the Baptist Church, to anyone willing to stop and give him a monetary donation.

A few minutes ago, just before we made it to Joe Elby Dixon's field, where Timmy is now relieving himself on a steaming cow pile recently deposited by one of the pasture's grain fed residents, we had passed the Byrd house while peddling through town. Jimbo Byrd had been rocking slowly back and forth on his porch swing, staring blankly off into the late summer sky. Jim hadn't even looked towards us when we had thrown up our hands and yelled, "Hey, Mr. Byrd," as we biked past. Even in the best of times, Jimbo was simply an accessory to Betsy Mae's vigor and vitality, but without her, he had become just another piece of wicker furniture decaying away on the Byrd home-place porch. He has never been the friendliest or kindest of the Freedom town folk, but seeing Jim in this sorry state only makes me want to bring that bastard Griffin Maynor to justice that much more.

"What say we head down to the creek, Timmy? I do some of my best thinkin' when I'm skippin' rocks out there away from everything," I suggest.

"Sure," Timmy responds, seeming enthused that my recommendation doesn't involve me continuing to wear his ass out searching all over Freedom for the green car. "I brought a peanut butter jar with holes poked in the top to catch some tadpoles. I was a hopin' that we might get down that way."

We have spent a lot of time at Mill Creek over the past few summers. The muddy water is overflowing the bank this year due to the torrential August rains. Back in June, shortly after school had let out for the summer, Timmy, his little brother Ben, sister Beth, and me had built a small dam of sticks, branches, and rocks where the creek bottlenecks before crossing under Route 23. In one afternoon, the four of us were able to create a pool of water the size of a small pond that was plenty deep enough to take a dip in. Beth, being nearly four years older than Timmy and me, hardly ever had anything to do with us guys, but on that rare occasion, she had not only tagged along with us, but had actively helped tote and construct the makings of our dam. The most memorable part of the day for me had been when Beth, well into developing a nice set of adolescent boobies, had dove into the still chilly June water in only her Moncross Junior High tee shirt and cutoff jean shorts. It was all that I could do to keep from starin' at her Sunkist orange shaped mounds under her sopping wet cotton shirt, and her wet butt that resembled two bear cubs wrestlin' in her denim shorts, as she had pulled herself onto a beach blanket on the damp creek bank to catch a few rays of early summer sunshine.

Today, Timmy and me are skippin' flat rocks across the swollen creek, seeing who can come the closest to breaking the empty Schlitz longneck beer bottle that we have positioned between two stones near the middle of the water. After juggling a few ideas around in my mind, I decide to let my buddy in on what I've been thinking, and say, "Tomorrow might be the best chance I have to find evidence to pin Ester Yoncey's murder and Betsy Mae Byrd's disappearance on Mayor Maynor." *The statement comes out a lot more matter-of-fact than I'm feeling, probably because I've been contemplating heavily on this idea since the Chevy Impala incident yesterday.*

"You oughta' tell your Pa if you ask me, Bubba," *Timmy responds with deep concern, and more than a little fear for my safety, in his voice.* "Maynor has already tried to kill you once, so it ain't no big stretch thinkin' that it's only a matter of time afore he tries to do it again. Either that, or I reckon' you could catch him in a public place and just up and talk to him. Tell him that you were severely mistaken, and that you done forgot everything that you THOUGHT that you saw."

"It's way too late for that now, Timmy," *I say, after briefly weighing the possibility of his suggestion.* "He already knows that I'm either too afraid to tell 'because nobody would believe me, or that I've tried to squeal and nothin' came of it. Knowin' those things, he is still tryin' to kill me. I just don't think having a conversation with the mayor is gonna help. It might even make him more aggressive if he thinks that I know more than I really do."

Pondering about exactly how to express the feelings that have been rollin' around inside of me since we passed the Byrd house earlier, wantin' to relay those feelings in a way that my best friend and confidant will understand, I continue, "Did you see how far away, no, that's not right, how EMPTY that Jim Byrd looked when we rode by and waved at him this morning? The mayor is willing to do that, or worse, to anyone in Freedom that gets in the way of what he wants. Remember when you and me took that dare from Davey Grater to go up and explore the top floor of the old elementary school? How that old area had seemed 'dead' like it was a place that everyone alive had forgotten? A kind of 'no place'? That's what Maynor is doin' to this town. With his control over everything and everybody, he is makin' Freedom into a 'no place'. And worse yet, because he has all of the control, he can do whatever he wants, have whatever he wants, and always get away with it." *Not sure if I've made my point, I look to Timmy for understanding.*

128

Timmy nods, then shrugs, "But you're only a kid."

I cut him off before he says somethin' that might persuade me to reconsider my plan, "The mayor has scheduled the school dedication for late tomorrow afternoon and the whole town will be there, 'specially since they'll have free food and drinks. He ain't likely to try anything before then 'cause it would only distract attention away from him and his ceremony." I consider not telling Timmy the plan, but decide that since he has put his own butt on the line to help me, he deserves to know what I'm thinkin'. Besides, he would poke and prod until he got the skinny out of me anyways. "When everybody is at the dedication, including Louise Maynor, which is a must, I'm gonna slip into Chestnut Hall and see if I can find anything in the mayor's desk, like a love note, or an entry in his appointment calendar, somethin' that might help me show the link between Ester Yoncey, Betsy Mae Byrd and the mayor."

Timmy's eyes are as big as saucers and he's shakin' his head quickly in disbelief, but when he doesn't say anything, I finish relating my plan, "Dad will be home from Aunt Jane's and Uncle Rick's tomorrow night. One way or another, with or without some kind of evidence, I'm gonna tell him everything. Best that'll happen is that I'll find somethin' to support my story, and maybe fib a little on how and where I got it. The worst case is that I'll get caught and be in a shit load of trouble with Pa and the law. Either way, Mayor Maynor ain't likely to kill me anytime soon after I spill the beans, and my mind will be eased knowin' that I've done everything that I could to make things right."

Exhausted from the stress of simply telling the plan, I look to Timmy for validation, but he doesn't appear to agree with my course of action in the least, "They'll send your ass up the river to Bankston Juvenile sure as shit if you get caught!"

"You got a better idea?" I angrily retort. "I'm a goner if I don't tell, and nobody will believe me if I do. Look, there ain't no good ending without me helpin' it along a little." I feel bad for jumping on my friend, but there just ain't no other way.

Then, as I feared, Timmy thinks on the situation for a minute, then states, "OK, I'll go with you, at least as a lookout while you're in the house."

Expecting this response, I supply a quick rebuttal, "Nope. I gotta do this alone." So that Timmy will let it rest, I describe where his value in the plan comes in, "Besides, I need you around to tell the story if I don't make it home tomorrow *afternoon." To tell the God honest truth, I would love to have him on my mission, but I can't ask him to risk everything to help me.*

"You're crazier than a shit-bug, Bubba Armentrout," was all that Timmy could muster as a reply, tossing a flat rock across the creek and shattering the beer bottle into a thousand fragments.

****

The last lawn party of the year is abuzz with the news of the Freedom Elementary school dedication tomorrow afternoon.

Although the remaining sidewalks, including the area leading to the playground, won't be poured until after school on Monday, following a week of sunny weather, the ground has finally dried enough to hold the mortar. The crowd at the lawn party is festive with gossip about the upcoming celebration surrounding the dedication. It is rumored that Johnny Miller and the 'Virginia Pickers' will be providing the musical entertainment, hamburgers and hot dogs will be grilled by the husbands of the Ladies Auxiliary and served free of charge, and that many of the small rides usually disassembled after the last lawn party of the year will remain in operation for the kids to enjoy. Even with all of these goodies on the slate of events, the largest buzz revolves around a time capsule, supposedly filled with items reflecting the progress of the town of Freedom since the Old Freedom School was built in the early 1900s. The capsule is to be placed in a vault mortared into the exterior wall of the steps leading up to our new school. A flagpole will adorn the area, along with a bench, and a memorial to Principal Ester Yoncey with a bronze profile picture like they have in Cooperstown for the baseball Hall of Famers.

Me and Timmy have been meandering about through the lawn party crowd, trying our skill at ring toss, where you could win a dollar bill for hooping the top of a Pepsi bottle. We also rode the small Ferris Wheel, and dunked Ronald Nockley, our new Freedom elementary principal, with a direct hit from a softball to the bright red circle of the dunking booth. Mr. Nockley gave us a sly grin, as he crawled back up on the platform above the water, and called, "You boys will pay for that!" Hopefully, he was just joshing us.

Circling the 'Guess Your Weight' stall, a new attraction catches our attention, and we decide to fork over a dime each to see the 'Rainbow Animals'. The sign outside of the trailer states, in bright colorful letters, 'SEE THE

130

WORLD-FAMOUS EXOTIC SHOW FROM THE DEEP, DARK CONTINENT OF AFRICA', with a picture of three wild baboons having multi-colored circles looping around their butt holes. The barker for this attraction is just about to take our dime and hand us our tickets when Leonard Byron steps up onto the makeshift stage, where the bingo caller had been shouting out letters and numbers minutes earlier, to make an announcement.

"Good evening, everyone!" Byron exclaims, feedback blaring from the microphone held too closely to his mouth. Tapping the top of the mike until he is comfortable that he can talk without the ear-shattering buzz persisting, he continues, "On behalf of our Freedom Town Council, I want to welcome you to our Lawn Party gathering tonight." After those words, Leonard receives a round of applause and a few whistles from the crowd. One good ol' boy out of eyesight yells, "How's about some free beer for everybody, Len?" and the crowd erupts in cheers. As the noise dies down, Leonard Byron picks up where he left off, "Our Honorable Mayor Griffin Maynor and his lovely wife, Louise, are home busily preparing for tomorrow afternoon's Freedom Elementary dedication festivities, but they asked me to remind you that it will be an event that you won't want to miss. Our Town Council looks forward to seeing everyone there. The fun starts at 4:00 with music, food and games. The mayor will commence the dedication and special ceremony at 5:30. So, have fun and enjoy yourselves this evening. Make sure that you try a slice of Lilly Buckwater's prize winning apple pie, sixty-five cents a slice or a whole pie for three-dollars. Remember, not only is the pie melt in your mouth delicious but, like all of tonight's proceeds, the dollars that you spend will go towards upgrades and renovations that we have planned for the Freedom firehouse." Then with a newly elected Richard Nixon-like wave to the crowd, a big grin breaking out on his face from ear to ear, and a few handshakes from those on stage, Leonard Byron hands the microphone back to the Bingo caller to begin a new round of the game.

Having visited the 'Rainbow Animals', I'm terrible disappointed that I wasted a dime on a monkey trailer. The animals look like every other ape that I've seen on television, except that these appear to have circles painted on their asses. I shoulda' learned my lesson two years ago when they charged a quarter to see the 'Headless Woman' in the glass case.

Supposedly, she had been in a wreck and was kept alive by a mass of tubes running into her headless neck. That was bullshit too; I saw the girl running into a portable john when she thought nobody was lookin', and she definitely had her head attached.

While waiting in line for cotton candy and frozen chocolate covered bananas, most likely a favorite of the Rainbow Animals, Terri Chandler, the prettiest girl at school, appears from the crowd, grabs me by the elbow, smiles brightly and says, "Bubba Armentrout, if I didn't know better, I would think that you have been avoiding me at school. You had promised me at the end of last year that you would eat lunch with me on occasion."

"Nope, Ms. Terri," I grin back at her, my heart fluttering like a baby sparrow is loose in my chest. She looks beautiful with her hair pulled back in a ponytail tied with a pink ribbon, and sporting the slightest bit of lipstick foretelling the coming of womanhood. "I just didn't want to get any more of my teeth knocked out." I tease her playfully, referring to the May Day incident with the playground swing.

"Now Bubba, you KNOW full well that was an accident. Besides," she says laughing, "almost no one in Freedom has their own teeth anyway."

Chuckling with her, I say earnestly, "It's really good to see you, Terri. I like your hair and lipstick. A lot!"

"Well, thank you, Bubba," she says blushing. "I've been looking for you because my mom said that I can take someone with me to see the new Disney movie, 'Rascal', starring Billy Mummy, tomorrow afternoon at the State Theater. Would you like to go with me?"

My heart sinks as the fluttering bird croaks. Remembering the task that I have planned for Sunday afternoon, but wishing I could forget, I reply dejectedly, "I can't, Terri. I've got somethin' really important that I gotta do. I promise you; I'd much rather be eatin' buttered popcorn and fizzle sticks with you, but I just can't tomorrow."

Terri feigns a pout, then says disappointedly, "I just can't imagine what could be more important than spending the day with me," then adds, grinning again, "but, I'll let you off the hook...this time. You will be at the dedication tomorrow evening, won't you?"

"Yeah, sure I will. Wouldn't miss it for the world," I lie, knowing that a 'maybe' would definitely cause more questions.

"I can hardly wait," Terri beams with excitement. "Everyone's talking about it! Mayor Maynor is going to unveil a plaque that has poor Principal Yoncey's likeness engraved into it, but the best part is going to be the time capsule. Folks

are saying that the vault will have something in it representing nearly every year since the old school was built in 1903. My mom and dad gave Louise Maynor a lapel pin from the 1904 St Louis World's Fair that my grandma visited as a little girl. She was in first grade at Freedom Elementary then, and brought back the pin for show and tell to her class. I can't wait to see what other people have donated."

"That's great, Terri," I say, pretending to share her excitement, but only able to think about the dangers I face tomorrow. "Listen, I gotta get home. Grannie Bess will be frantic if I'm not there by supper time. Thanks again for asking me to the movie."

Terri grabs my hand in hers and kisses me lightly on the cheek. We are both oblivious to Timmy Wyatt and Davey Grater walking towards us, side by side, holding snow cones with sticky red syrup spilling over the paper sides.

"You won't stand me up next time, right Bubba?" Terri states flirtatiously. Before I can answer, Timmy and Davey are ribbing us about the peck on my cheek.

"Well, now I know what's been goin' on since I been in Cloverdale," Davey chides.

"Yeah," Timmy adds light-heartedly, "Bubba's done give up fishin' for neckin'!"

Totally ignoring my two goofball friends, Terri spots Janet McCutcheon and her regular circle of girlfriends over by the rides, and gives me a brief wave goodbye.

"See ya later, Terri," I say dejectedly hoping that she'll ask one of the girls to go with her to the movie and not Wilbur Satterfield. Will's had a crush on Terri since first grade, and he's got a lot more popular since his dad got the head football coaching job at Moncross High. Shoot, I even heard that Lucy Lam let Will get to first base with her behind the bleachers at one game.

"Come on, Romeo," Davey quips, as he and Timmy start to make their way to the Spin & Win tent. "We're gonna win the big 'Tony the Tiger' that they got hangin' out front. So far, ain't nobody been lucky enough to win anything but a coupla' free ride tickets."

"You guys go on. I told Grannie Bess that I'd be home 'fore dark." Lost in my thoughts, somber and scared shitless, I walk down Schoolhouse Road towards home finalizing the specifics of my plan for tomorrow.

I've already made up my mind how to explain to Momma and Dad why I broke in to Chestnut Hall if I get caught or, God help me, somethin' worse happens. I'm going to write a note tonight telling them the whole story, beginning to end. I'll give the letter to Timmy for safekeeping, and tell him to hide the note in the busted television in the chicken house. Nobody will find it there, and he can get to it if need be. So far, it don't seem like the mayor thinks that my buddy is in on the whole story just because Timmy was with me the night that Griffin Maynor chased me through the Wyatt yard. Up 'til now, if the mayor does have suspicions, he ain't threatened Timmy or nuthin'. Course, Maynor might be waitin' until he offs me to go after Timmy, but I can't do a damn thing about that now. I've warned my buddy to always be on the lookout for the old bastard.

When I get home, Grannie Bess tells me that she received a call from Momma this afternoon letting her know that Uncle Rick's trial is scheduled to begin in early October, and that she and Dad will come home from Aunt Jane's late tomorrow night. The police are continuing to hold Rick until Aunt Jane and Dad can come up with two-thousand dollars for bail. Momma said that Dad might need to sell a coupla' of his hunting rifles being that Aunt Jane don't have nuthin' of much value, and all that Uncle Rick has is in hock for the washin' machine that he bought two years back.

Well, if everything goes to Hell in a hand basket at Chestnut Hall, at least they'll be back in town to do what they can. There ain't no choice at this point. As bad as the consequences might be for searchin' Mayor Griffin Maynor's house, finding something related to Ester and Betsy Mae, anything, that links him to the crimes seems like my best, and only, hope.

Chapter 12

Conspiracy at Chestnut Hall

Late Fall 2019

Reflection

Fifty years after the festivities surrounding the dedication of the new Freedom Elementary School, the day remains as vivid to me as if it happened yesterday. By 4:00 on that September afternoon, the activities occurring at the school were kinetic. Although the formal dedication wasn't scheduled to begin until 5:30, groups of townspeople had already began touring the reborn facility, burgers and hot dogs were being grilled and consumed in bulk quantities, beer and Coca-Cola were flowing from taps sprouting out of a Bankston Beverage Company truck and the children's rides on the lawn party grounds behind the Baptist Church were running noisily with every seat filled and long lines of kids waiting. Many in the large crowd had staked out the choice positions near the front steps of the school, laying down bulky blankets and unfolding lawn chairs so as to get a bird's eye view of the ceremony. The enthusiasm, excitement and energy generated from the mass of people emitted a perpetual, clamorous hum, as if creating its own form of electricity, that powered an even higher level of anticipation. There were carefree smiles on nearly every face, a sense of cheer and community from the crowd that belied the aura of dread that had enveloped me, as I had watched from the periphery of the commotion.

Then, time had screeched to a stop, the din of the crowd a few decibels lower, when the white Cadillac drove slowly towards the center of the event. The townspeople had fanned out in front of the vehicle as if Moses himself were parting the Red Sea. The mayor and Louise Maynor, Freedom's royalty, had exited the car with practiced panache to smiles, handshakes, cursory cheek kisses and hearty slaps on the back. As Mayor Griffin Maynor began to artfully work the crowd, there had been a brief moment when I had nearly turned and bolted for home. But, without an alternative choice to implicate Maynor, at least one that my young brain could construct, I instead mounted my trusty bike, inhaled a deep breath of cool September air to help calm my nerves and peddled like Hell towards Chestnut Hall.

****

Sunday September 7, 1969

Grannie Bess had carted me off to Freedom Baptist this morning, where I prayed feverishly for God to remember any good deeds that I had performed in my life. There weren't very many that I could recall, but I was hopin' that the Lord would give me the benefit of the doubt for anything that was close. Thanks goodness Golden Jennings ain't dead yet, because I definitely wouldn't want Jesus consultin' with her over the worth of my prayers.

During the service, I made an extra effort in singing 'What a Friend We Have in Jesus' loud and with conviction, and even burst out with an 'Amen' when Reverend Spicer concluded his sermon on 'Living the Path of Righteousness'. Grannie Bess had smiled broadly and given me a big bear hug thinkin' that all of this exposure to religion must finally be startin' to take hold.

I had been able to avoid the Maynors after the service by asking Grannie Bess if she wanted to kneel down with me at the communion rail, near the altar in the front of our church, to pray for Uncle Rick and Aunt Jane. Peeking through my semi closed eyelids, and seeing Mayor Maynor exit the vestibule in deep conversation with Stu Verner, I persuaded my grandma to leave through the rear door behind the choir so that we could see if anyone had started preparations for this evening's festivities next door. From there, we had walked down Schoolhouse Road, declining a ride from Elton Pratt as he passed by, and was talkin' about things that all Grandmothers want to know; like 'how is school going?' and 'what do you want for lunch?'.

It was mid-afternoon by the time that we finished lunch, and Grannie Bess was sacked out on the couch snoring in the living room. I had gone to my bedroom and pulled the letter that I wrote last night from between the mattress of my bed and the box springs. Double checking one last time to make sure that I had included everything that I needed to say, I put the note in an envelope, sealed it and wrote Armentrout on the outside. The celebration was scheduled to

136

begin in a half-hour, at 4:00, so I stuffed the envelope in the back pocket of my jeans, grabbed my pocketknife and watch from my bedside table, and headed for Timmy Wyatt's house to deliver the note.

He met me about halfway across his yard but, to his credit, didn't try and persuade me to forget my plan. I took the time to make sure that he understood that it was possible that the mayor might link him to me, specially since we had been together the night that I confronted Maynor. I told him that it is REAL important to get the note to my dad if he hadn't heard from me by 9:00 tonight, but to hide the envelope until then. Seeing that he was appropriately scared, tears welling up in the corners of his eyes, I had hugged Timmy and thanked him for stickin' out his neck for me.

That's how this pisser of a day has gone for me up until now.

Arriving at the school on my trusty Roadmaster, I find that the event is in full swing even though it's only a few minutes after 4:00. Food and drinks are being served, and the ticket line for rides is nearly thirty kids deep. Hot dog wrappers with mustard stains are blowing across the lot in front of the school, and a number of adults sit smoking on the steps leading up to the building talking about whatever it is that parents are interested in. I'm trying to stay outta' sight, because I don't want Terri to see me when she arrives with her folks. So, I'm monitoring the arrivals to the celebration from the cinder block wall that circles the back of Freedom Baptist. From here, I'm close enough to the parking lot and podium to see when the mayor arrives, and can also spot folks walking to the event from Schoolhouse Road.

The party is going full tilt at nearly 5:00 when the mayor and Louise Maynor drive their Caddy slowly through the crowd and park near the podium where Griffin is to address the crowd at 5:30. Knowing that I'm on the clock, time beginning to race forward like a stopwatch, I hop on my bike and peddle as hard as I can to the intersection of the school road and Route 23.

Ignoring the stop sign before the highway, horns blaring from slow moving traffic waiting to progress towards the dedication, I race over the bridge near Cline's Barbershop and leave my bike beside the creek and out of sight from traffic. I figure that it's safer to sneak through the open field and woods for the half-mile journey to Chestnut Hall, and I'm less likely to be seen by one of the few townsfolk not attending the celebration.

In circling around through the field, I can see the steeple of God's Witness Methodist Church over the trees bordering the Maynor's lot. I'm not sure if that is a good sign or a bad omen, but I do know that I've added about fifteen minutes to my journey in order to avoid prying eyes on Route 23. I'll still have slightly more than an hour, worst case scenario, if everything goes as planned, and will have cover from the trees until I get to the final acre leading to the Maynor's cleared backyard.

It seems like it took hours instead of minutes, but I'm finally stationed in a hunkered down squat, concealed below pine trees shading a brier covered neglected lot bordering the mayor's yard. From my vantage point, I have a clear view of the massive porch jutting from the rear of Chestnut Hall.

Shaking like a Chihuahua in an igloo, nervous sweat from my forehead burning my eyes, and my forearms and hands trickling blood from the brier scratches and mosquito bites, I double check to ensure that there isn't any sign of activity in or around the Maynor's house. Seeing none, I crawl, crablike, across the finely manicured lawn. I stop about halfway to the house in Louise's towering sunflower garden to both settle my nerves and to make sure that the coast is still clear. I nearly jump out of my skin when a rabbit bursts from a flower stalk directly in front of me, and scoots towards the woods that I recently passed through. That being the only detectable movement at Chestnut Hall, I continue to worm my way to a screened window on the side of the rear porch. Seeing it up close for the first time, the porch looks like a fairly recent addition to the mayor's house. The area is filled with wicker furniture, Griffin's smoking chair with a side table and ashtray, an unlit stogie waiting for his arrival, and a large wooden, circular table covered in books and magazines. Unfortunately, I can see through the window that there is a large wooden door leading to the main house from the porch. To get in this way, after prying off the window screen, I would need to be lucky enough for the inner door to be unlocked. Not great odds, and I don't have much time.

Looking for another, more direct, way to get inside, I circle the back steps to the shaded side of the porch. I get an immediate jolt of adrenaline when I notice that, catty-cornered to the porch, on the rear wall of the main house, a window is cracked open to allow in the fresh September air. The window is screened, and about eight feet off of the ground but, at least, it's open.

Perusing the yard, I see two wooden apple crates are stacked against a small shed, used to store tools, back near Louise's flower garden. Feeling like Lady Luck might just have decided to smile on me, or maybe all of that prayin' this morning amounted to somethin', I rush to grab the crates and position them end to end under the window.

The stacking is shaky, but balancing myself against the wall of the house, I'm easily able to pop the screen off with my knife, which I thoughtfully brought for just such an occasion.

Dropping the screen to the ground, I leverage my fingers under the slightly ajar wooden frame, and raise the window to a level wide enough to crawl through. I pull myself up the few feet to the sill, and stick my head through the thin, white drapes.

Surprisingly, I discover that I'm looking into the master bedroom, where the light had flickered on the night that Timmy and me set off the firecracker and started this crazy spying idea. I hold my breath, listening for any sound within Chestnut Hall, but all I hear is my heart pounding like an Indian drum at pow wow time, and a grandfather clock ticking away precious minutes somewhere in the mansion. Hoisting my butt over the windowsill, I drop and roll onto the newly waxed cedar hardwood floor of the Maynor's bedroom.

Even pressed as I am for time, I can't help but goggle at the magnificence of the room. It's decorated like Monticello, which I had a chance to see when our fourth-grade class made a school trip to Charlottesville last year. This room might even be nicer!

A gold-plated chandelier with drooping crystals hangs directly over the huge, cherry bed. A thick comforter, with pictures of Colonial times sewn into it, is turned down to reveal a satin bed sheet covering a fluffy, down mattress. A ruffled sham, tinted baby blue, adds a softness to the room, as it barely grazes the spotless floor.

Original, hand painted pictures in large, bulky wooden frames cover each cream-colored wall, a few depicting colorful flowers in large vases, while others look like they may be depictions of relatives long deceased. The largest painting, by far, is an oil rendition of Chestnut Hall that hangs directly above the massive headboard of the bed.

Finely crafted cherry furniture, with intricate designs identical to the bed, are positioned throughout the room. A three-drawer night stand, holding a multi-colored Tiffany lamp and cluttered with china figurines of dancing maidens and gentlemen in stylishly long coats, stands directly above my head, as I push myself up from the floor next to the window. This appears as good a place as any to start my search. It ain't likely that the mayor would have hid anything pertaining to Yoncey or Byrd so close to where Louise sleeps, but it won't hurt to take a quick peek in the bedroom drawers before I move to Griffin's office. Sometimes, it's the things that are right under your nose that can be the hardest to see.

Carefully opening the top drawer of the nightstand, I'm surprised to find that it only contains a few items; a silk kerchief with LM embroidered in bold, pink letters in its center, a set of earrings emblazoned with what looks like large, red rubies and a silver, heart shaped locket, unpolished and worn with time, on a simple gold chain.

I lift the locket from the drawer for closer inspection, and find a small latch protruding from its side. When I push the latch, and the locket pops open, two ladies' faces peer at me, one from each side of the silver heart. The woman on the left side of the locket has a stern expression, age lines flowing over regal features that might have once been labeled as beautiful, but time had won that battle. The drawn lips and humorless glare imply that little happiness was either extended or received in her life. Strangely, with the exception of her hairstyle and the antiquated attire visible in the small photo, she bears an eerie resemblance to Louise Maynor.

The face on the other side of the locket, although having the same bone structure as the first, exudes youth and vibrancy. She conveys a broad smile that almost radiates from the photo, and possesses bright, frolicsome eyes filled with a zest for life.

From the ancient hairstyles of the women, long braids wrapped into buns positioned on the tops of their heads, and the neckline of their dresses, frilly white with lace nearly to their chins, it is evident that the photos were taken a long, long time ago. Flipping the locket over, I can barely make out the worn inscription, 'To Louise on her 16th birthday, Mother'.

Mesmerized by how young and beautiful that Lady Louise had once been, I almost don't hear the key opening the door on the back porch where I had been scouting around minutes earlier. Once my confused brain makes the connection between the light footsteps making their way down the hall towards the bedroom and my continued well-being, I quickly close the window to the level that it was before my arrival, quietly shut the nightstand drawer, and slide under the big bed just as muffled voices sound outside of the closed bedroom door. Realizing that I still have Louise Maynor's locket in my hand, I jam the jewelry into the back pocket of my jeans, hoping to have an opportunity to replace it in the drawer before escaping the house. That is, IF I have the chance to get out of Chestnut Hall undiscovered.

Whoever has entered the house obviously doesn't know that they have an unseen visitor because they sound unabashed in their own activities. The passionate 'ums' and 'ahs', pleasurable moans and groans, that are accompanying the rustling noise of clothes being removed, are filling the room and giving me flashbacks of the nightmare at old Freedom Elementary. Although little light penetrates the sham around the bottom of the bed, there ain't much doubt about the act that's about to take place above me in the mayor's bed. Lifting the sham ever so slightly, and glancing out into the room, I can make out four feet shuffling awkwardly towards the down mattress, as a female voice exclaims impatiently, "Let me get it. The damn hook on this bra is impossible."

SHIT, my inner-voice screams, what in the name of creation are the mayor and Louise Maynor doing home? The dedication should just be starting!

"Elwood, Elwood, wait a second for God's sake. Let me get it off."

At first, I just think that I've heard wrong, then I nearly swallow my tongue when Elwood Breffton replies lustily, "C'mon, Lou. I want you NOW...it's been weeks since we done it."

Flabbergasted beyond belief, I'm trying to make sense of what's happening above me in the bedroom when a few more horny moans come from the pair. The lover's bodies plop onto the mattress with full force, their weight causing the old box springs to screech in agony, and drives one of the bowed slats on the underside of the bed to within a fraction of an inch from my head. I slide as quietly as I can towards the nightstand side of the bed, moving away from the action occurring in the middle, and watch fearfully as the springs bounce up and down, while the headboard bangs rhythmically against the wall. It's like listening to two mangy mutts, one ruttin' and the other in heat, pokin' in the trash bin behind Gee's Grocery. If they keep this up much longer, either the Cherry bed is gonna collapse and kill me, or the huge oil painting of Chestnut Hall above the headboard is gonna flop off the wall and crush Louise and Breffton.

Closing my eyes, and prayin' to Jesus for this to end soon, I hear a coupla' consummating gasps and pants as the dirty deed comes to a close. Having been spared from impalement by the heavy box springs, if not the nauseous mental image of a juiced-up Elwood Breffton poundin' away at the leathery Louise Maynor, I can only hope that the two of them will be on their merry way after finishing their adulterous rendezvous. From what I heard today, it looks like the mayor ain't the only guy fishin' for trout in another man's pond.

Unfortunately for me, after a minute of heavy breathing as they recuperate from their physical exertion, a winded Elwood Breffton pants, "Lou, you're the best."

I think, 'Holy Crap, hopefully they ain't settling in for a long session of pillow talk'. I check my watch and see that it's only about twenty minutes until the mayor's speech is scheduled to be done, and then folks will start adding their memorabilia to the time capsule. With all that considered, Griffin could be home in a little more than half an hour, forty minutes tops.

Then, Louise Maynor quells my fears of a prolonged after sex goo-goo session when she states, with no residual romance in her tone, "Alright, Elwood. Fun's over. We have some very important business to discuss."

"Can't that wait, Lou?" Elwood responds dejectedly, "We got a few minutes and, hell, I think I might even be able to go again."

"Listen to me, and listen close," Louise says curtly, "Stick your dick in your shorts, or you're going to be without one. We're going to talk NOW." There is a moment of silence, then some shuffling, as one of them moves towards the edge of the bed. I can see Elwood's swollen, varicose ankles and feet under the sham as they touch the floor on the opposite side of the bed from where I'm hiding. Louise Maynor continues speaking in a chastising tone, "If you hadn't fucked up taking care of that little shit Armentrout, we wouldn't be in this god damned predicament."

"Louise, I did what you 'tole' me," Elwood replies defensively. "I took a helluva risk hot wiring that car from the patient lot at Bankston Memorial Hospital to do the job. Far as I know, didn't nobody notice neither. I'd a gotten the little bastard too if that snot nosed shit from across the street hadn't pushed the tire in front of 'im."

"Excuses won't keep your sorry ass out of Federal Prison, Elwood, and I'm certainly not going to allow you to take me with you." Louise pauses to allow her stern rebuttal to sink in, then continues with escalating impatience and anger increasing the decibels of her voice, "Because YOU didn't finish the job, now YOU'VE got to get rid of that god damn tramps body TONIGHT!"

"I didn't have nuthin' to do with you killin' Betsy Mae Byrd, not a fuckin' thing!" Breffton screams, "That's on you, Louise. YOU!"

I nearly jump out of my skin, both at the revelation of Betsy Mae's murder, and Breffton's abrupt response. I come within a hair of bumping my head on the bed slat, an error that would certainly mean an end to me here and now.

Possibly seeing the situation getting out of hand, and needing to reel Elwood back in, Laura says softly, with full control of her emotions, "Do you really think that the police will believe that to be true after discovering that you strangled Ester Yoncey to death, and then burned down the school to cover your fucking tracks?"

On the verge of tears, Breffton replies more adamant than angry, "I did that for you, Louise. I would do ANYTHING for you."

These revelations are more than I bargained for when I decided to search Chestnut Hall. Time is running short on the mayor's dedication ceremony, but the story playing out between these two staples of the community has me stunned and mesmerized. If I could see myself, I'll bet that my mouth is open wide enough to drive a Greyhound Bus through. My God, what spurred all of this, and what possibly can they reveal next?

"I know that you would, Elwood. You've already done so, so much." A faux loving tone, stuffed with double-entendre coats her words, "That's why tonight, after Griffin and I leave the house for a benefit dinner in Bankston, you're going to come and get that slutty tramp away from Chestnut Hall, and bury her for good under where the sidewalk will be at Freedom Elementary. Griffin told me that the workers will be pouring the concrete after school tomorrow afternoon. Then, I'll be done with that bitch once and for all."

"But Lou, if I get caught moving..." Breffton's voice is quivering with fear, as Louise Maynor cuts him off mid-sentence.

"But nothing! I don't give a flying fuck how you do it, just do it! I swear to God, if you screw this up Breffton, I'll say ANYTHING to see that you get FRIED in the chair at the Penitentiary."

Allowing herself time to gain her composure, Louise continues, "I'll leave the back door unlocked. We will be out of the house by 8:00, and won't be home until around 11:00. We're having cocktails with the Vice-President of Colony National Bank after dinner, and you know how Griffin loves to talk to bankers. Look for the light on the front porch to be on. That way you'll know that we've left the house."

"What are we gonna do with the kid?" Breffton sighs, seemingly resigned to the fact that he will continue to be forced to do Louise Maynor's bidding.

"I would have thought that he would have told someone what he knows by now if he was going to," she says. "Or, maybe he has tried, and they figured that he was full of shit. Sooner or later, he probably will get someone's attention and they'll start snooping around. We can't take that chance. Get the tramps body disposed of tonight, and then we can see that Armentrout has an unfortunate accident in a couple of days."

Silence envelopes the room, and my stomach picks a terrible time to decide growl. I ball up under the bed to muffle the rumbling and, luckily, Breffton has more questions. "What about Griffin?"

"You let me worry about Griffin," Louise snaps. "All he knows is that the kid saw him banging that whore at Freedom Elementary. Just like everyone else in town, with the exception of that shit Armentrout, Griffin still thinks that his little tramp ran off with a lover, and that the school fire was a tragic accident." More forcibly, she adds, "And Elwood, it damn sure better stay that way. When you finish tonight, without fucking up, and YOU CAN NOT FUCK UP, that means staying away from the god damn bottle for one day, then we'll take care of the Armentrout kid and put all of this behind us."

"That ain't exactly what I meant, Louise," Elwood states meekly. "What about us? You gotta know that I been in love with you for years. That's why I've done all the things you asked me. You know I can take care of doin' away with the mayor too. Easy."

Louise's tone is furious, as she states bluntly, "What about us, Elwood? There isn't an us! Don't you ever confuse affection with necessity. You are my sometimes lover and henchman out of necessity...nothing more. Griffin is WHY I did these things. To protect his reputation, and to ensure that he didn't get some wild hair up his ass and run off with one of these little cunts." Seeming to recognize that she still needs to keep Breffton in her corner, she adds softly, "Look Elwood, you are special to me. Go do your job, do it well and let's see if we can't get through this nasty situation without spending the rest of our lives behind bars. There certainly won't be any afternoon flings from the joint. Sound good?"

Assuming the fragility of a chastised little boy, Elwood Breffton mumbles, "Yes, ma'am. Like I said, whatever you need."

Jesus, everything that I had believed about the murder, the fire, the disappearance...everything...has been turned inside out. Although Griffin Maynor isn't responsible, at least directly, for the murders, it doesn't make my

144

position any less precarious. Now I know the truth, but instead of setting me free, it's about to get me killed.

Louise pushes back the sheets and slides out of the bed. I hadn't seen her panties, frilly nylon for the occasion, lying under the edge of the sham until her hand reaches down to grab them, an inch or so away from my foot. Holding my breath, and praying one more time in a day filled with prayers, the panties disappear from under the corner of the bed without me being discovered.

"I've got to get back to the dedication," she says. "Griffin's speech will be done in a few minutes, and he'll be furious if I'm not there beside him, giving him compliments on his presentation, as he works the crowd. Here, help me pull up the sheets. He only conceded to let me leave during the dedication because I told him that I had forgotten to lay out his tux for tonight's benefit."

I can hear the two conspirators fluffing the pillows and patting the wrinkles out of the bedspread. "There," Louise surmises, "no indication of any illicit activity, except for the Jack Daniels on your breath. You have got to get off of that shit, Elwood. It's going to kill you. It also causes you to be sloppy. I would heavily suggest that you spend the rest of this evening getting preparations ready for whatever you will need to take care of our problem." I can hear Maynor's voice trailing towards the far side of the bedroom, and water splashing in a sink; probably an attached bathroom that I hadn't noticed when I dropped through the window.

Once finished in the bathroom, Louise's high-heeled feet can be seen at the bottom of the bed as she rustles through the closet. Laying clothes on top of the comforter, she concludes the rendezvous with a word of encouragement, "Elwood, I KNOW that you'll do well, darling. Now get the hell out of here. It's almost 6:00."

Breffton leaves without uttering another word, and Louise Maynor follows a minute later. Just before the rear door of Chestnut Hall closes softly, I hear her whisper 'idiot' to herself, and I'm left alone in the massive mansion as I had been before the couple's arrival.

****

I wait five long minutes before crawling out from under the bed, my thoughts racing like an Olympic sprinter. Breffton and Louise Maynor are good and gone, shoot, she's probably already back at the dedication by now. Since it's gotten so late, the ceremony has probably progressed to where folks are adding memorabilia to the time capsule. That means my planned time at Chestnut Hall is up, and the Maynors could be home at any minute. Seeing the mayor's tuxedo on the bed reminds me that they have another function to attend tonight, one more reason for them to get home quickly.

From the conversation that I just heard between Louise Maynor and Breffton, I know that Betsy Mae's body is somewhere in Chestnut Hall, but it won't be after tonight. Well, it won't be if Louise has her way and Breffton does what she asked. The problem is, there ain't much chance of me finding her before the Maynors get home. Heck, the mayor lives here and he ain't come across her body. Even if I did luck out and stumble across her hidden corpse, would the police even come if I called them? Could be that they'd chalk it up to a prank, and call the mayor to let him know that he had a kook in town.

Then it hits me. Yep, damn near slaps me in the face like a prudish prom date. I know EXACTLY what I need to do! Quickly sliding across the hardwood floor, I get to my knees and peek out of the window to ensure that the coast is clear. Pushing myself out and over the sill, I stand on the window ledge and squat down to grab the screen. Nearly losing my balance, I waver on the ledge until I can grasp the inside of the open window, and shift the screen into place. Jumping to the ground from the ledge, I grab the apple crates, and place them back by the woodshed before hauling ass like a banshee towards the woods behind Chestnut Hall. Even though I'm elated, and a little relieved, to have a plan, and a damn good one at that, I have less than a day to get everything ready to pull the idea off. And, I'll need help.

Lord, with what I learned today, this is my chance to bring everything out in the open. Failing ain't an option, because if I can't pull this off, I'm likely dead anyways. Reflecting on these thoughts, I'm not nearly so elated or relieved anymore!

Chapter 13

Sticks and Stones

Monday September 8, 1969

Monday afternoon, when the bell rings to dismiss school for the day, Timmy Wyatt and me fly by Mrs. Kent and blow through her classroom door in a flash. The cement masons have already arrived at the back of the school driving three large trucks churning huge canisters of the wet mix. In their preparations to complete the sidewalks, steps and platforms outside of Freedom Elementary, the workers have neatly organized metal trays, shovels, trowels and other assorted masonry tools around the school grounds. A massive plastic tarp is stacked near each wooden frame where, later tonight, the cement will be left to dry.

It has been damn hard for any of the students in our class to concentrate on Mrs. Kent's lessons today seeing how we had a bird's eye view of the activities taking place directly outside the window of our fifth-grade classroom. The commotion created by the trucks and workers, who arrived shortly after lunchtime, combined with all of the hullabaloo still on everyone's mind from yesterday evening's dedication, pretty much ensured that any serious learnings for the day would fall on deaf ears.

Terri Chandler cornered me in the cafeteria at lunch to give me the fifth degree for not showing up at Sunday's ceremony. I was well prepared and had earlier rehearsed a small fib detailing Momma and Dad coming home with bad news concerning Uncle Rick, his soon to be held trial date, and our cloudy outlook on how the judgment might play out. I had regurgitated the tale well enough to keep Terri from asking more probing questions. And, it's really not a lie, at least not a big black one; they really had come home late last night with that news. I had decided to mix a little more truth with the fib because I hate lying to Terri, so I added that we had needed to get Grannie Bess back home and settled in since she had been away from Granddiddy Robert for nigh on a week.

During recess, while both fifth-grade classrooms participated in a boring activity in the gym, flapping a piece of cloth shaped like a parachute up and down while circling the center of the basketball court, I had asked permission from Mrs. Kent to be excused for a restroom break. Instead, I sneaked out for a look at the new plaque, centered on the wall beside the steps leading up to the school. Seeing Ms. Yoncey's likeness, with the inscription 'Heaven's Most Valuable Educator. God bless you Ester Yoncey', the afternoon sun reflecting brightly around the outline of her face, bolstered my courage and strengthened my resolve to bring her killers to justice. But, first things first. I've gotta make sure that Betsy Mae Byrd's body gets discovered, otherwise, I'm right back where I started with my head on the chopping block.

****

Early this morning, before school, me and Timmy had hidden a burlap sack that Flo Wyatt used for gathering garden vegetables, along with a pair of Dad's quail hunting binoculars, near the dumpster at the rear of Gee's Grocery. Bennie don't take his trash to the dump but once a month and that's nearly always over the weekend. There ain't no custodian at the dump on Saturdays, and Gee can trash shit that he don't want nobody asking questions about; like stale dated meat wrappers and rats poisoned behind the food shelving. In carrying out my plan, I felt confident that we'd have time to retrieve the items, plus fill the sack, between the time school ends for the day and the cement masons finishing their work and leaving the school work site for the evening.

So here we are, partners in crime, a little after 7:00 in the evening with dusk about a half-hour away, sitting in our perch on the branch of an old oak tree a quarter mile from Freedom Elementary. I chose the location between Mill Creek and Freedom Elementary because of the cover the still leafy, now colorful, autumn oak provides and the straight-line visibility to the workers. Through the binoculars, I can see them smoothing the last, and largest, area of the newly poured cement with trowels, nearly finished with that phase of their job.

Our burlap sack at the base of the oak tree is nearly bursting with trash and debris. Empty milk cartons, tin cans, an antifreeze container, torn paper grocery bags, a sleeve of broken light bulbs, leaves and sticks are only some of the things stuffed in the sack. Anything, and nearly everything, that we came across on the way from Gee's dumpster to our perch is stuffed in there. With dusk approaching,

148

all we can do now is wait. Well, wait, and pray that the cement won't completely harden before we have time to put our finishing touches on the work.

****

Thirty minutes later, with the setting sun nearly hidden by the mountains, the workers have just completed pulling large tarps over the drying cement, and hammering stakes at each corner of the plastic to keep debris from blowing into the mixture. Since we settled into our position on the tree limb, I've been watching intently for any tell-tale sign that might indicate that the workers have uncovered anything out of the ordinary in, or around, the sidewalk forms. From the casual way that they're laughing and joking as they finish up the job, it seems that they don't have a care in the world.

When I'd gotten to school early this morning, directly after we had hidden the burlap bag and binoculars at Gee's, I had made a beeline for our classroom window that overlooked the playground. It was a long shot, but I figured that I might see some trace that Elwood Breffton had completed Louise Maynor's Sunday night disposal directive. The moist, red dirt inside of the wooden forms where the concrete was to be poured was as smooth as a baby's ass. Either Janitor Breffton had stayed sober long enough to not 'fuck up' the job, or he could count on Louise Maynor crushing his balls in her fists and feedin' them to the pigs.

Now, watching the masons complete their tasks, finally loading the trucks with their equipment and tools, then pulling away from the lot with headlights cutting through the quickly darkening evening, it's clear that they hadn't been suspicious of any tampering at the work site, whatsoever.

Every second that we wait after the truck's lights disappear over the crest of Schoolhouse Road allows the cement to harden. But we've also got to make sure that, once we start dragging the heavy burlap bag towards the school, none of the workers return for a tool left behind or some small, forgotten task. It also occurs to me that Breffton might want to show up at the scene of the crime to verify that the workers hadn't uncovered the nasty little secret that he had buried under the dirt of their wooden forms.

With our patience growing thin, and our nerves reacting like electric prods to every noise in the night, I slide off of the limb and scan the school one last time for signs of movement. Freedom Elementary is engulfed in darkness, with the exception of the emergency exit lights casting an eerie red glow through the windows at each end of the new building. It isn't hard to imagine Ester Yoncey and Betsy Mae Byrd peering through those windows, urging us on, and eternally searching for a way to leave the building. STOP IT, BUBBA! It ain't ghosts that you need to be afraid of; it's the live ones that'll do you harm.

Me and my best buddy slowly and as stealthily as possible make our way across the open field towards our destination. Taking turns dragging the heavy burlap sack, trying and failing miserably to avoid groundhog holes and deep ravines cut in the dirt by the summer rains, we stumble and fall numerous times before reaching the work site. Without using a flashlight to lead the way, fearful that someone from a neighboring house or cleaning people at the Baptist Church a short piece away might spot us, the quarter mile trek takes an eternity to cover.

Nearly exhausted from my turn toting the sack, the knees of my jeans grass-stained and muddy from tripping and falling in the field, I drop to the ground beside the closest tarp covered form. Timmy, already recovered from his stint lugging the bag, leans over and pats me on the back. "I was watchin' for anybody while we covered the last hundred yards. Catch your breath, Bubba. I think we're in the clear, so far."

Eager for this to be over and done, I pant, "Let's start with the platform over there," pointing to an area lit only by the glimmer of moonlight. The largest tarp covers this newly cemented area, located at the bottom of a small railing beside three steps leading to the playground. "Breffton would have needed a space big enough to bury Betsy Mae's body in, and that's the only area where she'd fit."

"What if he cut her up to stuff her in a freezer or somethin'?" Timmy said, grimacing as he visualized the thought.

"I guess that's possible," I respond, craning my neck to look at the other tarps. "Just to be sure, we'll jam some trash in the sidewalks, too. That way, if she's in pieces, they'll still be more than likely to find her." Thinking out loud, I deduce, "You know, even if she is in one piece under the biggest block of cement, stickin' trash everywhere there's new cement poured might lead 'em to think that it was vandals that caused this mess, and that findin' Betsy Mae was just blind luck. That would make sense, wouldn't it?"

Timmy immediately drags the burlap sack over to the large tarp covered form, reaches inside the bag grabbing three long branches, an armful of leaves and two pork and bean cans from Gee's trash bin, saying excitedly, "You got it, Bubba."

Having regained my energy from dragging the sack, adrenaline throwing some internal switch that sets the body's control panel to hyper-focus, I jump up and hustle over beside my friend. After pulling one end of the plastic from the stakes, and folding it back to reveal the thickening cement underneath, I take the three branches from Timmy and ram them as deep as I can into the center of the mixture. I want to penetrate the ground if I can so as to force the workers to dig as deep as possible to remove the damaged cement. Damn... I would swear on the bible that I hear the faint sound of plastic tearing when I give an extra push on the longest branch, a four-foot-long dogwood limb that had fallen off the bed of Cesar Riley's truck after he had cleaned up the grounds around the cemetery. "Did you hear that?" I whisper, knowing full well that it could be my imagination runnin' off on me.

"Hear what?" Timmy murmurs, turning in a full circle and looking for any movement near the school. "Let's get this done and get the hell outta' here. This place is givin' me the creeps. I 'bout shit myself every time I hear a cricket chirp!" Driving the trash deep into the platform is easy work with the cement havin' the consistency of wet mud. But, by the time that we finish the sidewalks, the mixture is hardening and beginning to set near the forms, making the job of gettin' the debris to the ground under the walks a challenge.

Completing the task that we came for, and having used everything in the burlap sack plus a huge rock that we found nearby, we stand side-by-side in the dark and peruse our work by the light of the September moon. Seeing the mass of cans, leaves, bottles, sticks and the bowling ball size rock embedded in the newly poured foundations, it's obvious that it will take a jackhammer to undo the damage that we've created this evening.

I won't lie, there's more than a sliver of guilt welling up inside of me for destroying what so many folks, including myself, are so proud of. I just gotta believe that, if Betsy Mae really is buried here, the results will outweigh any trouble that we've caused.

I turn to Timmy, and sheepishly grin, "Only one more thing to do here." I hadn't planned this, and really didn't come up with the idea until, still sitting on the branch of the tree, I told Timmy to be careful not to get a foot or hand print in the cement, right before we drug the sack across the field. Picking up a small twig from the ground, the only unused remnant from the sack, and walking back to the large platform where Betsy Mae HAS to be, I squat and look for a small section of undamaged cement.

Grinning at my buddy, knowing that this is right up his alley, I carefully write, 'PEANUT C.-1969' in huge capital letters across one entire chamfered edge of the wet cement.

"Timmy," I cackle, "paybacks are hell."

Laughing, while grabbing the burlap sack and binoculars, we dart back across the field towards the cover of the trees before making a direct beeline for home.

Chapter 14

Judgment Day

Tuesday September 9, 1969

I couldn't sleep for worryin' about whether or not Breffton had buried Betsy Mae under the cement forms. Another reason for my restlessness was my lying to Momma, sayin' that I'd been with Timmy up at Davey's house watchin' television last night. I'd missed my 9:30 curfew by ten minutes, but caught a break when Momma was on the phone with Aunt Jane as I slipped in.

When I finally did doze off in the early hours of Tuesday mornin', I dreamed that Timmy, covered in dirt and sweat, was digging in a wet cement grave on Cemetery Hill. Elwood Breffton and Louise Maynor were watching him shovel out the heavy mixture, as an approaching car's headlights cast shadows across the morbid scene. Momma woke me for school just as the mayor pulled up in his Cadillac at the graveyard, opened his car door, lit a cigar and told Breffton, "Help the boy, Elwood. There's no telling what goodies he might find at the bottom of that hole." When Breffton joined Timmy at the lip of the grave, the ground collapsed, and sucked both of them under like quicksand. A small air bubble burped to the top of the wet cement grave as Elwood, only one hand visible, made a last grasp at the freezing night air.

I nearly knocked Momma in the chin with the top of my head when I jumped up from her shaking me awake. Trying to get ready for school had been like swimming in molasses, the dream continuing to circle in my head and anxious as heck over what today had in store. Last night, I was prepared to change clothes in the Wyatt chicken house before heading home. Both Timmy and me had hidden a clean shirt, jeans and shoes in the building after I had told him the plan on Sunday, but our assessment on the trip back had been that we weren't any dirtier than normal, and besides, we had been runnin' really late.

This morning, the same clothes that I'd worn last night are strewn over the wooden chair in the corner of my bedroom, with no overly visible signs of our grimy, destructive adventure. I find a fresh pressed shirt in my closet, change socks and underwear and grab a Pop Tart on my way out the door to school.

By the time that I enter Mrs. Kent's classroom, shortly before the morning bell, every kid in the room is lined up at the window overlooking the playground. "What's goin' on?" I inquire to no one in particular, pretending that I don't have a clue as to what they are gawking at on the other side of the glass. "Someone made a terrible mess of the new sidewalks last night!" Janet McCutcheon responds, teary emotion and anger fill her voice. "Yeah," Davey Grater chimes in, hypnotized by the scene outside, "when I got here, Principal Nockley and the teachers were just startin' to cover the walks back up with the tarps. There are all kinds of shit stuck in the cement; sticks, bottles and other stuff. Trash is jammed in 'bout every square inch."

"Who would do such an awful thing?" Terri Chandler adds, nearly crying. "It must be a really bad person that doesn't care at all about anyone else!"

I'm feeling about as low as a pimple on a snail's butt, watching Principal Nockley, along with about every other teacher at Freedom Elementary, finish pulling the thick plastic covering over the platform and sidewalks. A few of them start to reinsert the stakes to hold the tarps in place, but finding the task difficult without hammers, the teachers forgo their effort.

We can see side conversations occurring between the Freedom Elementary staff, but can't hear what they are discussing through the thick glass window. Most are shuffling around like zombies, uncertain of what to do to help, while others are having the same angry and tearful reactions as the students.

Brian Nockley is standing off to the side of the platform nearest the school talking to his Secretary, Fran Singleton, who is feverishly taking notes on a small writing pad. Principal Nockley, never one for splurging on his attire, is donned in his typical brown khakis, short sleeve white shirt and nondescript clip-on tie. He is a bear of a man, probably 6'5" if he is an inch, with a physique that, at forty, is beginning to turn to paunch, but still retains some semblance of the champion boxer that he had been while serving a tour of duty in the Army.

****

One winter day last school year, while we were still attending classes at Freedom Baptist Church, Nockley had sent his secretary to pull me out of Mrs. Lamplier's room during the middle of a math quiz. Scared to death, with Fran Singleton refusing to give me a reason for his summons no matter how hard I pleaded, I marched down the hall to his makeshift office figuring that some recent misdeed of mine had finally come to roost. Having spent enough time in Ester Yoncey's domain to be considered a permanent resident, this was my first visit into Principal Nockley's realm. It hadn't looked at all like I had expected.

The walls were covered with black and white photos of a younger Brian Nockley standing over bleeding and beaten boxing competitors. A number of small, framed cases hanging beside the pictures held medals and ribbons from the winning matches. The area over a large wooden file cabinet displayed two faded Country music posters; one promoting 'Mr. Love Sick Blues' Hank Williams at Rob's Place in Robstown, Texas from 1952, and the other highlighted Roy Acuff and The Smokey Mountain Boys at the Armory in Charlotte, North Carolina from 1957. Photos of an attractive brunette, and two late-teen boys sat in a gold-colored frame on the corner of his desk.

Sandy Williams had been setting on a wooden stool in the corner of the room, his Gibson guitar balanced on one skinny knee. Sandy, a sixth grader, had been taking guitar lessons with me from Johnny Miller on Saturday mornings before my fingers got so sore that I quit the program.

As Mrs. Singleton led me into the office, Nockley had said enthusiastically, "Bubba, Sandy here has been telling me about you and him doing a little picking together over at the Miller place. I'd appreciate a demonstration on what you've learned if you're up for it."

That, in a nutshell, is Brian Nockley. He's a straight to the point guy that runs a tight ship. But, he's also kinda' impulsive, and usually seems to have some mischief stored under that thick layer of toughness. Principal Nockley is as quick to slap you on the shoulder and say 'good job', as he is to slap you on the ass and say, "don't you ever do that again."

While Sandy had flawlessly picked 'The Wildwood Flower' and I had half-assed strummed rhythm on Nockley's cheap off brand guitar that he kept in his office closet, our principal had tapped his size 13 foot and hummed along to the chorus. From that day forward, even with my too regular transgressions, Brian Nockley always waves and smiles when we cross paths. And, if there's any *semblance of wiggle room, will give me the benefit of the doubt when a classroom dispute with a teacher arises.*

****

    A seemingly bewildered and agitated Mrs. Kent enters her classroom after the congregation of teachers and staff break away from the vandalized playground. Everyone, especially me, is in our seats and quiet as mice when she arrives, sensing that our teacher will have little, or no, patience for questions about what she knows, or tolerance for any disruption in class. She stoically calls roll, then braces herself with both hands firmly on the corner of her large, wooden desk. Doris Kent is a big woman, and she uses her size to be intimidating when necessary. Her blue, tightly pinned hair, streaked with gray, does little to soften her sour appearance. She reminds me of Ma' Barker from pictures I've seen of the Barker Gang crime family.

    Mrs. Kent stares intensely at our class for a moment, seeming to make eye contact with everyone in the room at least once, and growls, "In my thirty years of teaching, I thought that I had experienced everything, but today beats all. Obviously, having seen you gawking out the window, you've seen the damage that someone has caused to our beautiful, new school. I pray to goodness that none of our students are responsible for this heinous act."

    Bart Heatwole raises his hand, and starts to blurt out a question, but Doris Kent cuts him off at the pass. "Now is not the time for questions. We'll learn more in the next few days. Principal Nockley has contacted the police and they will investigate this afternoon before the workman arrive later today to fix this mess."

    Circling around her desk, and walking down the middle aisle of student seats, Mrs. Kent's tone becomes even graver, "If any one of you has any idea who is responsible for this vandalism, it is your civic obligation, your DUTY, to come forward and inform Principal Nockley. I am going to pass a basket around the room, as are teachers in the other classrooms," she says direly, pointing to a wicker tray on her desk that she uses to hold excuses for absences, "so, please take a blank sheet of paper from your binders, and write 'yes' if you know ANYTHING about what happened last night on the playground, or 'no' if you don't. Fold the paper over and place it in the basket as it is passed to you."

156

Mulling over how best to proceed, she nods her head with resolution and states, "I want you to understand completely. If you know something and don't tell, you are just as guilty as the individual that performed this act." She pauses for emphasis, and I see Davey, in the row beside mine, looking around the room expecting someone to falsely identify him. "Class, is that clear?"

There are scattered nods, and 'Yes, Mrs. Kent' from around the room, so she turns and hands the basket to Jamie Gleason in the first desk to her right. Every nerve in my body is tingling with guilt, and nearly uncontrollable fear of being discovered is welling up in my chest. I'm like a buck caught in the headlights with the car speeding towards me; I'm almost ready to initiate the inevitable. I contemplate writing 'yes' on the blank sheet of paper in front of me, just to get this nightmare over with.

Ultimately, I reconsider, knowing that spilling my guts now about the mayor, Lady Louise and Elwood Breffton will only distract from what I pray will tell its own story when the workers dig up the cement. I had hoped, unrealistically, that the police wouldn't be involved until Betsy Mae's body was discovered, but they are, so I'll need to lay extra low for the time being. There is one positive. If I'm this antsy about the police, the workers, and getting caught, I wonder how Janitor Breffton and Louise Maynor are feeling this morning.

Retrieving the basket, now overflowing with folded notebook paper, Mrs. Kent says, "Take five minutes to review your spelling words before the quiz." She then eagerly starts pulling one note after the other out of the wicker basket, and glances at what is written on each slip of paper. The one opportunity that I chance to peek up at her from cursorily reviewing my spelling words, I find Mrs. Kent still setting behind her oak desk, scanning the classroom like a perched eagle, searching for its next tasty rabbit. Fortunately for me, she is staring at Davey picking his nose and wiping the bugger on the bottom of his desk.

My heart skips a beat, wondering if she received any 'yes' responses, as she returns to the front of the room. An unintended sigh of relief escapes from my chest when Mrs. Kent instructs the students, "Please place your spelling books under your desk, closed, and get out a clean sheet of paper from your notebooks."

Hesitating while she peruses the room for compliance, seeming satisfied, she continues, "The first word is CON-TEM-PO-RAR-Y, meaning current or modern. Using this word in a sentence, 'My sister lives in New York City, and recently moved into a contemporary home'." If any of the kids in the classroom had indicated that they knew anything about the vandalism, Mrs. Kent is doing a fine job of not letting on.

Directly before lunch, Principal Nockley looks in our fifth-grade classroom door, and asks for Mrs. Kent's permission to disrupt her lecture on the duties of the United States Congress and Senate. If there's one thing that Doris Kent likes more than boring lectures on government, it's anything to do with Brian Nockley. She purrs like a kitten anytime that he is in the vicinity. I'm surprised that she doesn't shit in a litter box and rub up against his leg when he steps into the room. She, of course, relinquishes control of the class to him and, surprisingly, Principal Nockley's address to our class doesn't feel like an interrogation at all.

"Thank you, Mrs. Kent, for allowing me a minute with your class." Nockley is unusually low key and consoling, as he begins, "I am speaking to each class this afternoon because I want you to know that everything is going to be alright. I will get to the bottom of the vandalism that occurred last night, and guarantee that the individual, or individuals, responsible for this crime is punished appropriately. But...I want you to know that there is nothing that you kids need to concern yourselves with. My only ask is that you feel comfortable in coming to me if you hear anything from your classmates, other children at school, or others outside of school about who caused this destruction." Nockley pauses, and smiles warmly, trying to reduce the tension in the room. From the looks on the faces to my left and right, small nods and slight grins, I think that he's been successful.

"I know that the last two years have been very tough for many of you. Between the fire, losing Ms. Yoncey and needing to attend classes at makeshift locations, you kids have done an admirable job of adapting...as well as excelling in your studies. Whoever vandalized the school grounds not only dishonored Freedom Elementary, but the memory of Ester Yoncey as well." With words exuding sincerity, and a stoic gaze of determination, Principal Nockley puts an exclamation point on his message to the class, "You have my total commitment, and promise, that I will take care of this issue, but even more importantly, the teachers and I will take care of you."

The principal's comments have made me feel about as low as a snake's belly, especially the ones regarding my dishonoring the memory of Ester Yoncey. That's the exact opposite of what I've been tryin' to do! I guess I didn't think it through how everybody was a goin' to react to what me and Timmy did, not that I coulda' come up with a better way.

With guilt and uncertainty causing me to fight back tears, I listen to Brian Nockley attempt to conclude his serious address on a lighter note, "Bubba Armentrout, I guess it's a good thing, but you hardly ever visit me in my office anymore. I've still got that beat up old Harmony guitar in the closet if you get the itch." He gives me a huge grin, and I take my best shot at returning the gesture.

"Don't you kids fret. Just let me know if you hear anything. Thank you, Mrs. Kent."

He smiles at our teacher, who abruptly pushes a loose strand of blue hair back into the bun, and leaves the room. Seconds later, our classroom still totally silent, we hear the principal knock on Mr. Glick's door across the hall. I guess Timmy will be hearing the same speech next. I sure hope that he don't feel as bad as I do about what Nockley says. This whole mess has been my idea, and I've just drug Timmy through the mud to help me.

I couldn't feel worse if Principal Nockley had come in to Mrs. Kent's room and slapped handcuffs on my wrists. In trying to incriminate the mayor and his clan for their wrongdoings, and get poor Betsy Mae Byrd discovered, I've created another disaster for Nockley, the teachers and my classmates. I shoulda' realized this was comin'. Man...as Momma would say, "I've made my bed, so now I gotta sleep in it." Well, there ain't no way to change course now, so alls I can do is ride this out and hope to heaven that the mason workers find Betsy Mae's body.

****

Our class has been a mausoleum the entire day, and Timmy, at lunch, said theirs was the same. I'll bet that's the case with the whole dang school, 'cept maybe the little kids in first and second grade that don't know what's goin' on. I saw the Bankston police walking around the school grounds with Principal Nockley about an hour ago, and now, the workmen have finally arrived to try and clean up the mess. Shortly after lunch, seeing that both teaching and learning was a lost cause, Mrs. Kent had told us to use the last two periods before school ends for the day as study time.

From my desk across the aisle from a somber and studying Jan Breeding, I can peer over her head at the workers laying out jackhammers, shovels and other tools, as they prepare for breaking the cement that they poured yesterday. I feel

159

even shittier, and I didn't believe that was possible, when I notice that no cement truck is on site to replace the demolished walkways. Only a truck loaded with 2X4s, 'Jackson's Lumber Company' painted on its sides, is parked near the workmen. I guess that they're gonna use the wood for temporary planks across the churned-up ground, and to build new forms before they can pour the replacement sidewalks. From the look of things, it's gonna be quite a while before any of us kids will be using the new playground.

I can't help but wonder, again, if Timmy is feeling some of the same guilt that's got me so down. He doesn't ever express his worries like I do, and maybe that's a good thing.

After an eternity of waiting for the police, Principal Nockley, or Satan himself to walk through our fifth-grade door and haul me off to Hell, the end of the day bell rings and I'm nearly startled out of my skin by the broken silence. I mope out of the school, head dangling like a whipped pup, without speaking to anyone. The workers are just getting into the job, jackhammers beginning to vibrate in unison across the playground now that school's out, but at least there ain't no police in sight. Too distracted with my own thoughts to seek out Timmy to get his perspective on everything, I unhitch my bike from the metal rack, and head past a waiting line of parent's cars and busses idling in the circular drive connecting Freedom Elementary to Schoolhouse Road.

With all of the other depressing events that have happened today, every bit caused by me, it doesn't come as no surprise, and is just icing on the cake, when I see Principal Nockley's red Mustang parked outside of the Cheatum residence a few blocks from school. It had seemed like a dang good idea last night to write Peanut's name in the nearly dry cement; now it feels like a vengeful act that I know better than doin'. There's probably a prime corner in Hell for the likes of me.

But what's done is done, and there ain't nothin' gonna change it. All that I can do for now is hope that Breffton didn't bury Betsy Mae's remains too deep for the workers to find it. The last thing I see as I crest the hill above the school is a big, yellow front-end loader plowing through the moist ground, churning up broken slabs of cement.

Pulling my bike up beside our porch, and dropping my math book on a stand inside the back door where Momma keeps her new 'Good Housekeeping' magazines, I take a second to consider an additional outcome that might have played out over the last two days. I don't know what's worse, the workers not finding Betsy Mae because she's buried too deep, or that Elwood had fucked up and not buried her at all. Either way, my skinny ass is on the line with Louise and Mayor Maynor, Elwood Breffton, the Bankston police and every citizen of Freedom. And that don't even include what happens when Momma and Dad find out! Lord, help me, somethin' good has got to happen soon.

Part 3
Bubba's in Deep Shit

Chapter 15

Fading of Friends

Late Fall 2019

Reflection

In fifty years, Ester Yoncey hasn't aged in the least. The still familiar eyes staring back at me from the bronze plaque retain the same knowing gaze that they had conveyed the last time that I had peered into their depths; not on the handcrafted memorial, but as she pondered forgiving two young boys for their foolish and mischievous deeds that she perceived as a rite of passage. The plaque fails to capture the smirk that she would project, lifting 'Big Baby' from its prominent place on her office wall, hiding a smile of satisfaction, knowing that the fear of the punishment was twice as effective as the whipping itself.

Ester had few traits that aligned with the malevolence of my hometown. The one attribute that she did share, the willingness to take risks involving social taboo, ended up getting her killed. Her willing relationship with Mayor Griffin Maynor, igniting the fierce jealously and possessiveness in Lady Louise, now, looking back, seems more a product of naivety and need for human connectivity rather than some covert, seedy attempt to destroy another's marriage. She was a lonely aging woman, residing in a rural mountain community, barren of opportunities for meaningful companionship. And she, obviously, got in way over her head. Even so, those needs, and her choices made to accommodate them, can hardly be considered a major character flaw.

I blame the mayor, even more than Louise and Breffton, for the dark aura that enveloped Freedom, and the demise of Ester Yoncey. Griffin operated like the abductor, manipulating his victim into absolute reliance. As time passes, reality blurs for the captive, and is redefined. The captor becomes the sole source of reference and, consequently, the means by which the prisoner retains existence. At some point, the prisoner no longer considers themselves a captive, and the relationship is bonded.

I don't believe, now, that Ester had an endgame plan with Griffin. Her infatuation with 'belonging', outside of her work environment, blinded her to the peril that ultimately consumed her on that cold winter night five decades ago.

Unlike Ester, the town of Freedom is showing the decomposition of time. As new subdivisions with backyards bursting with children, and chain grocery stores promoting organic produce spring up in neighboring towns, our hamlet has been content to allow mother time to chisel away at its rough facade, one fading memory at a time.

In 1969, Sly Stone lyrically described the plights and conflicts of 'Everyday People'. Freedom Virginia was a microcosm of those internal cultural battles; long hairs and short hairs, rich ones and poor ones, the fat ones and the skinny ones, and, prominently, the white ones and the black ones. Different strokes for different folks. Most of those cultural divides remain, no matter how stringently the God-fearing denizens deny it, even though many of the 'Everyday People' from my childhood have passed on.

****

Feeling, more than visualizing, my past while I cruise by structural artifacts that continue to stimulate childhood recollections, I remember that I had planned to stop by Peg Lipsay's house before I leave town. Mom had mailed me a copy of Jack's obituary from the Post & Courier sometime around the late '90s, and I didn't take the opportunity to tell Peg, at the time, what a positive influence that her dad had been to me and many of the other kids around town. Jack had slowly withered away from the effects of alcohol, diabetes and Alzheimer's; one of Freedom's Everyday People.

At least Jack Lipsay lived a full life. A few of my Freedom Elementary classmates didn't make the journey to, or through, adulthood. Laura Jenkins, who had blushed when Ms. Huckman captured the innocent love note addressed to me, didn't survive the '70s. Shortly after inviting Bobby Braxton to the Sadie Hawkins dance at Moncross High during our sophomore year, 'Super Snatch', as she was fondly labeled by the football team because of her bowed legs and naive promiscuity, died when Bobby's souped-up Datsun Z swerved into an embankment on State Republic Road on the outskirts of Freedom. With her hair up in curlers and her pants to her knees, as the John Prine song laments, Laura was discovered by paramedics when they scissored her date's car in half to free her body. Tommy Jones and The Shondels 'Crimson and Clover', Laura's favorite song, and one that she danced to an hour before the accident, played softly at her funeral. Bobby, a year older, knocked up a girl from Roanoke his senior year and moved to somewhere in Western Virginia.

Jimmie 'Rattler' Solomon died of a drug overdose on his seventeenth birthday while experimenting, for the first time, with heroin. He had acquired his nickname from his hobby of catching and killing rattlesnakes, then attaching the rattles to clothing that he wore to school.

Dwayne Moobray fell off the back of the high dive at Franklin's public pool in Elmont, hitting his head on the cement platform at the bottom of the ladder. He was in a coma for nearly a week, and eventually died from swelling of the brain. The doctors said that he had a seizure of some sort, causing the accident.

As for the folks that were prominent in Freedom during those scandalous years of the late '60s, the Verner brothers, town icon and barber Marvin Cline, Bennie and Em Gee, Bob and Flo Wyatt, and Jimbo Byrd are long dead and buried. Reverend Ross Spicer lived to be ninety-seven, dying in Sunnyside Nursing Home where he continued to try and save resident's souls until the second that he took his last breath.

I had a chance encounter with Timmy Wyatt at a Denny's in Bankston on one of my Christmas visits to Freedom a few years back. When we were in sixth grade, Flo Wyatt, who was significantly older than Bob, had suffered a stroke, as she pulled weeds in their garden. Because of the care that she required, the Wyatt family had moved to West Virginia to be close to Flo's sister and brother. When she died a few years later, Bob came back to Freedom, and Timmy followed after he graduated from high school.

I hadn't seen Timmy since his family had rented a U-Haul and driven down the gravel driveway that he and I used to try and escape the mayor on that warm summer night long ago. At the restaurant, Timmy had looked much more tired and worn than his age would warrant, but justifiably so after five failed marriages and six kids that he had supported through the needs and challenges of growing up. Although the gray aura of our escapades involving Mayor Griffin Maynor hung over our chance meeting like a thunder cloud engulfs a humid Southern evening, verbalizing those thoughts remained in hallowed, unmolested ground. That evening, Timmy and I parted ways with the perfunctory 'stay in touch' sentiments reserved for acquaintances that have long ago depleted any emotional attachment, or current relevance.

One night while channel surfing and landing on CNN, Davey Grater's mug with 'DAVID M. GRATER, US FOREST SERVICE' captioned below it popped up on my screen. He was being interviewed by a young, Hispanic man dressed in a bright, yellow turnout coat and over pants and was answering questions pertaining to a spreading Northern California wildfire. Heavy smoke was billowing through the trees behind Davey's leathery face and bushy, blond mop of hair that had just begun to recede up his sunburned forehead. Spouting a Virginia drawl that would have made him easily recognizable, even without his name emblazoned on a metal tag under the breast pocket of his turnout jacket, Davey told the reporter the number of acres that had been consumed by the fire, and his prognosis of what the Santa Anna winds might do to the firefighting efforts.

Davey and I graduated together in '77, but hadn't been close since our freshman year of high school. His German Shepard, Luke, had sent me to the emergency room for fourteen stitches from slightly above my ankle to the back of my knee. We had been playing flag football in Davey's grandmother's backyard with a couple of other kids from Moncross Junior High when Luke broke free of his collar and the metal chain attached to a stake beside his pen. As fate would have it, at the same moment that I tackled Davey to the ground with a thud, unable to get the sock that we used for a flag from his pocket, his dog pounced on me from behind and began ferociously gnawing on my lower leg like it was a fried pork chop. Luke probably thought that I was attacking his boy, so it was all Davey could do to drag him off of me. Blood was soaking through my torn jeans, and my calf was too stiff for me to walk by the time that his Grandma Grater called my mom, who fussed about their carelessness as she loaded me in the car for a trip to Rockland County Hospital. The bites were relatively shallow, so I had been lucky that the damage wasn't any worse than the stitches.

As to the break in our friendship, my guess is that Davey's parents, still struggling from the bankruptcy associated with their failed bait and tackle shop, feared that my mom and dad were going to hit them with the medical bill from the incident.

In truth, Mom fumed with Dad over that topic for a couple of months after the incident, but he insisted that his insurance had covered most of the cost, and that the Graters had been through enough. After that day, I was never invited back to their house again, and Davey and I didn't have any classes together at school, so our friendship had simply grown apart.

Two folks that were important to me during that period of my adolescence were Lou Anne 'Bounce' Verner and Terri Chandler. Although I haven't spoken to either of them in over forty years, I've tried to keep tabs on them through family members.

Lou Anne, the golden goddess, had briefly realized her dream of 'turning on, tuning in, and dropping out' at Woodstock, but the experience had been short lived. On day two of the event, during Country Joe McDonald's performance of 'Rockin' All Around the World', Bounce had been busted for possession of a controlled substance; the substance being heroin that was possessed through a needle in the vein of her left arm. A few years later, Lou Anne had gotten the monkey off her back and her life under control. Following a short, abusive marriage and a nasty divorce, she had raised twin daughters while managing the daily operations of the Verner farms. Dad told me many years ago, when her twins were still in high school, that Lou Anne was President of the Moncross PTA and was a significant voice against condom distribution in the schools. He had heard at church that she had joined a pro-life group from Richmond, and was an active protester of abortions during rallies at the State House. Sometimes, 'Everyday People' change in ways you would have never anticipated.

Terri Chandler, the flame of my childhood, is more difficult to keep track of since she is one of the few Freedom natives, including myself, that was able to break the culturally sheltered gravitational pull of our upbringing. Even though she was able to distance herself, literally, from Freedom, she wasn't able to avoid the ethical vortex that can, for some, suck the virtues from the upwardly mobile affluent and deposit them in a morally bankrupt black hole.

After attending William and Mary on scholarship, and marrying a New England blue blood that she had met at a Fraternity/Sorority mingling party, Terri acquiesced to serving as the little homemaker as her husband, Randolf T. Robbins III, rapidly progressed to a senior level executive position at a burgeoning energy and commodity company based in Houston, Texas.

Unfortunately for Terri, that company's name was Enron, and her husband was nabbed for diverting company money to personal offshore accounts. For that transgression, Randolph T. Robbins III was awarded a ten to twelve year, all-expense paid vacation to Beaumont Federal Prison, or Institute if you're in the don't call me Randy crowd. Much of the 'pump and dump' money accumulated by Terri's husband that was the foundation of their wealth had been civilly forfeited to the government when Randolph III was sent up the river. Mom told me that the last that she had heard about Terri was that she had remarried, a state trooper, and was living in a nice middle-class neighborhood in Upstate New York; just 'Everyday People'.

****

There is a message on the Methodist Church marquee, as I drive by the sign on my way to Freedom Elementary. Under the message, 'Those That Sin Are Welcome Here. You Will Have Good Company', is the notice that Reverend Sandy Williams will be leading a gospel music sing-along directly after his 11:00 service on Sunday. I wonder if the late Brian Nockley, who partook of one too many unfiltered Camels, will be tapping his size 13s and humming to the chorus in heaven.

****

In retrospect, I can't say, with any real certainty, why that I didn't tell my dad about the potentially lethal dilemma that I had been facing concerning the Maynors and Elwood Breffton.

Especially considering that Arle Armentrout was always the guy that had gotten my scrawny ass out of a barrel full of scalding water whenever I had needed him previously; including an incident that began on my way home from school in the second grade. While cutting through the Thompson's front yard, a shortcut that provided me direct access to the shrubs behind Ms. Leity's house, their fifteen-year-old daughter, Shelia, had screamed, "Get out of my yard, you little shit."

Without hesitation or thought, and certainly not considering the potential consequences, I had retorted, "Go to hell you fuckin' bitch." Now, 'fucking bitch' was a term that I had recently learned from a group of sixth graders, as they described their teacher after a failed history test. Because of Dad's beagles, I was aware that a bitch was a female dog; I wasn't nearly as certain what fucking meant at the time.

170

Shortly thereafter, Sheila Thompson had called my mom, repeated what I had said, and adamantly conveyed that I was the most rude and foul-mouthed brat in Freedom. Mom, in turn, too angry and embarrassed to address the situation herself, had turned me over to Arle when he arrived home from work. As was customary when there was an ass whipping in order, he led me by the collar of my shirt to his work shed behind our house for the formal ceremony. When we arrived at the shed, he unstrapped his leather belt and asked me if what Sheila Thompson said was true. I had ashamedly replied, "Yes, sir, it is.", then he inquired if I knew what a 'fucking bitch' meant. Through heavily flowing tears, I had defined a bitch as a female dog, and honestly relayed that I wasn't positive about the 'fucking' part.

Surprisingly, Dad's face had broken into a huge grin. He slapped me on the back, and chortled, "Bubba, Sheila Thompson IS a fucking bitch. You got that right. It's just that, sometimes, we can't say what we're thinkin'. You and your daddy, unfortunately, have got that in common. I trust that you won't make that mistake again. Am I right?"

I had vehemently shaken my head yes, and rubbed the tears from my eyes on the palms of my hands. Arle had said, "We'll discuss what 'fuck' means when you're a little older. For now, keep bawlin' your eyes out and go straight to your room. We want your momma to think that I whipped your ass good. If she asks, tell her the truth. If she doesn't ask, don't make it a point to volunteer." To Dad's credit, Mom never knew that he hadn't carried out her edict.

Dad always seemed to have the perfect punishment to fit the crime, and he never stayed angry after dolling out the discipline. Once, after discovering that I had shot out streetlights along Route 23 from our front porch with a BB gun, he had me mow our neighbors' lawns for an entire summer to pay for the damage. After I had paid my debt to society with hard labor, Arle never mentioned the streetlight scandal again. Well, unless he was drunk at a Christmas party.

Maybe it was because of those wise fatherly acts of love, and not in spite of them, that I hadn't told him about my dilemma. At a time in his life when he had needed a youngster that was seen, and not heard, predisposed as he was with the enormous responsibility of managing the affairs of his older brother, I couldn't drop another truckload of shit onto his mounting pile of emotional garbage.

At least, that was probably part of my reason for silence. I also continued to fear that no one would believe me, at least, without some hard evidence to validate my accusations. After causing the destruction at the school, if I squealed about what I knew without proof, then I would have been the only person implicated in a crime. Whatever the reason, or combination of reasons, rational or irrational, that evening in September, while waiting for any semblance of news from the schoolyard, had been agonizing.

****

The atmosphere at home had been thick with tension on the evening that the cement masons had dug up the damaged sidewalks and platforms at Freedom Elementary. My parents were so spent from their activities during the prior week concerning my uncle that no one had looked up from their supper plates to strike up a conversation during our evening meal. The news about the school grounds hadn't made its way to our house at that point, and the solemn mood at the table hadn't facilitated any current event discussions. Flo Wyatt mustn't have realized that my folks were back in town, otherwise, she would probably have been sitting at the head of the table spreading the gossip of what she knew, and some things that she didn't. Mom and Dad hadn't noticed my self-absorption and anxiety, as I had guiltily replayed the school day over and over again in my mind. I remember vividly, as if it happened this morning, how desperately I felt the need to bike to school before dark to see if there was any indication that the vandalism that I perpetrated the night before hadn't been performed in vain. So, when I had lied to my mother after supper, professing that I thought that I had forgotten my math book and homework assignment by the bike stand when I left school, she had given me a brief nod of her head and said, "Just be home before dark, Bubba."

Prior to leaving the house and starting my trek back to the Freedom Elementary playground, I had already resigned myself to the fact that I would need to tell the entire story to the authorities if the workers didn't uncover the evidence of Betsy Mae's demise. I had pulled a duffel bag from the top shelf of my closet and packed a few necessities: a change of clothes, underwear, socks and my Fantastic Four comics, for what I had been certain would be a visit to Bankston Juvenile if my plan failed. After hiding my packed bag under the bed, I had headed to the recreation room in our basement to call Timmy Wyatt. I was hoping to tell him to keep his mouth shut, and that I wouldn't mention his involvement if I had to go to the police. The Wyatt phone had rung for nearly a minute before I had put down the receiver, assuming that there was no one home.

There wasn't but a few hours before dark, and I didn't have time to waste in tracking him down.

Mom and Dad had been discussing serious matters on the couch in our living room when I shot out of our back door, hopped on my bike, and peddled hard down Schoolhouse Road towards the destination that, in all likelihood, would determine my immediate future.

Chapter 16
Trailing the Janitor

Early September 1969

Was it just wishful thinking, my imagination or had I actually heard sirens while I distractedly attempted to finish my English homework on the small card table in the corner of our kitchen before dinner? The adjective and verb identification homework that Mrs. Kent assigned could just as well have been translating Vietnamese for all the success I was having at completing it; keeping my mind on my work and off of the workers at the school playground was nearly impossible. And, I hadn't been the only distracted Armentrout. Watching Momma cook supper from my perch near the living room door, a vantage point from which she could ensure that I was at least pretending to be engaged with my studies, I had observed her staring blankly at the boiling pots on the stove, her thoughts seeming to be a million miles away. It's clear that she's worried about Dad, my Uncle Rick too, but mostly Dad. She keeps telling him to let the lawyers do their job, and to take some time for himself, but that ain't Dad's way.

That's when I heard, or at least thought I heard, a siren. If the brief squawk had penetrated whatever land Momma was drifting away in, it sure didn't register on her face. I know I heard somethin'; Jimbo Byrd and his Fire Department guys would sometimes wash the squad trucks in the afternoon, and then test the equipment afterwards, but that activity was always reserved for Saturdays when most of the volunteers were off from work at their regular jobs.

Neither Momma nor Dad had mentioned hearing anything about the vandalism at Freedom Elementary during dinner. Heck, they didn't say two peeps about anything, and I wasn't about to call that topic to their attention. Ain't no doubt, Flo Wyatt will get the word out to everybody and their brother soon enough anyways.

Now, after lying about my math book, trying to stomach our evening meal, and peddling towards school, I wonder if today can get any worse. Jesus, I don't even want to think about what it's gonna put my parents through if I have to tell 'em that I'm the one that destroyed the school grounds. And that don't touch the shit storm that will be blowin' in when I proceed to tell them the tale about the mayor, Lady Louise, Elwood Breffton, Ester Yoncey and Betsy Mae Byrd. What an ungodly mess, and to think, all I wanted to do was to get my belongings from Ms. Huckman's desk.

If it ain't enough being responsible for your family gettin' thrown to the wolves, as they surely will be once everyone in town hears what I done, there's also Timmy Wyatt to consider.

Once he gets wind of me in juvenile detention, more than likely, he'll fess up to helpin' me and get his ass thrown in the can too. And, I'll never be able to face Terri Chandler again, not that she'd be interested in a common criminal anyways. It's a pretty damn good bet that I won't be tradin' Swizzle Stick smooches with her at the State Theater. Shoot, she'll probably pretend that she don't even know me if somebody mentions my name.

Totally absorbed in churning up all of the negative things that are inevitably going to happen to me, and half-heartedly listening for any small sound that could signal somethin' important happening at the school, I crest the hill above the Cheatum place. If 'Peanut' has another tire to roll in front of me, I probably deserve it this time for writing his name in the vandalized cement at school.

It's not the youngest Cheatum that causes me to shake my head to clear my vision and nearly piss myself with excitement when I reach the top of the hill, but seeing two squad cars parked end to end in front of the Breffton house. Anticipation rises to a frenzy in my chest, as I slow my bike to a crawl halfway down the slope. Wanting to see as much as I can, I figure that my choices are to cruise by the Breffton house on my bike and briefly try to take in what's happening, or ditch my ride and sneak up on foot to get a closer, more detailed look. After little deliberation, I decide that there ain't no reason to start bein' cautious now, and choose the second option. I have come this far takin' risks and carrying out my plan, I can't see throwin' in the towel now, and goin' home to wonder all night why the police have paid a visit to Elwood's house. Shit, for all I know, Nance Breffton coulda' suffered a massive heart attack, or Elwood mighta' gone down with a bad case of liquor poisoning.

I lay my bike over in the high grass beside the culvert next to the Denniston's mailbox, out of sight, and trot down the remainder of the hill to the woodpile beside the Cheatum house.

With a slight flash of guilt, but not too much since Peanut rolled the tire in front of me from this very spot, I think about Principal Nockley's visit here earlier today. The Cheatum's place is directly next door to the Breffton's home, and the Lee Roy Randle family live one house down from the Brefftons. The memorial to Ester Yoncey and, at the top of the steps, the double doors at the entrance to Freedom Elementary are located directly across Schoolhouse Road from the Randle place.

Crouching down on my haunches behind the Cheatum's woodpile, out of view from both the road and the goings on at the Brefftons, I take a few deep breaths hoping that my thumping heart will quiet down enough to let me hear what's goin' on next door.

With the sun beginning to droop towards the top of the mountains, shadows growing from the nearby elms like tentacles reaching out to pull me from my hiding spot, the wind picks up and blows down Schoolhouse Road towards Gee's Grocery. If there are sounds to be heard at Elwood's house, they are drifting away from me on the heavy breeze. Every few minutes, I can see a blue, Bankston police hat pop up over the honeysuckle covered wire fence between the Cheatum's lot and the Breffton's detached garage, about fifty feet from where I'm hiding.

I consider that I just might be able to get within hearin' distance, and possibly even get a glimpse of what the cops are doin', if I can make it to the fence undetected. But that's a BIG if. Although there ain't no evidence of the Cheatum clan being home, and I would think that ol' one arm Ray and his boys would be out in the yard gettin' a snoot-full of gossip if they was, gettin' caught by them, in their backyard, would more than likely mean getting my ass pelted with a load of buckshot or worse. Being that I'm already here, that's a risk that I'll just have to take.

The thick, tangle of vines provide the deepest cover near the front of the Breffton's small, detached garage. Though tough to break and clear away without shears, the vines are pliable enough to allow me to push the flowery branches aside and position myself next to the wire fence with a view of the squad cars, garage and the front of the house. Two young police officers with starched white shirts, sharply creased blue trousers, and flattop crew-cuts are carrying

176

boxes, tools, and stored household items from the garage and stacking the stuff up on the gravel driveway next to the Breffton house. A much older cop wearing the same style starched shirt, except that his has a black and yellow striped patch on each shoulder, and it clings too tightly to an enormous beer gut that lops lazily over his black leather belt, is standing on the porch next to a weeping and wailing Nance Breffton. All of this activity is taking place within spitting distance of my hiding place.

Nance appears feebler and more decrepit, if that's possible, than when I saw her standing behind the yellow 'DO NOT CROSS' barrier tape the night of the fire. With her wispy, thin, gray hair dangling down on her shoulders and matted to her brow below her elongated forehead, and her emaciated and withered face displaying protruding bloodshot eyeballs, she looks eerily similar to the Crypt Keeper on the cover of the magazine that arrives in our mail once a month. A feeling of regret stabs at me, as I wish that I had ordered the X-Ray Specs advertised in that same magazine. If the testimonials are true, I would be able to look through the garage wall and see what the Bankston cops are so doggone interested in. The picture in the ad showed the wearer of the glasses looking at the bones in his hands, AND through the skirt of a lady walking down the street.

At that moment, the fantasy of peering into the Breffton property, and potential ability to ogle female classmates at school is shattered when one of the young cop's darts from the garage yelling, "We found the trash bags, Chief!"

The large cop in command gently pats Nance's forearm, excuses himself and lumbers towards where the policeman is standing on the driveway. Before the 'Chief' reaches the younger cop to see what he has uncovered, I hear a rustling noise on my side of the honeysuckle fence, coming from the furthermost corner in the rear of the Cheatum lot. Startled, and fearful that one, or all, of the Cheatum boys have been viewing the proceedings from another section of the fence, and that they are now heading towards where I'm hidden to get a better look, I quietly burrow myself deeper in the flowery vines. Nature's camouflage should be enough for me not to get noticed if whoever is coming isn't looking for an intruder. I'm shit outta' luck if they find this section of the fence as suitable for observing as I do, and decide to pull the vines back for a quick look-see.

Balled tightly in the brush, I chance a glance over my shoulder in the direction of the Cheatum's yard, and am startled to see a slouched, creeping Elwood Breffton slithering by my hiding spot without stopping, close enough for me to smell the Jack Daniels seeping out of his pores like he had used the liquor

177

as a splash on cologne. Elwood is toting what appears to be an empty feed sack over one shoulder, as he quickly reaches the end of the fence only a step or two from Schoolhouse Road. Dropping to his hands and knees, Breffton pulls the honeysuckle branches on that part of the fence aside, and peers at his yard to assess the activity taking place.

Evidently determining that all three cops have moved inside of his garage to discuss what they've uncovered, Elwood stands and staggers as fast as his drunken wobbly legs will carry him, across Schoolhouse Road and disappears into the heavily tree lined area beside the circular bus drive next to Freedom Elementary.

Contemplating what to do next, wishing that the cops would have seen him before he reached the trees, and getting a sick feeling in the pit of my stomach that Breffton is in the process of trying to hide evidence, I reluctantly decide to follow him, at a sizable distance, to see what he is up to. I've come this far in my efforts to unravel his and Louise's evil plan, now I just need to stay back far enough to avoid detection. Once I see what he's doing, I'll run and get the cops. I ain't gonna let curiosity kill this cat! By the time that I reach the end of the fence where Elwood Breffton had knelt on all fours a few minutes earlier, the 'Chief' is leading a shriveled Nance Breffton into her house with a meaty, consoling, and stabilizing arm around her shoulders. I can hear one of the officers rummaging through the garage, and see the other young cop sitting in the squad car, facing away towards Gee's Grocery down Schoolhouse Road, talking on a two-way radio. With the coast as clear as it's probably ever gonna get, I dash across the road to the trees following Elwood's exact path.

Making myself as invisible as possible behind a thick tree trunk, and taking a quick look under an eye-level branch to make sure that Breffton isn't stationed in the same area, I take a deep breath and prepare to slide across a heavy rug of pine needles to an area of the woods with a better view of the school building. Before I can churn up enough courage to make my move, a flurry of activity commences in the circular drive close to where I'm hiding. Lying on my stomach, and pushing myself forward with my elbows, it's only a few yards to the edge of the pavement. Still under the cover of brush, I can see a stretch ambulance, identical to the vehicle that had whisked a dead Ester Yoncey away from the same spot the night of the school fire, idling with its rear doors flung wide open. Two guys in white coveralls are leaning against the side of the ambulance sharing a cigarette, and looking anxious, as they make small talk while

178

constantly glancing back towards the school. Finally, an older gentleman carrying a brown, leather satchel and note pad, and wearing a wrinkled dark suit and tie, comes into view, walking from behind the school towards the ambulance. Dark suit guy takes a white handkerchief from his back pants pocket, dabs at the sweat bubbling up on his forehead and dripping onto his collar, and says, "You can take the body to the morgue now. We're done here." With that, the guys in coveralls slam shut the rear doors of the vehicle, crush the cigarette butt, quickly jump in the ambulance's front seats, and speed off around the circular drive and onto Schoolhouse Road. I hear them blast the horn and siren a few moments later as they reach Route 23 on their trek to Bankston.

The dark suit guy begins to walk towards the Breffton house but, first, stops at a late model Ford parked alongside the road, and tosses his bag and notebook in the backseat. From there, he continues to the Breffton's front door, knocks and enters.

Initially mesmerized by the action at the school, the heavy sound of shuffling boots and tree limbs being pushed aside breaks my trance. Carefully cocking my head to the left, I can see Elwood Breffton break cover about thirty yards from me, then linger at the edge of the woods, searching the school grounds for signs of any remaining people.

I'm dang lucky that the ambulance had caught his attention, as it did mine. Otherwise, I would have probably run up his backside before I had even known he was there. Well, I guess there surely ain't no doubt now that the workers have uncovered what's left of Betsy Mae Byrd's body, the only uncertainty is what Breffton has in the sack, and what he's a gonna do with it. I wonder how in the heck the cops know that it was Elwood who buried her?

The sun has become a red ball as it dips further in the sky, with black storm clouds beginning to gather in the West. At best, I've got about forty-five minutes if I'm gonna make it home before dark. But I've seen it through this far, and I have to know if he's tryin' to cover up somethin' before the police can find him.

With these thoughts rumbling through my head, and common sense telling me that following Breffton is bat-shit crazy, Elwood runs from the trees and makes a beeline for the door at the rear of the school. From his gait, I can tell that his drunk ain't wore off much, but I'll still need to keep a safe distance between him and me so as not to get discovered. That bastard has already sent one person to meet the Almighty, and helped with another's early departure; I don't need to make it easy for him to complete the trifecta.

As Elwood plods across the playground towards the rear door of the school, I slip out of hiding and shoot towards a bus parked near the back of the circle. I skid to a stop, perched behind the rear bumper of the vehicle, when Breffton reaches the yellow 'DO NOT CROSS' tape circling the hole where Betsy Mae was evidently buried. Breathless, he stops briefly, cranes his neck and turns his head from side to side, searching one last time for any remaining workers or policemen. Finding none, he clumsily ducks under the tape, and bolts for the school door.

Concerned that the door will lock behind him, I sprint from my hiding place at the rear of the bus, heading for the corner of the school adjacent to where he's standing but still not within eyesight of his position. I probably wouldn't have been quick enough to make the building undiscovered, except that Breffton tripped over a chunk of the broken cement, and fell a few feet short of the entrance before pushing himself up and staggering the remainder of the way.

He drunkenly sorts through the keys hanging from a metal loop attached to his belt, then makes three attempts to find the one that fits the lock. Finally, successful at finding the correct combination of lock and key, Breffton fumbles with the handle before angrily throwing open the heavy metal door and lunging into the building.

Fortunately for me, the new school has hydraulics installed that slowly pull the door closed each time someone enters or exits the building. I can see the metal arm above the frame beginning to close, as I dart towards it from my hiding place thirty feet away.

Reaching the door, my index finger barely catches, then nearly slips from the handle just as the mechanism begins to latch. Panting for air, I stand silently outside of the school holding the door slightly ajar.

Giving Breffton enough time to move down the hallway to wherever it is he is going; I take a nervous look around the destroyed grounds. In the hours since school let out for the day, the police have completed investigating the scene. In addition to the tape circling the dig site, barriers, cones and small flags mark areas where evidence was discovered. Hopefully, it was only Elwood Breffton that left any traces on the grounds and not two youngins' that would prefer to remain anonymous.

Moments before deciding that now is the right time to enter Freedom Elementary, I realize that if I follow Breffton into the building, nobody is within shouting distance if he catches me and I try to call for help. Wanting desperately

180

to let go of the door handle and haul ass for home or, at least, run to get reinforcement from the police questioning Nance Breffton, my instincts tell me that the janitor is trying to hide something that will tie him further to the crimes. I'm standing here, pissing away the last bit of daylight, while Breffton could be fucking up my plans to finger him for the dirty deeds he's committed. Reasoning and rationalizing, again, that I won't get too close, AND that Elwood is totally shit-faced drunk, I decide that what I WANT to do and what I NEED to do are two totally different animals. My burgeoning sense of obligation has finally overtaken the shame and guilt that I had felt watching my classmates mourn this morning. Hell, without my involvement, the Maynors and Breffton would have pulled off these murders without anybody ever knowing shit about it. I've managed to keep my plan on the road up until now, and I ain't about to let the wheels careen off after getting this close.

So, against my better judgment, and with every nerve cell in my body sending me warning pangs, I pat the phantom vice squeezing my stomach muscles with the palm of my sweaty hand, and slip through the doorway into the dark and ominous maw of Freedom Elementary.

Chapter 17

Making the Connection

Late Fall 2019

Reflection

When I close my eyes today, I can still feel the cold emanating through that thin cotton t-shirt, as I leaned against the metal door of the school. Initially, I hadn't been able to see anything down the hallway, but faint patches of the late evening sunset filtering through open classroom doors at the opposite end of Freedom Elementary helped my eyes adjust to the minimal light. Thankfully, none of the rays penetrated the dark pocket where I had stood, anxiously praying that Breffton wasn't aware that I was trailing him. The oncoming rumbling of a storm, as it made its way over the mountain, and the lack of light to validate my safety in the hallway had allowed my imagination to run free. It created ghostly hands reaching out in the darkness, searching to wrap my throat in a vice-like grip and strangling the breath from me. Then my memory flashed to the bedroom conversation between Louise Maynor and Elwood Breffton and I became certain that the janitor had somehow gotten behind me in the darkness, and was waiting for just the right moment to grab my throat, the same way that he had smashed Ester Yoncey's windpipe on the night of the fire.

All of the self-induced hysteria had created a sense of panic that made it difficult to think. Growing thunder broke the trance, and I had been able to haphazardly rationalize my options; remaining motionless at the door only left me vulnerable like cornered prey, a captured rat about to be bundled in Breffton's sack, while progressing down the hallway might possibly draw the attention of the predator. Ultimately, I had decided that I didn't want to be Breffton's last act of murderous revenge before the police caged him, but that I still needed to ensure that he wasn't able to avoid their grasp by burying evidence. There seemed little choice for my ten-year-old mind, tears of fear streaking down my face, as a loud clap of thunder and flash of lightening pushed me forward down the hallway.

September 1969

Shit, there ain't nuthin' good gonna happen if I keep screwin' around here like a scared rat on a sinking ship. Breffton's eventually going to finish whatever it is that he's up to, and then head back this way to escape being seen by the police. As it is, I might as well just package myself up with gift wrap and a bow, and yell, "Hey, Elwood! It's me, the lil' bastard Bubba Armentrout. Come and get me!"

Not only is it getting dark outside quick, there's a damn toad strangler of a storm a comin' too. With no alternative other than tucking my furry tail between my legs and making a mad dash for the safety of home, an act that will almost certainly allow Breffton to hide evidence and have a second chance to do away with me later, I gather what little gumption that I can muster, and force my scrawny legs to start shuffling down the hallway.

Creeping quietly from doorway to doorway, I find the darkest spot where I can perk up my ears and listen intently for any sign of movement from within each classroom. When satisfied that the janitor isn't occupying a room, I take a quick look to ensure I am right, and then slip to the next darkened area further down the hall.

My angst is near fever pitch by the time that I reach the first-grade rooms, next to Principal Nockley's office, at the front of Freedom Elementary. I sure am glad that Timmy and Davey ain't here to see how I got tears runnin' down my face like a baby. I ain't never been so scared in all my life.

The last orange glow of late evening light tinged with the deep purple of the approaching storm clouds is filtering through the shades beside Secretary Fran's desk, as the entire school grows darker. Again, I get the uneasy notion that Elwood Breffton suspects that I'm following him, and has hidden in one of the classroom closets, waiting to silently stalk me from behind. I cautiously turn on my heels to check the path I've taken, and throw my arms in front of my face expecting a blow. When none comes, I peer between my elbows and see only a tunnel of darkness.

Sighing to release the anxiety that has built up in my chest, I'm almost certain that I hear a noise coming from the vicinity of Principal Nockley's office.

Wanting to be sure, I hold my breath and stand as still as my thumping heart will allow. There ain't no doubt, a creepy sound is coming from that direction. Listening intently, the noise resembles a loose shutter blowing back and forth in a soft evening breeze. The methodical creak, creak, creak seems to keep time with the only other sound in the school, the ticking of the wall clock in one of the first-grade classrooms.

Trying to devise my next move, I contemplate if it could be Breffton creating the creaking sound. Freedom Elementary has those new-fangled tilting windows that are made for easy cleaning, and I'm pretty doggone certain that the builders didn't install shutters over those. And even if the office windows are different from the classrooms, they'd be latched so as not to be blowin' in the wind as the storm approaches.

Dropping, I crawl on my hands and knees across the shiny new tile floor, stopping again to listen, finally reaching the corner of the administrative office. Still, no movement in the room except for the sound that sorta reminds me of the metronome that Johnny Miller uses to keep his students on strumming pace during his guitar lessons on Saturday mornings. Whatever is causing the noise, it is definitely coming from Nockley's inner office, past Secretary Fran's desk area, in the adjoining room. If I can sneak behind the Secretary's desk without being discovered, and the principal's door is open, then I should be able to see what Breffton is up to without needin' to get any closer. One thing's for certain, and I've definitely made my mind up on this, if I can't see what I need to from there, I'm gettin' the Hell outta' Dodge.

Slithering on my stomach to Ms. Fran's desk, the bristly carpet in the administrative office pushing up my shirt and scratching my belly, I can almost see Principal Nockley's entire office through his open door. Nothing is stirring in the room except for a foggy, indiscernible shadow swaying back and forth across the wall, and the soft, slowing, creaking sound. Elwood Breffton's sack, and a broken whiskey bottle lay beside the rolling wheel of Nockley's leather chair, but there is still no sign of the janitor. A simultaneous loud clap of thunder, spray of rain and bright flash of lightening cause me to scoot back towards the hallway, sure and certain that Breffton is about to grab me.

The second that I turn my head to escape, I glimpse a pair of dangling feet that I hadn't been able to see from the corner of Ms. Fran's desk. Brown, mud-stained work boots hang in mid-air, barely visible in the afterglow of the lightning strike.

Squinting my eyes to get a sharper view, I'm able to determine that the boots are attached to limp, jean covered legs swaying to the rhythmic sound that I had heard coming from the office. The shadow on the principal's wall has now totally blended into blackness as the stormy night falls across Freedom.

Stunned and confused, it takes a few seconds for my brain to register what my eyes are tellin' it. Sure, I recognize the boots from when they shuffled past my hiding place over an hour ago, but that alone doesn't convince me that this ain't no trap.

I edge my way forward, towards Nockley's office, on hands and knees and look up at the ceiling. I can't suppress the 'YELP' that springs from my throat when I see Elwood Breffton hanging from a metal ceiling beam by a thick, hemp rope around his stump-like neck. Broken portions of the white ceiling tile that had once covered the beam now litter the top of Nockley's desk and the floor around his chair.

Certain, now, that the janitor ain't followin' me, and won't be ever again, I switch on the desk lamp beside the principal's nameplate, and pull it to the floor to try and keep the light from being detectable from outside of the school. Although the glow is faint, I can tell that Elwood's face is the black, purple of the storm brewing outside. His eyes are bulging in their sockets, with blood filling both eyeballs. Worse yet, there is a strand of spittle leaking from his puffed, cracked lips onto the front of his yellow work shirt, and his blackened tongue has pushed out his lower dentures. His heavy body is as limp as a forgotten rag doll.

Well, there ain't no doubt that Breffton's dead. I never seen but one dead body first hand, my Great Aunt Sarah on Grandma Armentrout's side of the family, laid out in the center of her living room the night before they buried her. I fussed when Momma and Dad asked me to sit up with her, like she was a goin' somewhere, but Dad knew it was only because I was afraid. He told me, "Bubba, it ain't the dead ones that you ought to be scared of. It's the live ones that'll do you in." With those words of wisdom in mind, and Breffton recently being introduced to Satan, I'm pretty damn certain that he ain't about to do me no harm.

After all that I've been through, fretting over what Elwood **might** do to me, it's no surprise that I'm not afraid of being alone with his body, dead and hanging from the ceiling. But, shit in a shoe box, there is still an alive and kickin' Louise Maynor, and maybe the mayor too, that has a damn sharp ax to grind

185

with me. *Fearful that someone will see the glow from the light in Principal Nockley's office, I flip the switch off and return the lamp to his desk.*

All in all, Breffton's suicide ain't done much to calm my discouragement and fear. I slide over to a corner of the office nearest the shaded window to assess my still shitty situation. That son-of-a-bitch Breffton knew that his ass was cooked when the police arrived at his house. I don't know how they knew that he buried Betsy Mae, but they did. And Breffton knew that they did, too. So, he went and hung himself to protect the love of his life, Lady Louise.

Jesus, that means that the involvement of the Maynors in Betsy Mae Byrd's murder will go to the grave with the janitor, and few, if any, questions will ever be asked. Oh, they'll be lookin' for a motive, but if one ain't apparent, then they won't look long.

Breffton's death also means that Ester Yoncey's murder and the school fire will go unsolved. Yeah, the police might make a connection since they somehow know that Elwood buried Betsy Mae, but there ain't no proof without Louise Maynor or the mayor being implicated. About the best that I can hope for is that the police will put the blame for the school fire on Breffton's shoulders, too.

Lady Justice might have tipped the scales and crushed Louise's foot soldier and lover, but she and the mayor will be scot-free to continue to run Freedom into the ground while working outside of the rules that apply to everybody else. And worse yet, for me, there's about three good reasons that Louise Maynor will still want to see me sinkin' to the bottom of the Shenandoah River in the near future; Ester Yoncey, Betsy Mae Byrd, and Elwood Breffton. I'm the last link to her involvement, and she's already tried to have me killed once. As it stands, the best-case scenario is that I tell the police my story with no real evidence to back it up, and maybe that'll keep her off my ass for a spell. Even to buy that time, I'll need to admit to breaking and entering, and vandalism.

Lost in thought, and on the verge of giving up, I slide over the floor on my butt to lean against the wall and ponder my hopeless situation. No sooner than I've scrunched up my legs, and brought my crossed arms and chin to my knees, deep in thought, I'm jolted back to the present by a sharp object digging into my ass through my worn jeans. That's all I need is to have a sliver of Breffton's broken Jack Daniels bottle stuck in my crack from sliding across the floor in the dark. Shifting from sitting flat on my butt cheeks to balancing on my left hip, the sharp pain immediately subsides.

Knowing that I gotta get home before Momma begins to search for me, but feeling like there's got to be an answer that will get me out of this pickle, I drift back into thought forgetting about the broken bottle. Contemplating about saying nuthin' and then needin' to look over my shoulder every second for some goon that the Maynors have hired, or spillin' my guts and draggin' my parents through the ringer for the chance at borrowed time, I realize that there just ain't no good answer to come up with.

My thoughts are chasing their tail like a beagle with the mange, the same circle of unanswerable questions churning around in my head, when I feel the sharp pain again. Mary, mother of Jesus, whatever it is that keeps pokin' me in the ass feels like it's about to break skin. Sliding my back up the wall to a standing position, I search the floor where I had been sitting, but don't see anything sharp in the bristly new carpet. Rubbing my butt with my palm through the thick material of my jeans, I feel the outline of the hard-edged object that has been causing the prodding pain. Reaching into my back pocket, cautious in case it's a piece of glass, my fingers touch a coiled chain attached to metal. Holding the object near the office window, and slightly opening the shades, the faint glow of a streetlight across Route 23 through the pouring rain provides enough illumination for me to recognize the item.

The locket and chain that I found in the bedside table at the Maynors is softly reflecting in the dim light through the shades. The keepsake, with Louise's picture inside, along with the inscription from her mother, feels massive in my hand; heavier than its weight would warrant, like an archaeologist discovering a small but vital piece of ancient artifact.

I had stuffed the locket in my back pocket as I slid under the bed at Chestnut Hall, anxious to avoid the afternoon rendezvous between Louise Maynor and the recently deceased Elwood Breffton. With everything that I had heard and learned during their pillow talk, I had totally forgotten about Louise's necklace when I slipped back through the window on my way out of her house.

Gazing at the silver locket on the gold chain lying in my palm, barely visible in the scant light, I have an idea. Thank you Heavenly Father; I don't know if finding this is a godsend, but it sure is a small ray of hope in the darkest of times.

Without hesitation, I pull my thin cotton shirttail out of my jeans, spit in my right palm where the locket is lying, and wipe the silver dry holding the object firmly in the cloth of my shirt. Repugnantly grabbing two of Elwood Breffton's sausage link swollen fingers, I press their tips to each side of the locket with my

187

shirt covering my hand. I need to get his prints on the locket without getting mine on there as well.

Feeling secure that Elwood's prints are on the locket, I push Principal Nockley's leather chair directly under Breffton's hanging body with my elbows. Carefully crawling onto the seat, standing, then balancing with legs splayed on the chair, I hook the gold chain around the janitor's bloated neck, just above where the rough noose has cut deeply into his skin. It's a damn tight fit, but it would have hung nicely before his pooled blood increased his collar length by two sizes. I carefully lift his shirt collar, and shake it slightly until the locket drops towards his chest, so as to appear that he had been secretly wearing the keepsake.

After replacing the rolling executive chair to where the janitor's feet had pushed it when Elwood jumped from the seat to hang himself, I wipe the leather seat with my shirt in case I left any fingerprints. Looking around the office for anything that I might have caused to be out of place, and seeing nothing that I had missed, I run from the office towards the rear of Freedom Elementary. By God, the Crypt Keeper himself would be proud to describe the grisly scene that I have left behind.

Bursting through the rear door, rain pelting my face, I retrace my steps through the woods all the while pondering how the police will react to the locket. Finding the keepsake may not incriminate Lady Louise, but it sure as hell will cause some pretty direct questions to be asked. I've always heard that dead men tell no tales, but I've got a feelin' that Breffton just might be an exception to that rule with a little help from the locket that I left hanging from his neck.

The police cars are still sitting outside of Nance's house when I reach Schoolhouse Road. One of the young crew-cut officers has a flashlight and umbrella, and is loading sealed evidence bags into the back of his vehicle. He closes the trunk and shouts towards the porch, "I've got the pieces of the trash bag loaded, Chief. I'll get them to the evidence locker before I head home for the night. Spenser said he'll tote the other stuff that you wanted fingerprinted."

The Chief must have been standing at the screen door, because he immediately responds, "Thanks, Mikey. I'm headin' out now, too. Tomorrow's gonna be a long day. I've got the coroner at 6:00 am, and then a meeting with the press after that. Mitchell and Davidson are searching Breffton's local haunts in case he shows up, and Daugherty is gonna watch the house and the school. I *just talked to him on the phone at the station in Bankston. He's on his way. Let's get some sleep while we can."*

After waving his acknowledgment to the Chief, the young cop drives away. The Chief and the remaining officer follow a few minutes later.

Watching from the cover of the trees, and seeing that the coast is clear, I run up Schoolhouse Road, jump the ditch in front of the Denniston's house and grab my bike from the weeds. Just as I begin peddling towards home, I see the lights of my Dad's pickup truck crest the top of the hill.

Soaked to the gills, and prepared to get my backside tanned for being late, I still smile to myself, as I throw my bike in the bed of his truck, thinking that whatever punishment that Dad doles out, tonight's accomplishments are well worth it.

Part 4
Reaping What Is Sowed

Chapter 18

Breaking News

Late Fall 2019

Reflection

Not surprisingly, I had slept fitfully that night after getting a stern lecture from Dad and being sent straight to bed for riding my bike after dark. The few times that I did doze off, I had dreamed that Elwood Breffton was looking for me as I hid under Louise Maynor's bed. His head was swollen to the size of a pumpkin, eyes bulging to the point of being unable to blink, and the necklace around his bloated neck was so tight that it was causing thin rivulets of blood to drip onto the meticulously waxed cedar floor of Chestnut Hall. His sausage like fingers, with a crusty black substance under the fingernails, were slapping at the floor attempting to catch my T-shirt in their grip. I could hear Louise Maynor screaming from somewhere in the bedroom, "You've fucked up again, Elwood! How could you be so stupid that you screw up killing yourself?"

Each time that Breffton's fingers neared my throat, I would wake up in a cold sweat, and discover that only twenty minutes had passed since the last time that I had looked at my bedside clock.

I hadn't even dozed after midnight, so I had been awake for hours when our phone rang at 6:00 am. Mom, already up and preparing breakfast for Dad before he headed off to work, answered the kitchen phone after the fourth ring. I could hear her shifting pans off of the burner, before irritably barking,

"I'm coming! Hold your horses."

The call had been brief, and impossible for me to hear Mom's part of the conversation from my bedroom, but within a few minutes, she was talking in a soft tone with Dad in their bedroom across the hall from mine. "Arle," she had said, concern radiating from her voice, "I just got a call from Fran Singleton at the school. They've canceled all classes today. She said something about vandalism the night before last, and workers needing to clean up the mess today. Fran is calling all the parents, so she said that she didn't have time to answer any questions. I can't believe that Flo Wyatt hasn't shown up on our doorstep bearing bad tidings. Maybe she's still sick. Jen Hemmings told me over the weekend that Flo had been down with the crud that she caught from one of her kids."

I could hear Dad grunt, and start to respond, but Mom hadn't given him the opportunity. With an air of impatience, evidently his level of concern hadn't matched hers, she worriedly whispered, "I was so dog-tired last night that I went directly to bed after checking on Grannie Bess. Did Bubba say anything to you about something happening at the school?"

"Not about the school," Dad responded immediately this time, "but after I scolded him last night for not being home before dark, he told me that on his way back from getting a soft drink at Gee's Grocery, it had started to rain and he waited the storm out under a tree at the church. While he was there, he saw police cars at the Breffton's and was afraid that either Nance or Elwood might have had a heart attack. No ambulance ever showed up, so he figured that everything must be OK. I didn't go too hard on him; just sent him to bed. You were already asleep when I came in to tell you that I was going looking for him."

The next few days had been filled with breaking news.

****

Wednesday September 10, 1969

Rumors are running rampant all over Freedom. Timmy Wyatt called around lunchtime to let me know that gossipers from Flo's grapevine told her that workmen repairing the vandalism at Freedom Elementary had found an unidentified body buried under the cement. "Ain't that sumthin'?" My friend chuckled, feigning surprise. And, unbelievably, that wasn't the biggest slice of juicy news. Timmy could hardly contain his excitement, as he dropped the next bombshell. Flo's source, the wife of a City Tax Clerk that plays poker with a cop that works for the Bankston Police Department, told her that Elwood Breffton was discovered last night around midnight hanging by the neck dead in Principal Nockley's office at the school. "How about them apples, Bubba?" Timmy anxiously inquired, obviously searching for a response from me on what I knew about the janitor's untimely demise. Fortunately, while I was tryin' to think of

194

exactly how to answer, I heard Flo in the background yelling at Timmy to get the hell off the phone, that she had an important call to make. It sure didn't take a mind reader to guess what that call was about.

"Listen, I gotta get off now. Mom is having a hissy 'bout the damn phone," Timmy groaned. "Come on over this evenin' if you can."

Knowing that I would need to spill the beans to Timmy on what had happened yesterday evening with Elwood Breffton if I went by his house tonight, I made an excuse to at least delay that discussion for another day. If questions started to be asked, I wanted him to know as little as possible. I'd already dragged him in to trouble neck deep. "I gotta do chores around the house all day 'cause I got grounded for not being home on time yesterday. I'll give you a call tomorrow. Thanks for lettin' me know about Breffton! Do you think it's true, I mean, about him hangin' himself?"

"I don't know, but I'll call you if I hear more," Timmy replied, abruptly hanging up the phone before Flo could slap the back of his head.

****

Thursday September 11, 1969

Excerpt from the front-page headline story in the Bankston Post and Courier, Morning Edition:

**WORKERS UNEARTH DECOMPOSED
BODY AT LOCAL
ELEMENTARY SCHOOL
JANITOR FOUND HANGED AFTER BODY
DISCOVERED**

Freedom – Bankston Police Chief Robert 'Bud' Burns has confirmed that the unidentified body of an adult female was unearthed Tuesday evening as workers repaired the vandalized grounds of Freedom Elementary School. Information is limited at this time, but a school administrator that we contacted regarding the incident told the Post and Courier that classes have been canceled for the remainder of the week to accommodate the police investigation, and to reduce

195

the student's exposure to the situation. As of this morning, Chief Burns was unable to provide an estimated time of death for the deceased.

In a bizarre twist to this story, the Post and Courier learned, just before this edition went to press, that a few hours after the body was unearthed on school grounds, Elwood James Breffton, a custodian at Freedom Elementary for over twenty-five years, was found hanged in the school administration office.

The Bankston Police Department and the School Principal, James Nockley, had no comment as to any connection between the unearthed body and Mr. Breffton. Chief Burns did provide that the death of the female is being treated as a potential homicide, while there is no indication of foul play regarding the custodian.

The new Freedom Elementary School opened earlier this month after a December 1967 fire destroyed the previous structure, resulting in the death of, then, School Principal Ester Yoncey.

As our paper reported on Tuesday evening, recently poured sidewalks and bench areas were destroyed at the school on Monday night, which required extensive repairs on Tuesday afternoon.

The Post and Courier is actively following this story, and will detail additional findings as we learn them.

****

The news of the scandal has been the one and only thing able to break the trance that Momma and Dad have been mired in while helping Uncle Rick and Aunt Jane with their legal and financial troubles. During supper, I pretend that all of the patchwork of information circulating from the newspaper, television news and word of mouth that they are sharing is as surprising to me as it is to them. After days of not eating, I'm suddenly feeling hungry, nearly starved, for the first time since my near collision with Breffton's stolen vehicle across from the Cheatum house. I cautiously ask questions and probe for information on how much that my parents know between mouthfuls of meatloaf and mashed potatoes. Momma simply shrugs her shoulders, and says, "I guess that we'll find out soon enough," when I ask if they have any idea who it is that the workers found. But I see her cast a glance at Dad, so I'm pretty sure that they've already shared their suspicions with each other. Dad is more willing to provide his views when I ask, "Golly, I heard tell that Mr. Breffton had a drinkin' problem, but he always seemed like an OK guy to me. Do you reckon' his suicide has anything to do with the body that was dug up?"

"Bubba," Dad looks over at me slyly, and points the end of his fork that has recently skewered a mass of peas, "Yogi Berra once said that some things are too coincidental to be a coincidence. I think that this happens to be one of those things." From my perspective, that about sums up everything.

There is one tidbit of information, discussed during chocolate pudding, that Momma received from Flo Wyatt, and the news gave my guilty conscience a needed boost of relief. "Martha Spurlock told Flo," Momma begins, passing the Reddi-Wip can, "that the police questioned Peanut Cheatum and Ray about the vandalism at the school. She said that there was a name, or initials, I'm not sure which, left in the cement that made the cops think that Cheatum was involved."

"Wouldn't surprise me none," Dad says with emphasis. "All those boys, including the old man, are bad news."

"Well, supposedly, not this time," Momma quickly interjects, "or at least, not according to Martha Spurlock. Seems that they have an airtight alibi. Ray and both boys were up in Salisbury at a Klan meeting on Monday night. Lonnie Hammer from down on the river road was more than willing to vouch for them."

"Now ain't that a big, damn surprise," Dad quips, as he gets up from the table, kisses Momma on the cheek and thanks her for supper.

****

Friday September 12, 1969

Excerpt from the front-page headline story of the Bankston Post and Courier, Morning Edition:

FREEDOM ELEMENTARY SCHOOL JANITOR TIED TO MURDER
UNEARTHED BODY IDENTIFIED

Freedom – The remains of the body unearthed by workers while repairing the vandalized grounds at Freedom Elementary School have been identified as those of Mrs. Betsy Mae Byrd, 33, a Freedom resident missing since February of 1968. From preliminary coroner findings, the cause of death was likely poisoning. A toxicology report verifying that assumption is due back from Richmond early next week.

Bankston police have confirmed that Mrs. Byrd's remains were found buried in an industrial trash bag identical to those used for refuse by county schools. Each school in the district has its name printed on the bags in order to be tracked at the county landfill for expansion purposes. A crate containing unused trash bags assigned to Freedom Elementary was found in the garage of Elwood J. Breffton, the custodian who was found hanged in the School Principal's office the night that Mrs. Byrd's body was discovered.

Chief Robert 'Bud' Burns of the Bankston Police Department, lead investigator of both the Byrd homicide and the Breffton suicide, would not validate if the deceased custodian is the primary suspect in Byrd's death, or if others are potentially involved.

In a brief statement last night, outside of his downtown office, Chief Burns did indicate that there is another party of interest to be questioned once the medical findings are complete.

The Post and Courier will be providing additional information, as it becomes available.

****

Well, well, well, it seems like ol' Elwood Breffton has done reached up from Hell and grabbed him some potential company. The newspaper article made it pretty clear that the police have questions for at least one more person about Betsy Mae's death. Hopefully, Louise Maynor's locket has given them a valuable clue on where to look first. That alone should keep her and the mayor off of my ass for a while.

But there is one more thing to do that I just can't leave to chance, and I gotta do it quick!

With a grin of satisfaction plastered on my face, I set out to do my task.

Chapter 19

And That's the Way It Is...

Late Fall 2019

Reflection

The week after Betsy Mae Byrd's body was found was a miasma of fact, half-truths, and outlandish conjecture, randomly brewed adding various quantities of bullshit in Freedom's cauldron of community gossip. From barbershop to beauty shop, and communion tables to dinner tables, all conversations led to the 'Freedom Elementary School Scandal', as it was dubbed in the daily press releases and news broadcasts across the state. Newspapers and television stations in Bristol, Richmond and Fairfax had mercurially assigned reporters to cover the story locally, and the smaller town papers across Virginia immediately utilized the larger agencies' reports once they were released.

With the uncommon attention from outside our community, the townsfolk responded to their ten minutes of fame by developing hypothesized assumptions and creating outright fabricated stories that they concocted from bits of fact, fiction and rumors that they heard from neighbors, family and friends.

The most widespread and popular, though short-lived, tall tale involved Elwood Breffton threatening the mayor when the janitor became aware of Griffin Maynor's affair with Betsy Mae Byrd, whom Breffton was supposedly infatuated with. Many around town found this story feasible because there had been rumblings among the women of the Lady's Auxiliary about how Betsy Mae was always 'all over' the mayor at every town event. As the sensationalized story spread, it expanded to having Jimbo Byrd, in a fit of rage, killing his wife when he caught Breffton, in some tales, and Mayor Maynor in others, in the sack with Betsy Mae.

Ultimately, the yarn weavers assessed, Elwood couldn't live with himself harboring the guilt of her demise, so he had made the decision to do a little rope swinging at the local elementary school. Though the story didn't correlate to the facts surrounding the case, many spouted the tale, in various versions, as gospel.

Another variation of the fable had Breffton offing Betsy Mae because she had scorned his advances, while another story involved a mysterious drifter hired by Griffin Maynor to 'take care' of the two locals, Betsy Mae and Elwood Breffton, because they knew of the mayor's sexual indiscretions and were about to ruin him politically or through extortion. An alternative version of this theme had the mayor's motivation being the loss of Louise's family money if she divorced him after finding out about his affairs.

Each of these yarns, and many more, were mixed, matched and expanded on without anyone, well…almost anyone, knowing the real story. That is, until Jack Lipsay provided the skinny on how each of the events surrounding the scandal had played out from the wooden bench in front of Gee's Grocery on a bright, but chilly, Sunday afternoon in September 1969.

****

Sunday September 21, 1969

After church, my parents and me drove to Grandma Bess and Granddaddy Robert's house for Sunday dinner. The same as everywhere else in town, all we talked about was the scandal.

Nobody knows exactly what to believe from all the stories circulating around Freedom. And, you can't throw a rock without hittin' a dang newspaper or television reporter. One thing's for certain, everybody in town is shook up about the murder.

Jimbo Byrd hasn't shown his face in town for two weeks, not that he's been particularly outgoing since Betsy Mae's disappearance anyways. Some say that he is being held in connection with her murder, but I think that he might just have left town to get away from all the questions and attention.

It was real interestin' this mornin' when the Maynors didn't show up for church. I can see how they'd be embarrassed from all the gossip circulating around town. Nobody, and no story, has mentioned Louise Maynor's locket, so I don't know if the police didn't make the connection, or if they did and are holding that piece of evidence tightly. What I do know is that I ain't seen hide nor hair from Griffin and Louise Maynor since the dedication, and I just hope that it stays that way.

Once we finished Sunday dinner, everyone retired to the living room where Granddiddy Robert immediately went to sleep in his leather La-Z-Boy recliner with a lit stogy burning between the index and middle finger of his right hand. Grandma Bess is all nervous about his upcoming cataract surgery, and Momma tells her that she'll be glad to stay with them a spell until he starts to heal. Dad's tryin' to manipulate the rabbit-ears on top of the television so that Johnny Weissmuller's Tarzan doesn't swing through a jungle snowstorm, and I'm lying on the couch with Cindy Lou, Grandma's overweight Dachshund, playfully fighting for possession of a Bullwinkle chew toy. I usually like my time with my grandparents but, today, I can't seem to keep my attention on any one conversation.

Eventually, the jitters get the best of me as I roll off of the plastic covered couch and ask, "Momma, are you OK if I walk to Gee's and get a soft drink? I'm gettin' antsy bein' inside all day."

"It's alright with me, as long as your dad's good with it." Momma responds, looking over to Dad, who's still fidgeting at the television.

"Yeah," he replies, finally giving up and changing the channel, "just be careful. There's lots of Sunday drivers on the road today. We're probably gonna be heading out in a half hour or so, anyway."

After hugging Grandma goodbye, and Dad reminding me to thank her for dinner, I put Cindy Lou out to pee and start my trek to Gee's Grocery.

****

About a block from the store, I can see a group of men gathering around the bench near the front steps of Gee's. As I get closer, I hear the gregarious voice of Jack Lipsay shootin' the shit with a number of guys I recognize, and a few that I don't. I wedge my way to the front of the dozen or so fellows and find Jack sittin' on the wooden bench, a Dixie cup propped between his legs and a Red Man chewing tobacco pouch in his right hand. He sticks a plug of the dark tobacco in his mouth, spits out a stem, and grins at me.

"Well, if it ain't Bubba Armentrout," Jack says jovially, always receptive to a larger audience. "What the heck are you doin' being seen with a pack of mongrels like this bunch?"

"Hey, Mr. Lipsay," I respond, knowing that an amusing story is forthcoming as it always is when Jack finds a crowd. "I just came by to get a Coke."

"Well, I'm about to tell these fellows what I know about the scandal, and it might be a little rough for your ears, Bubba."

"I'd really like to listen if you don't mind, Mr. Lipsay. It probably won't be any language that I ain't heard before."

"Alright," he says, nodding his head, "but if Anna asks, you be sure and tell her that I gave you full warning." Skillfully spitting a thick brown spew of chewing tobacco into the Dixie cup, Jack begins to weave his tale.

****

"Now boys, me and Chief Bud Burns go back a long way. We went to school together at Bankston High in the late '30s, and the both of us played on the district championship baseball team. I was a pitcher, and he was our catcher...and a damn good one, at that. Some folks say that he coulda' made the Majors if he hadn't torn up his knees blockin' my wild pitches. Anyway, we've had some dealings over the years when he would clue me in on a story to pass along to the news folks at Channel 2, or if the Chief needed contributions for the Child's Hope Orphanage that he's been so involved with. So, yesterday, I saw my good friend Bud Burns outside the liquor store, he was off duty mind you, and asked him about all this horse shit that's been flowin' about town. He gave me the facts, straight upright from the horse's mouth."

Looking around at the crowd of men circling the bench, searching to see if he had caught their attention, Jack sees nods of acknowledgment, as the crowd leans forward with interest.

"I'm sure that by now all of y'all have read in the Post and Courier that there might be another 'party of interest' that the police were interested in questioning. Well, that line of questioning, that's what Bud called it...line of questioning... came from a woman's silver locket that they found around Elwood Breffton's neck, that's the school custodian for any of you that don't know, when they found him hanging from the beam in the principal's office at Freedom elementary."

A few of the folks in the group gasp with surprise, 'What?' upon hearing about the locket, but Jack ignores them, and continues.

202

"So, obviously, Burns asks Nance Breffton, Elwood's wife, about the locket and the pictures inside. From Burn's first observation, neither picture looked like Nance or any of her relatives. One picture was of an older woman that might have once been attractive, but was showin' her years, and the other photo was a young lady that was as pretty as a new born filly. Nance Breffton had cried when Bud showed her the locket, and she said that she had never seen that particular piece of jewelry in her life. Wiping away her tears, and ogling the locket again, Nance made the observation that the older woman sure did bear a strong resemblance to Louise Maynor, the mayor's wife, and damn if it didn't! And you know what else, the inscription inside read, 'To Louise, on her 16th birthday. Mother'."

With perfect timing, like he had been standing inside of the grocery's door listening for a break in Jack's story, Bennie Gee pops out to the top step leading down to the bench, fakes a scowl, and barks loudly, "Are any of you fuckin' vagrants gonna buy something, or are you just gonna hang around my store all day and run off my payin' customers?" Jack smiles, and teasingly replies, "Bennie, if it weren't for us, you wouldn't have any damn customers."

"Go on with your story, Jack," one of the old guys snorts from the center of the crowd, then turns to Bennie Gee and asks, "You got any more of that horse piss that you pawn off as beer in that there store of yours?"

"Yeah, Lem, I got a fresh batch that your wife squirted in a pail for me this mornin'." Bennie retorts gruffly as he stomps back into his grocery. "Now, where was I?" Jack contemplates. "Oh, yeah, the locket".

"So, the cops decide to pay a visit to Chestnut Hall to ask Louise Maynor about the jewelry. Well, low and behold, when questioned about the necklace, Louise informs the police that she and the mayor had discovered their back door swinging wide open one night a month or so ago when they got home after an evening out. They had decided not to report the incident to the authorities since they hadn't found anything stolen from the house. Louise said that she hadn't thought about the locket in ages, and didn't even realize that it was missing."

Lipsay picks up the Dixie cup, spits a wad of juice into it, adjusts his crotch, then casually continues, "The Chief said that he figured that Louise Maynor's explanation was reasonable enough, that was, until his investigative boys discovered coal soot on the trash bag that Betsy Mae Byrd had been buried in. As you probably already know from readin' the papers, those of you that can read, the trash bag was labeled as 'Property of Freedom Elementary School', and matched perfectly the ones found in Elwood Breffton's garage. The perplexing problem for the Chief was that the Brefftons don't have a coal bin or furnace; their house has radiator heat."

Jack pauses to ensure that the onlookers understand the importance of the Chief's findings, and seemingly satisfied that they realize the significance by their wide-eyed gazes, he continues, "So Bud chose to do a little follow up inspection work himself by making an unannounced visit to Chestnut Hall. After strolling around the property and takin' in the lovely flower gardens, what did the Chief find but the chute to a coal bin at the rear of Griffin Maynor's house. Well, by golly, it just seemed natural after finding the chute for Burns to ask the mayor what kind of heat a beautiful, old home like Chestnut Hall used in the winter. Griffin told him, proud as punch, that electric heat had been installed back in the late fifties, but that he kept a coal octopi's furnace in working order that he and Louise used on real cold days, or when snow and ice knocked out the electricity. 'Well, wasn't that just the smartest thing', the Chief had told the mayor, and then Burns asked Griffin if he could see the furnace being that the Chief might consider getting his old furnace up and running for such a severe weather event too."

"You know, there's one thing that gets Madge Burn's goat," Bud had confided in the mayor, "and that's a cold chill in the main floor of the house."

"Chief Burns told me," Lipsay continues, "that the only thing that nagged him so heavily after discovering the chute was that Mayor Maynor was so doggone enthused to show him the furnace; Griffin wasn't reluctant at all! You would think that if a dead body had been stored in your coal bin, especially one that you put there, that you might be somewhat apprehensive about showing said bin to the Chief of Police."

Bennie came back out of the store with a frosty six-pack of Pabst Blue Ribbon and hands them to the fellow that he had called Lem, pulling off one can from the plastic yoke and sitting it beside Jack's spit cup. "Y'all be careful that don't nobody see you drinkin' from the road," Bennie warns. "You know it's Sunday, and we still got the Blue Laws."

Jack reaches over and grabs the 'church key' hanging off of a nail next to the bench, pokes two holes in the can, takes a gigantic swig, and continues his account of Chief Burn's story, "Nope, the mayor wasn't hesitant at all. At least not until Bud started to dig and poke around in the coal bin. That's when Griffin puffed up like a Macy's Thanksgiving Day balloon as he's prone to do when he's *pissed, and asked Burns just what the fuck he was up to. When the Chief informed the mayor that his boys had found coal dust on the trash bag that Betsy Mae Byrd had been buried in, he said that Griffin turned as white as a Klansman's sheet, and told Bud Burns to get the hell out of his house. Maynor was as purple as a preacher's pecker when he angrily told Burns that the police would need a goddamn warrant delivered personally by fuckin' Governor Mills E. Godwin Junior before he would ever allow any cops to set foot in Chestnut Hall again."*

"But gentlemen, the mayor's threats came too late. Unbeknown to Griffin Maynor, Chief Burns had already found a small piece of torn plastic in the coal bin, and stuck it in the back pocket of his dress pants for the boys back in the Bankston lab to match up to the trash bag that Betsy Mae was recovered in."

The afternoon sun is beginning to heat up the day, and rivulets of sweat are beginning to streak down my cheeks. Jack Lipsay's information that he gathered from Chief Burns is even better that I had hoped. Jack wipes his brow with a handkerchief pulled from his shirt pocket, guzzles the remainder of his beer, crumples the can in half and tosses it in the waste basket next to the steps of the grocery.

"We ain't seen nuthin' in the paper about that, Jack," rebuts Franklin Swathers, a taxidermist and self-proclaimed Civil War historian that is always a contrarian in any discussion where he isn't the deliverer of the facts. "Are you sure that Bud Burns ain't pullin' your leg?"

"Just 'cause you ain't read it in that bird cage liner that you call a paper, Franklin, don't mean it ain't fact. The Chief didn't want any of this evidence available to the public until his investigation was complete. And for your information, the torn corner of plastic found in the Maynor's coal bin matched perfectly with the trash bag that Betsy Mae Byrd was discovered in."

"But Jack," Franklin begins to counter, but before he can get another word out of his mouth, Bennie Gee says, "Shut the fuck up, Franklin, and let Jack tell his story. If we want any shit outta' you, we'll squeeze your damn head."

"It's alright, Bennie," Jack interjects, "what I'm tellin' is a lot to take in. But it IS fact. Just wait 'til you hear the rest."

"Anyways, Chief Burns had his boys bring in Griffin Maynor for questioning. Pulled him over on his way to a meeting in Front Royal, and left his treasured Cadillac setting right there by the side of the road. Once they got him to the station house, Griffin said that he wasn't going to say shit until his fancy lawyer from Richmond arrived. Chief Burns wasn't surprised by that development, but

what did come as a shock, and this will blow your drawers off like a beanie-weenie fart, before the attorney arrived, Louise Maynor burst into the police station where Griffin was being questioned, and screamed, 'Let my husband go! I'm the one you want. I killed that goddamn floozy, and I would do it again if I had the chance!' Gasps of surprise, disbelief and utter astonishment flow from the crowd of townsfolk circling Jack Lipsay. The Post and Courier had alluded to another 'party of interest' to be questioned, but the rumblings around Freedom were that the Police Department's investigation was focused on Jimbo Byrd, Elwood Breffton, or an unknown accomplice. There hadn't been any speculation that I'd heard regarding Louise Maynor's involvement.

Needless to say, my ears perk up like a goosed Chihuahua at this news. I had hoped that the locket might prompt the police to question the Maynors, but this development is an answer to my prayers.

"Hold tight, folks," Jack says slyly and winks at Bennie, "if you think that's somethin', this next part will make your bladder splatter. Bud Burns says that there's also a connection twixt Betsy Mae Byrd's murder and Principal Yoncey's death in the school fire. And that connection was made by Louise herself."

Johnson Greeley mumbles skeptically through the mechanical hole in his throat from the pack near the end of the bench, "We ain't heard hide nor hair of Louise Maynor being involved, Jack. And this Ester Yoncey thing, that's been a closed case for goin' on two years now."

Lipsay eyes Greeley steely over the silver rims of his bifocal glasses, and states irritably, "Some folks won't believe lard is greasy. Listen up, Louise Maynor's story to the Chief went somethin' like this:"

My heart is racing, and I'm leaning forward to hang on every word that Jack relays. The entire crowd of men, now grown to more than twenty, are so engaged that Jack could have charged admission.

"Lady Louise received a phone call from Ester Yoncey late in the evening on the night that Freedom Elementary burned to the ground. Yoncey was so blazin' irate that she was damn near incoherent. You can bet that Louise Maynor was all ears when Ester told her that that she had caught Mayor Maynor in one of the classrooms gettin' a ten-dollar blow job from that whore, Betsy Mae Byrd, after everyone had gone home from the December Town Council meeting."

For once, no one interrupts at this point in Jack's story. You could knock the whole crowd over with a puff of wind, and if their gaping mouths could collect bugs, then Bennie Gee wouldn't need fly paper in his store for a month. It's clear that Jack is enjoying our suspense, by the grin spread across his face. Although there had been small rumors of the mayor's flings for years, none of the boys in the crowd expected what came next. Well, with the exception of me.

"So, Bud Burns asks Louise if Ester Yoncey said anything else, and he said that Louise Maynor got this devilish smirk on her face, venom ready to spew from bared cuspids, and spit out, 'Oh yes, Ester said AND JUST SO YOU KNOW, LAURA, I'VE BEEN SLEEPING WITH THE OLD BASTARD FOR THE LAST YEAR MYSELF'!" The collective intake of breath from the listeners could have sucked the milk from a twenty titted Guernsey, and they all hold that air for fear of missing one word of Jack's story.

"Well, it seems that Griffin Maynor had led Ester Yoncey to believe that he just might be willing to leave Louise for the School Principal. Ester was a bit gullible in the arena of love, being that she was never married except to her work. Most women would have realized that he was just leading her on in order to get in her drawers, but Ester didn't. Louise, when Ester called, was more than willing to provide the principal with that insight."

"Ester, even more pissed by Louise's unexpected response, told her that she was making the call so that Louise would know what a goddamn heel she was married to, and that she, Ester, was going to do everything in her power to ensure that the entire town of Freedom knew what the 'PRICK' Griffin had been doing, too! Ester told Laura that she didn't give a damn whether it cost her the principal position at Freedom Elementary, or not, because her sole goal in life would be the ruination of Mayor Griffin Maynor. Then Ester had slammed down the phone without waiting for a response."

"Now, we all know that hell hath no fury like a woman scorned, and Louise would have probably realized that Ester's ire, at least at its current level, would eventually dissipate. Except that, Louise had real concerns about the safety of her marriage when it came to Betsy Mae Byrd."

"Louise told Chief Burns that she had suspected the mayor's side tryst with Ester Yoncey, but had shrugged it off as a temporary mid-life fling. Griffin had been unfaithful a few times in the past that she was aware of, but his interest in 'the other woman' had always waned after a month or so. What Louise hadn't known was that the mayor was banging Betsy Mae Byrd, and she was afraid that 'big titted, hot-twatted piece of shit trailer trash', as Louise referred to her, really might steal Griffin away."

"Although devastated by the news of the affair with Byrd, Louise told Chief Burns that her first objective was to strongly discourage a scorned Ester Yoncey from blabbing about Mayor Griffin's sexual indiscretions to the entire town of Freedom."

"Louise said that being the town mayor meant more to Griffin than anything else in the world because ancestors of his had held that position since the town's inception. If Ester were to run her big mouth, the mayor could lose his job, and then she, Louise I'm talkin' about here, almost certainly would lose her husband."

"Are y'all still with me?" Jack inquires sheepishly to the clearly mesmerized crowd.

The townsfolk gathered around Lipsay are so enthralled with his masterful weaving of the tale that they hardly notice that Bennie Gee is passing around stale baloney and cheese sandwiches. I've never seen Bennie give anything away for free, so the meat and bread must be out of date. Ignorin' the fact that I'll probably be pukin' my guts up later tonight, along with the rest of the men gathered at Gee's, I unwrap the deli paper and take a cautiously sized bite of the hardened bread.

Jack rubs the stubble on the side of his face with one hand, removes his glasses with the other and attempts to wipe them clean with his sweaty handkerchief. He passes when Bennie offers a sandwich, but doesn't add a smart-ass comment about the quality of Gee's produce, as he normally would. Lipsay ponders for a moment, seeming to be trying to decide how best to move forward with the story, and is only pulled from his thoughts when Butch Harnsburger chirps, "Jack, you gonna sit there all day with your finger up your ass, or are you gonna finish tellin' the story? Ain't none of us gettin' any younger."

"Hold your horses, Butch. I'm gettin' to it," Jack replies.

"This next part has a little hair on it. You see, the Chief thinks that Louise Maynor told him pieces of the truth, but wouldn't come totally clean with everything that she knows. So, it's best, I think, if I tell you just the way he told me."

"Elwood Breffton had made a few unsolicited romantic passes at Louise Maynor in the past, and she knew that the Brefftons were strapped for cash. So much so, that Nance Breffton had recently asked her who she needed to talk to in order to get a job in the school cafeteria. So, Louise figured that a little cash *and feigned attention towards Elwood just might go a long way in persuading him to have a talk with Ester Yoncey on her behalf."*

"The same evening that Ester calls her about the mayor, the night of the fire, Louise contacts Elwood Breffton and tells him about Ester Yoncey's threat. Now, she knows this is a risk, but Louise tells Breffton that if any of this gets out, he'll lose his janitorial job and any other employment opportunity that he might stumble across in Freedom. Once Maynor was sure that she had Elwood's undivided attention, she flatters and flirts with him a bit before offering five-hundred dollars in hard, cold cash to play the heavy with Ester Yoncey. Louise wanted him to warn the principal of what COULD happen to her if word of the mayor's affairs were to get out around town. As expected, Breffton jumps at the opportunity to please Louise and make a bunch of easy cash at the same time. The deal having been agreed to, Louise tells Elwood that he's to have the conversation with Ester that same night, and that she'll leave him the cash under the front seat of his unlocked pickup truck in the school lot the next day."

"Chief Burns asked Louise straight out if Elwood Breffton killed Ester Yoncey, and then set fire to the school. Louise said that, as far as she knew, the fire was an accident, just like the papers reported. Bud Burns, like anyone with any sense, figured that the fire was a terrible coincidence, too big if you were to ask him, but Louise Maynor refused to change her story. She said that she left the cash in his truck the next day. It was parked in front of his house since the school lot was blocked because of the fire. And, that she didn't know about Ester Yoncey's tragic death until Mayor Griffin Maynor told her once the coroner had contacted him. Louise told Chief Burns that everything happens for a reason, and that maybe Ester Yoncey had it comin', but that she hadn't spoken to Elwood Breffton again until the night that she directed him to bury the body of Betsy Mae Byrd on the school grounds."

****

Sweat is startin' to run down the crack of my butt, and the top of my underwear is rubbin' me raw. I ain't sure whether it's the heat, or my dang nerves. As Jack Lipsay tells this part of his tale, I want to scream 'Oh, she knew! She knew for sure! I heard them plottin' about what happened to Ester and Betsy Mae after they screwed on the mayor's bed'. Thank goodness, good sense prevails, and I keep my mouth shut.

209

Knowing that Breffton strangled Principal Yoncey, that he had burnt down the school to cover his tracks, and that Breffton and Louise were fuckin' wasn't goin' to make any difference in bringing Louise Maynor to justice. Besides, there might be another way to get that part of the story told. I've done a pretty doggone good job at bringin' their crime of killing and disposing of Betsy Mae to the light of day, there ain't no cause for gettin' myself in the spotlight now.

****

"Chief Bud Burns called bullshit on this part of Louise's confession, but she maintained that she didn't know a damn thing more about Ester or the fire. About that time, her lawyer arrived and advised her not to say anything more, but Louise said that she needed to ensure that the police understood that Mayor Griffin Maynor had nothing to do with the death of Betsy Mae Byrd."

If a pin had dropped outside of Gee's, it would have sounded like an atomic explosion. Although a few listeners whispered to themselves 'well, I'll be damned' and 'Holy Mary, Mother of Jesus', the vast majority of the townsfolk stand stunned trying to comprehend how the events that Jack is describing could happen in their little mountain hamlet.

"Are y'all boy's hearts up to hearin' the rest of what Burns told me?" Jack says, grinning widely. Grabbing another beer from the new six-pack that appears beside him on the bench, he pulls the plug of tobacco from his jaw and drops it in his spit cup.

"Go on, Jack," Lem prods anxiously.

"OK, let me see if I can wrap this up for you."

Clearing his throat, Jack continues, "Louise told Chief Burns that the mayor didn't know nuthin' about Yoncey's call to her on the night of the fire, either. The 'accident' had eliminated one of her concerns, the spreading of the gossip about Griffin's affairs, but her major issue still existed; Griffin Maynor's growing obsession with Betsy Mae Byrd. She told Bud Burns that she believed that the affair was getting more heated with every day that passed. When he came home from an overnight meeting in mid-January of '68, and said that he was moving his sleeping arrangements to the upstairs bedroom at Chestnut Hall, Laura was frantic that he was about to demand a divorce. Her fears were enhanced when she saw Jimbo Byrd at the Post Office, and he told Louise that Betsy Mae had been spending quite a few nights at her sick mother's house in

210

Nelson County. Jimbo said that Betsy Mae was tryin' to make the thirty-mile trip at least every Wednesday, and that she'd sometimes spend Thursday night as well. Louise told Bud that she found it pretty damn interesting that many of those nights Betsy Mae spent with her momma were the same nights that Griffin was out of town on business. Now, Griffin hadn't yet brought up the 'D' word, and she still hadn't been positive that he would let his position as mayor go for a two-bit whore, Louise Maynor's words, not mine. I don't speak ill of the dead. But she was scared that her marriage was dissolving. Anyway, Louise told Burns that at that point, she had reached her limit, and was willing to do whatever was necessary to keep Betsy Mae away from her husband."

"The morning of the Negro Minstrel Show, the day that Betsy Mae disappeared, Louise Maynor saw Betsy Mae cattin' around at the Moose Lodge in Bankston when she went to deliver brownies and cupcakes for a bake sale to help out that kid with Leukemia in Cloverdale. What's her name? You know, the kid whose picture is on all them mason jars in the stores, shit, I'll think of her name in a minute. Burnette, that's it. I'd forget my dick if it wasn't attached. Anyway, after delivering the baked goods, Louise waited in the parking lot of the Lodge for Betsy Mae to finish her crotch grabbin' inside, and called to her when she was gettin' in her car to leave. Louise acted surprised to see Betsy Mae, and told her how fortunate it was that she had run into her that morning. As many of you may already know, Betsy Mae Byrd had been directing the Minstrel Show for years, and Louise Maynor determines how best to spend the proceeds."

"Sometimes, it's to help folks that can't afford to pay their water or heating bill, while other times it's for playground equipment and the like. So, Louise invites Betsy Mae over to Chestnut Hall for lunch so as they could discuss the finishing touches on that night's show. Louise Maynor said that Betsy Mae was initially hesitant, too busy with last minute details of writing her introduction for the show, but conceded when Louise told her that she would add a little brandy to their afternoon tea to get the ideas flowin' freely. Maynor suggested that Byrd walk the few blocks from her house to Chestnut Hall because she, Louise, wouldn't ever want Betsy Mae to run into any trouble with the law from drinkin' and drivin'."

"You see," Jack emphasizes, as if he is talking to a group of dunces and, to a fair degree, he is, "Betsy Mae had no idea that Louise Maynor was on to her and the mayor's escapades. She had simply been droppin' her panties for the mayor the same as with some of the bucks at the Moose Lodge. Bud Burns made a point of tellin' me that it was Griffin that was getting serious about their relationship, and not Betsy Mae. And even the mayor's infatuation with her, like his other flings, would probably have burnt off after a while."

"So, as Louise had suggested, Betsy Mae hoofed on over to Chestnut Hall for her lunch appointment with Maynor. Louise told the Chief that they had talked about many things over pimento cheese sandwiches and macaroni salad. Betsy Mae had talked about Jimbo, and how much additional work his new supervisor job required, that his hours had increased to almost sixty per week, and that if they didn't get a piece of quarry digging equipment repaired by late afternoon how Jim might be late for the Minstrel Show that night. Well, all of this information fit perfectly into Louise's plan. When she poured the brandy to cap off lunch, Louise added a significant dose of arsenic to Betsy Mae's drink for good measure."

Jack is really rolling now. He lowers his voice an octave or two, as if telling an unmentionable secret to a lost lover, slides forward on the bench to gain intimacy with the group, and slowly reveals each tawdry detail of how Betsy Mae's demise had played out. "With the mayor's lover dead on the dining room floor of Chestnut Hall, Louise told Chief Burns that she hadn't thought, at that point, of how to dispose of the body. Bud Burns believes that she elicited the help of Elwood Breffton, again, but Maynor swears that she hid the body herself. Betsy Mae Byrd only weighed about ninety-five pounds sopping wet, so I guess it's possible, but not likely."

"Louise told Burns that Betsy Mae had passed pretty quickly from the heavy dose of poison. After a few sips of brandy, she had complained of stomach cramps, but before she could get to the toilet, she had turned purple and grasped her chest. Bud Burns told me that she could have suffocated from the neck swelling, or even had a heart attack caused by the arsenic."

"The mayor was scheduled to be home in the early evening from a golf outing, and Louise rightly knew that he wouldn't take too kindly to finding his pokin' buddy laid out dead as a doornail when he arrived at Chestnut Hall. So, Louise wraps Byrd's body in plastic sheeting that they had stored in their basement, something that workers had left when they painted the place a few years back, and drags the body to the coal bin under the house. Louise said that it took her the better part of two hours to get the body well towards the bottom of the bin, and that she had been as black as the participants at the Minstrel Show when she finished. Louise felt comfortable that the mayor wouldn't *discover Betsy Mae in the bin, especially since she was stored so deep under the coal. She told Burns that she knew that the body would need to be moved and buried eventually, and thought that Breffton might be able to help her once everything calmed down from Byrd's disappearance."*

"Well, time went by, as time does, and Louise got more and more anxious about having Byrd's body in her basement. Everyone, especially those who knew her, assumed that Betsy Mae had runoff with an out-of-towner, but were just as confident that she would eventually return to Jimbo when she went out of heat. Obviously, she didn't return. Louise said that early last year was warm enough that they didn't use any coal, but she started to get concerned as record low temperatures hit Freedom last fall and into the winter. Then, as summer approached, she and the mayor started to get a whiff of what the mayor thought was a dead rat. At that point, it became an obsession of Laura Maynor's to get rid of Betsy Mae Byrd's body. As the new school was nearing completion, and the sidewalks and playground platforms were about to be poured, Louise knew that this would be her best opportunity to get the job done, and she was running out of time."

****

I could tell from Jack's story, of Louise Maynor's confession to the Chief, that she was trying to make herself the victim in the eyes of the police and, ultimately, the town. Philandering husband, loving wife, what else was she to do when she was about to lose everything? What she didn't want Burns, the townsfolk, and the mayor to know about was her sexual trysts with Elwood Breffton. It was clear that Louise thought that if she could avoid being held responsible for Ester Yoncey, hide her affair with Breffton and make Betsy Mae Byrd's death appear as an act of passion, then she might receive a load of leniency from the police and the town. After all, she was Lady Louise Maynor.

From what Jack says, it seems to me that Chief Bud Burns is comfortable enough with Louise Maynor's explanation since it includes a confession to Byrd's murder. As long as she refuses to tell him more, only Louise Maynor and me know the story from beginning to end.

****

Jack Lipsay is Freedom's Uncle Remus, spinning his yarn in a way that captures our attention and imagination. But even his ability to weave is beginning to waiver as he approaches the end of his tale.

"*According to Louise, it was time to call on someone to help, and who better than her accomplice from before that already knew her secrets, Elwood Breffton.*" *Interesting word that Jack uses in describing Elwood as an accomplice, almost like he suspects there's more to the story than Louise is telling. My guess is that Chief Burns has the same suspicions.*

"*Louise explained to Breffton how she had poisoned Betsy Mae, and how she planned to hide the evidence. All that Breffton needed to do, for a thousand dollars in cash, was to bury Byrd deep enough not to be discovered by the workers pouring concrete into the wooden forms at Freedom Elementary the next afternoon. Chief Burns had chuckled when he described this part of Louise Maynor's plan. Bud said that everything about Louise's confession involved somethin' gettin' laid. Get it... concrete, laid, the mayor... oh, whatever.*"

Upon garnering a few polite laughs and a bunch of groans from his audience, Lipsay continues, "But, Breffton says he don't want nothing to do with being an accomplice to murder, and flatly declines her offer. Maynor told Burns that she had needed to remind Elwood that she was aware of his heavy drinkin' on the job, and how that just might have been a major contributor to the Freedom School fire. Cold feet or not, that was somethin' that Breffton didn't want anyone digging into any more than they already had."

"*The evening of the school dedication, when Ester Yoncey was memorialized for her work in developing the minds of Freedom's children, Elwood Breffton was removing Betsy Mae Byrd's body from the rotting plastic sheeting at Chestnut Hall, and placing her remains in an industrial trash bag for burial on school grounds later that night. And you know what? That plan would have worked to perfection if the new sidewalks and platforms hadn't been vandalized the following night. Louise Maynor told Chief Burns that she didn't have a clue who pissed in the punchbowl; maybe it had been a nosy neighbor that saw Breffton digging in the wooden frames, or simply some kids up to mischief. Whoever it was, they sure fucked up a well-conceived plan!*"

"*Bud Burns said that you could call it karma, or just blind luck, but it was the one thing, the only thing, that had set the wheels in motion for the guilty to be brought to justice.*"

I can't suppress the huge grin that breaks out across my face after hearing the Chief's comments recounted. It's such a big relief to learn that the havoc that me and Timmy caused when we vandalized the cement was worth all the troubles and tribulation that we had put the townsfolk through.

Something else Jack said caught my attention, and I couldn't wait until we were alone to ask the question. I raise my hand, like I'm in a classroom, and wait for Lipsay to call on me.

"Bubba, by God, you're the only one with any manners at all around here. Whatcha' got on your mind, buddy?"

"Mr. Lipsay," I say sheepishly, "you mentioned when you first started that Chief Burns found a piece of trash bag in the coal bin, and eventually matched it to the bag that Mrs. Byrd was buried in. And I think that you said that the police found the same type trash bags labeled 'Freedom Elementary School' in Mr. Breffton's garage."

"OK, Bubba, right so far. What's your point?"

"Well, if Mrs. Maynor wrapped Mrs. Byrd in painter's plastic, and Mr. Breffton didn't put her in the industrial trash bag until the night of the dedication, then how did a torn piece of the trash bag get into the coal bin? It would seem to me that Betsy Mae musta' been in the trash bag in the bin before bein' moved to the school grounds."

Jack seems surprised that the question was asked, but not necessarily by the question itself. Doing his best to avoid a detailed conversation about my inquiry, he simply states, "Well, that's a question that I didn't think to ask, Bubba. I'll have to run that one by Chief Burns and get back to you. Maybe he'll have an answer." Satisfied that others in his audience didn't realize the implications of my question, and spent from his efforts in providing his fellow townsfolk with Chief Burn's account of the events surrounding the Freedom Scandal, Jack sighs and says, "Now you folks know as much about what's been goin' on as I do."

Somehow, I don't think that is necessarily true.

****

Jack Lipsay pulls me aside, as the crowd begins to disperse. A number of the men that had been in attendance slap him on the back, and one even calls him a County Treasure. I'm just happy to call Jack my friend.

We walk towards the old town bridge, and Jack puts his arm around my shoulders, "Bubba, that question that you asked about the bag. I told a small fib when I answered your question, and I'm goin' to ask your forgiveness, 'cause it's hardly ever right to lie. I want you to know why I did."

"When Louise Maynor confessed to Bud Burns, there were a number of inconsistencies in her story. One was her involvement with Breffton, especially concerning Ester Yoncey's death and the school fire. Other things that didn't match up perfectly were her not having contact with Elwood Breffton again until she asked him to bury Betsy Mae, and Bud finding that piece of trash bag in the coal bin at Chestnut Hall."

"Bud told Louise Maynor that if she pleaded guilty to second-degree murder, not premeditated, with a twenty-five-year sentence with no probation, then he would consider the case closed. You see, Bubba, there wasn't much more justice to be doled out. Breffton was dead at his own hands, and Louise would spend the rest of her life, or the best part of it, behind bars. No expensive trial for the County, and Louise gets the satisfaction of knowing the mayor won't be prosecuted, at least by the courts. Burns couldn't find any angle that implicated the mayor in murder."

"But what about justice for Ms. Yoncey, Jack?" I ask passionately. "Everybody, forever, is gonna think that her bein' dead, and the school fire, was just an accident. From what Louise Maynor told the Chief, Ester was willin' to put her reputation on the line so as the town would know exactly what kinda' man we have as a mayor."

"I hear ya, Bubba," Jack counters, "but here's the thing. The official release from the Bankston Police isn't gonna provide specific details about the call from Ester Yoncey to Louise Maynor. It was in Burn's agreement with Louise Maynor for her confession, and he figures that there ain't any need to soil the reputation of Principal Yoncey or, for that matter, make life more difficult for Nance Breffton. The parties responsible for the crimes, Elwood Breffton and Louise Maynor, receive the ultimate punishment. Bud Burns will make a statement to the press this week that Louise Maynor had concerns that her husband was having an affair, of which there was no specific proof, took matters into her own hands in killing Betsy Mae Byrd and then hired a long-time loyal County worker to dispose of the body. Elwood, distraught over what he did, and the police finding evidence in his garage linking him as an accomplice, took his own life."

"What about the locket that you mentioned?" I frustratingly ask, not angry with Jack but at the injustice to Principal Yoncey. "The papers are gonna want to know what caused the police to question the Maynors in the first place."

"Bubba, sometimes you're just too damn smart for your own good. If pressed, Chief Burn's response will be, like Louise Maynor told him, that their house was broken into weeks before Betsy Mae was murdered. He'll make a potential connection saying Breffton may have been infatuated with Louise Maynor, but no one will ever know for sure, and Elwood can't speak for himself."

"Seems pretty convenient," I say resignedly, "that the mayor gets off the hook, and he's the one that started all of this trouble."

"Life works that way sometimes, Bubba," Jack replies sagely. "Look, we don't know anything for sure, and neither does the police, other than Louise killed Betsy Mae Byrd, and that Elwood Breffton buried the body. There isn't solid proof of the mayor having a fling with anyone. This could have totally been concocted in Louise Maynor's mind, and carried out by Breffton because he had a crush on her. That's all that we know for certain but, in this case, that's enough."

Although feelin' like shit because Ms. Yoncey, in death, is gettin' a raw deal, and knowin' that Mayor Griffin Maynor is never goin' to get what he deserves, I do appreciate Jack workin' to teach me a life lesson.

"Thanks, Jack. I appreciate you takin' the time to spell this out for me."

"Always a pleasure, Bubba. You got more sense than the biggest part of the adults here in Freedom. Why don't you let me buy you a drink for your trip home?"

****

Jack and I step through the screen door at Gee's and find that the other townsfolk have already gone their own way. Bennie is slipping a stained apron over his head, revealing an even more tattered and greasy T-shirt underneath, when Jack says jovially, "Bennie, Bubba is gonna get a Coca-Cola and peanuts. How much do I owe ya'?"

"Twenty cents," Gee replies gruffly.

"Twenty cents," Jack pretends to be stunned, and lays a quarter on the counter, "that's highway robbery, Bennie. I only want a pack of nuts, not the whole goddamn can."

Reaching into the ice chest at the front of the store, and pulling out a near frozen Coke, I hear Bennie ask, "So, Jack. Who do you think vandalized the playground at Freedom Elementary, and what woulda' caused 'em to do it?"

*"I don't rightly know," Jack replies, shaking his head in puzzlement. "Probably **WAS** those Cheatum boys up to mischief, but the police will never be able to charge them as long as that fuckin' river rat, Lonnie Hammer, continues to lie for 'em."*

Jack contemplates for a second, then provides another possible culprit, "Could also be that disgruntled mason that the company fired for being late to work on the afternoon that the cement was poured at the school. I heard tell that he doesn't have a verifiable alibi for that night, but the cops can't place him at the scene neither."

Pointing at the rack behind Bennie's head, Jack says, "Grab me a pack of Pall Malls, will ya' Bennie. I believe that the connection between the vandalism and the workers uncovering Betsy Mae's body was just a fortunate coincidence, or an act of God, but I don't rightly know. Probably never will."

The whole time I'm thinkin', 'I sure hope that's the case'!

****

Late Fall 2019

Reflection

Those next few days in September of '69 are permanently imprinted in my memory as if carved in stone. The news that had broken in the paper and on television the following Monday was reported exactly as Jack Lipsay had said that it would be. The fire at Freedom Elementary was mentioned only as a chronological set piece illustrating the challenges that our town had endured over a two-year period of time. Although I considered myself fortunate to not have been mentioned in Louise Maynor's confession to the police, as that would have opened a whole other can of worms for her and me, I had been devastated that the truth regarding our sleazy, immoral mayor was buried deeper than Betsy Mae Byrd's remains.

Like most scandals, tongues wagged and hyperbole abounded for a few months. But, by the time that the spring of 1970 arrived, most of the conversation surrounding the murder had dissipated to whispers around card tables at Bingo night, and the story became another frayed thread in the tapestry that comprises my hometown of Freedom.

Louise Maynor had served only two years at a low security women's prison in West Virginia when she developed pancreatic cancer, and a few months later was transferred to a hospice facility that catered to the incarcerated. Mayor Maynor, it was rumored, had asked for her to be released to his custody, but she had died while awaiting the decision. Karma is a bitch but, so was Lady Louise Maynor.

Chapter 20

Bubba's Other Doings

Late Fall 2019

Jesus. Where has the time gone?

Sitting on the steps leading up to Freedom Elementary, directly under the plaque of Ester Yoncey and the time capsule scheduled to be opened tomorrow, I surprisingly realize that the evening sun has dropped behind the Blue Ridge mountains. My memories of Freedom and its inhabitants have been so engaging, not necessarily in a good way, that I've been sitting for hours replaying the 'scandal' as if it were a miniseries on Netflix. My stomach is grumbling, providing critical feedback that my breakfast of watery eggs and burnt toast at the Train Stop Cafe, a greasy hole-in-the-wall diner beside the railroad tracks halfway between Cloverdale and Freedom, had been fully digested hours ago.

When I checked into the Fountain Pen Inn, formally the Bankston Sheraton, near the Shenandoah Regional Community College last night, the bored and detached SRCC student working the front desk informed me that I had to let her know by six o'clock this evening if I planned to spend another night at the hotel. Supposedly, there is a Seventh Day Adventist convention in town and the rooms are filling up fast. I'll call from my cell I left in my car, otherwise, I'll be spending the night in the Lexus.

My plan is to stay in Bankston overnight, stop by and see Mom and Dad in the morning, and then attend the fifty-year celebration of Freedom Elementary School tomorrow afternoon before heading back home to Charleston, South Carolina as fast as the State Police will allow.

I might even drop in on Uncle Rick and Aunt Jane if I have the energy left from making excuses to Mom on why I've been in town for a day without letting her know. Last I heard, neither Rick nor Jane was in good physical health. Rick has late-stage Alzheimer's and Jane nearly died of a heart attack a few years back while mowing the grass. My Uncle, in the early phases of the disease at the time, and always a penny pincher, had refused to pay a local kid five dollars to do the chore.

They both must be nearing their mid-eighties by now, so, I guess that the stress of Rick's incarceration five decades ago didn't knock too many years off of their lives. God only knows what would have happened to them if he would have been convicted of the embezzlement that he was accused of. Days before Rick's case went to trial in October 1969, the Directors of the First Baptist Church of Elliston uncovered an interesting bit of information that the good Reverend Seymour Tasker had surprisingly failed to mention to them. Tasker had signed a contract with a local television station to begin a Saturday night gospel ministry program in the summer of 1967, and had needed eight-thousand dollars of his personal money immediately to get the evangelism show up and running. Coincidently, eight thousand dollars was the exact amount of money that was missing from the tithes fund that Rick was accused of stealing. I never heard whether it was ever proven that Tasker had taken the cash, but the fact that the good Reverend couldn't demonstrate where he had acquired the money from more than created the reasonable doubt necessary to end my Uncle's legal troubles and, Reverend Tasker's religious career.

****

After calling the hotel to book an extra night, and deciding that a dish of Sesame Chicken might hit the spot for supper when I get to Bankston, I turn up the volume on the XM station, 70s on 7, and sing along with Gallery's 'Nice to Be with You'. A one-hit wonder, but a definite goody. I remember seeing the band perform on American Bandstand as a kid, and thinking, I know those three chords. Why couldn't I be in a band?

So, in 1975, I had gathered up all of my friends with any musical instrument talent whatsoever, and created a garage band. Banging out limited chords on an acoustic guitar, an electric piano, a base, a set of drums and a bit of skill on the electric guitar, we practiced covering early '70s Rock in the basement of Donnie Devin's house on weeknights after school. Donnie, Buck Matlin, his brother Travis, Hondo Harlin and I, from some awful stroke of genius, collaborated to name our band 'Wizard' when we felt that we were ready to hit the big time.

And big time to us was our freshman year at Moncross High School. We would play tunes from Cream, the Doobie Brothers, Don McLean, and other Top 40 bands for high school dances, Moose Lodge shindigs and Ladies Auxiliary meetings dressed in worn blue jean dusters and platform shoes…sans the goldfish. The music wasn't actually too bad, so we would drown out the off-key vocals with riffs blaring from our Marshall speakers that we purchased from two grubbily attired entrepreneurs selling musical equipment from the trunk of their Dodge Charger that needed money fast…no questions asked.

One summer night, when I was sixteen, the 'band' as we informally called ourselves, decided that a drinking binge pilgrimage down by the Shenandoah River was definitely in order. We borrowed Donnie's Mom's, Sandra, brand spanking new Chevrolet Camaro by lying to her that we were heading out to the Kenny Burger in Cloverdale to grab a bite to eat with friends and 'No, Mrs. Devin, none of our friends drink alcohol or smoke pot'. On the way to the river, Donnie had us pick up a local girl, Sami Crawford, with a reputation for low moral standards and a high proclivity for sexual activity, that had been wanting to jump Donnie's bones since she heard the band at school. Shortly after building a small bonfire to light the one huge joint that Travis had buried in the bottom of his backpack, and drinking the two six-packs of beer that Jim Ray Gee, Bennie's grandson, had sold me, Buck threw out the brilliant idea of driving Sandra Devin's Camaro to the Stop 'N' Shop near the Community College in Bankston, where they didn't card you as long as the purchaser was old enough to say 'beer'. Buck persuaded us by calling our attention to the fact that Donnie and Sami had crawled off into the woods to perform their primordial business, and the car was just setting there being useless to anyone with the keys hanging from the ignition. His reasoning, at the time, made sense, so with none of us particularly adept at driving a stick shift, and high on life, beer and pot, we incautiously hit the road in search of booze, broads and trouble. Unfortunately, the booze and trouble were pretty easy to obtain.

The four of us had downed another twelve pack of Stroh's in a dark corner of the Shop 'N' Stop parking lot, listening to ZZ Top's 'La Grange' eight-track and smoking Marlboro cigarettes.

Once that was completed, Travis made the suggestion, and we all agreed, that we should visit the dorms and bars near the college to see if a few of the younger female students might believe a concocted tale of how 'Wizard' was on the brink of hitting the big time; "Haven't you heard of us? We're big on the

222

college circuit." The ruse had worked once before when we had crashed a prom party after playing a gig at a local high school, so feeling pretty brazen from the beer, we were set to move forward in stepping up our game.

As chance would have it, before we ever made it to the dorm rooms, I had needed to relieve myself of a full bladder of Stroh's behind a car in the center of the College campus parking lot. As my other buddies strolled towards the dorms, I was nabbed with my pecker in my hand by a not so friendly campus cop. The reason for his lack of cordialness, in part, may have been the result of me pissing on his pant leg and leather shoes when he surprisingly sneaked up behind me from between two other parked cars and roughly grabbed me by both shoulders. Who wouldn't have jerked around, startled, by such an inopportune annoyance?

Nonetheless, the campus police had allowed me to call home and plead for help, and Dad, angry as a banty rooster in a South Carolina cockfight, had come to pluck me from the college detainment area, or jail as it's referred to in certain socioeconomic circles. Upon promising the cops that I would never again frequent their institution of higher learning, and that there was a major ass whipping on the horizon for one Bubba Armentrout, they had released me and my buddies to Arle with a simple warning.

After dropping Buck, Travis and Hondo off in their respective driveways, Dad had waited outside of Sandra and Doc Devin's house when he sent me inside to explain what the 'band' had really been up to that evening. Mrs. Devin fussed and cussed, and swore that I was a terrible influence on her baby, Donnie.

Sandra hadn't allowed Doc, her husband, any questions or input when she informed him that he had best get his ass on down to the river immediately to get her baby back home safely. Good judgment on my part, for the first time that evening, made its presence known when I kept Sami Crawford out of my explanation to Mrs. Devin about the night's activities. I did give Doc a heads up as he got in Dad's truck for the trip to the river, but he seemed more concerned on how to get his wife's Camaro back home from the college.

When Dad, Doc and I arrived at the spot where we had left Donnie and Sami earlier, the campfire had dwindled to glowing embers and there wasn't any sign of the two young lovers.

Hearing frolicking sounds coming from near the water, we made our way down the muddy bank of the Shenandoah, and found the two of them still going at it hard and heavy in Donnie's sleeping bag; oh, the stamina of youth. I remember seeing Doc grin at Dad before proceeding down the embankment and grabbing Donnie by the short, curly hair on the back of his neck, and dragging him out of the bag buck naked. Donnie turned as pale as a ghost when he saw Doc, and could only stare, hands covering his Johnson, as his dad looked down into the stunned face of Sami Crawford and politely said, "Get dressed young lady. We're takin' you home."

What brings this story to mind, as I drive to my supper destination, is what happened about a month after the incident on the river. Town rumor was that Sami Crawford had strolled past Chestnut Hall in red, hot pants and a tight halter-top on the way to pick up a delivery of Tupperware products for her Mama at the Freedom Post Office. Supposedly, but never officially confirmed, the Honorable Mayor Griffin Maynor, seeing her cute little body walking alone while retrieving his daily paper from the front of his house, had offered Sami twenty dollars for sex.

This encounter could have ended with Sami's decline of his offer, except that she was only sixteen and made a beeline home to tell her PaPa about the lecherous old son-of-a-bitch that was offering her money to get in her pants. Even in light of the scandalous events that had happened a mere five years earlier, Griffin hadn't changed one iota; when there was a pretty girl involved, he was never able to keep his dick in his pants.

The part of the rumor that was confirmed, primarily by the bruising on Maynor's face, was that Gentry Crawford had beat the shit out of the mayor on the front porch of Chestnut Hall, and that Griffin had never pressed charges. We always figured that there was money exchanged since the Crawfords didn't notify the law of Maynor's indiscretion, but it may have been that Gentry felt like he had succeeded in administering due process on his own.

****

Fifty years after that scandalous time period in the last days of the Sixties, this visit to Freedom has helped me to realize that this town will always be a significant part of me, as intrinsic a fundamental element of my being as any X or Y chromosome in my genetic makeup. But, for me to reconcile with Freedom, debts need to be paid in full.

When the news about Betsy Mae Byrd's murder, and Louise Maynor's arrest, broke, I hadn't had many options to bring all of the facts to light. Jack Lipsay may have been right, at the time, when he told me that some information is best left undisturbed to protect the reputation of the innocent. Where he was wrong, somewhat unknowingly since he hadn't seen what I had observed, was his assessment that justice had been served. Ester Yoncey had been murdered for greed, jealously and retained social status. She had told Louise Maynor, during that last phone call, that she was willing to risk her reputation in the community, even her job, so that Griffin Maynor wouldn't prey on other gullible women. The school had been burned to the ground to cover the tracks of the guilty, more interested in personal gain and loss than in the life of a pillar within our community.

History reflects that Freedom Elementary School burned accidentally from an overheated boiler, and that Ester Yoncey was a casualty of that tragic mishap. I have lived with that injustice for fifty years.

Sometimes, history needs to be revised when previously unknown facts are uncovered.

I'll stop by and say a brief hello and goodbye to Mom and Dad tomorrow, pop in on the fifty-year celebration and vault opening at Freedom Elementary, and then get the hell out of Dodge. Hopefully, leaving with a lighter conscience than when I arrived in town.

Epilogue
Making Things Right

October 1969

Boy, plans don't always go the way you expect but, sometimes, they still work out OK.

The mayor had made a big hullabaloo at the dedication ceremony over all of the nostalgic items that the crowd had brought for the time capsule. And, rightfully so. There were pictures, a watch, coins, a confederate infantry patch, a 1920 yearbook, a recent 1969 Sports Illustrated magazine with Joe Willie Namath on the cover, a Patsy Cline guitar pick, a worn American flag with forty-eight stars, arrowheads, a family bible, even a doll that was supposedly owned by Dolly Madison. These, and tens of other trinkets, were brought to the event for their inclusion in the capsule. Conspicuously absent, at least from my perspective, was a token in respect to, or about, Ms. Ester Yoncey.

Since I had been prowlin' around Chestnut Hall when the formal ceremony took place, Timmy Wyatt had provided me the details of the dedication. He said that Secretary Fran was logging the gifts so as there'd be a record, and then the vault would be sealed by the mason workers when they came by to remove the tarps from the sidewalks later in the week.

Those plans went awry when there was vandalism at the school, and the masons weren't able to complete the job until the end of September. Finally, nearly a month after the start of the new school year, they placed and sealed the capsule vault for its fifty-year hibernation until the next scheduled ceremony in the following century.

After listening to Jack Lipsay's account of how the Bankston Police were going to break the story of the scandal to the press, and before the worker's labors were complete, I figured that I might still have an opportunity to set things right.

226

Since Ms. Yoncey didn't have an item dedicated to her from the ceremony attendees, I asked Secretary Fran if I could add a note to the historic contents. I told Ms. Fran, and truly so, that I loved Principal Yoncey and missed her terrible. I said that I thought it would be a good idea to have a remembrance like that for folks to see when the vault is opened in fifty years 'cause we'll all probably be dead by then. Well, Ms. Fran said that was about the sweetest thing that she had ever heard, and that she would be happy for me to add my note to the other items in the capsule.

Setting outside of the administrative office that afternoon, I had written my dedication note to Ester Yoncey, and tape sealed the envelope with supplies borrowed from Secretary Fran. I had asked her to keep the letter sealed 'cause, you know, it's a little embarrassing for a fifth-grade boy to write about how much he loves his principal. Ms. Fran said that she understood completely, and included my letter in the contents of the box, updated the log and thanked me for my kindness.

The workers, having finally completed the walkways, sealed the time capsule vault on the last day of September this year. I can't remember the note word for word, but this is pretty close to what I wrote:

September 25, 1969
Folks,

I been living with a secret for almost two years and I gotta find some way to share it. Telling the secret ain't to benefit me, but it's a story that a great woman wanted told. What I'm about to tell is the whole truth, so help me God. I'm sure that you have heard about Louise Maynor poisoning Betsy Mae Byrd. Most of what's been said about that happening is true. I want you to know what ain't been told.

In December of 1967, I got stuck in Freedom Elementary (the old school) during the Town Council Meeting. I won't go into details on how I got penned in there late, but just know that it was my fault for misbehaving earlier in the day. I was in the 3rd grade and was scared to death that I would get in even more trouble if I got caught still in the school.

After the meeting, I thought that everybody was gone except for Principal Ester Yoncey, so I was gonna sneak through the library and out of the school. I ducked into one of the classrooms on the way out, and seen Mayor Griffin Maynor having sexual relations with Mrs. Betsy Mae Byrd. I wasn't the only one

227

that saw them. Principal Yoncey came in and saw them too. There was a bad argument between the mayor and Ms. Yoncey, and she said that she was a gonna tell Louise Maynor that the mayor had been having relations with both her and Betsy Mae Byrd. Now I was hiding during this, but I could tell that Principal Yoncey was mad as hell.

That very night, the old Freedom Elementary School burnt to the ground and, come to find out, Ms. Yoncey burnt up with it.

It wasn't but two more months, and Betsy Mae Byrd disappeared right before the Negro Minstrel Show. That's what sealed it for me. I knew that something bad was happening here in Freedom.

I was afraid to tell anybody about what I seen, and there wasn't any way for me to prove it anyways. I did a couple of things that I ain't proud of, and I'll probably need to answer to the Good Lord someday for doing them, but they did make it possible for me to confront the mayor about what I knew. His actions all but told me I was right.

It wasn't but a short while later that a car tried to run me over on the way to school. If you don't believe me, you can ask Peanut Cheatum. He saw the whole thing.

After that, I knew that the mayor was trying to kill me, and that I needed to take drastic actions. I decided that I had to find evidence that I could show the police.

During the dedication ceremony at our new school, I snuck into the mayor's house looking for something to tie him to Ms. Yoncey and Mrs. Byrd. Anything that would help me prove what he done. I know this was wrong, but I just knew that I was gonna get killed if I didn't do something.

While I was digging through the mayor's belongings at Chestnut Hall, Louise Maynor and Elwood Breffton came in through the back of the house. I was able to hide under the bed afore they knew I was there. They had sexual relations and talked. I know this is hard to believe about a proper lady like Louise Maynor, but it is fact. Mrs. Maynor talked about how she killed Betsy Mae, and how she wanted to get rid of the body. Mr. Breffton didn't want to do it, but Louise said if he didn't, she was a gonna tell how he killed Ester Yoncey and burnt down the school. You see, Mrs. Maynor was scared of Ester Yoncey telling everyone about her affair with the mayor, and about Betsy Mae Byrd having relations with him too. That's why she paid Mr. Breffton to kill Principal Yoncey, *and why she killed Mrs. Byrd herself. They even discussed how they were gonna do away with me after things calmed down.*

There's something else that I need to get off of my chest. Knowing that Breffton was burying the body at the school from the conversation that I heard, I was the one that vandalized the school grounds. I couldn't think of any other way to get their crime discovered. I'll find some way sometime to pay for the damage. I feel really bad about it, and am truly sorry for what I done.

There are some other things that happened, but they ain't nearly as important as what I wrote so far. Ms. Ester Yoncey was a great woman, and I'm sure that Betsy Mae Byrd was good too. Louise Maynor and Elwood Breffton were responsible for the crimes, but Mayor Griffin Maynor set them to it by his actions and the way he treated people.

Principal Yoncey wanted this known. She said so herself that night at the school. Hopefully now, she can rest in peace, and Mayor Maynor, the devil reincarnated, will be long dead.

I'm sorry for all of the things I did wrong. I hope you and God understand.

Bubba Armentrout
Schoolhouse Road
Freedom, Virginia

The outside of the envelope read:

To: Principal Ester Yoncey
From: Bubba Armentrout
With Love

****

Late Fall 2019

It was good to see the family today. Everyone is getting older, and I don't expect that Uncle Rick, or Dad for that matter, will see too many more winters. I'll stay a bit longer on my next visit.

The Fifty-Year Celebration is bustling, as I park at the Ruritan Hall and make my way through the growing crowd of aging residents, and visitors from surrounding towns packing bulky strollers and hyperactive adolescents. There is

229

no longer any room for rides, but vendors are set up along the street selling hot dogs, French fries and cotton candy. The podium from which the mayor will make his speech and display the contents of the time vault is decorated with school banners and bunting, and the microphone is being tested before he steps to the stand.

There are a number of folks attending the event that look vaguely familiar, but none that I could name as old classmates or friends. I haven't been to a reunion since I graduated from Moncross High forty-some years ago, so I'm clearly not making this trek to renew relationships. I'm here for one purpose, and my wait is about to come to an end.

A thin, well dressed woman steps up on the podium and removes the microphone from its holder. She begins to talk with no sound, then a lanky kid in faded jeans with greasy hair helps by stepping beside her and turning on the sound switch.

"Ladies and Gentlemen," she enunciates each word as if they're paying her by the syllable, "thank you for coming out on such a beautiful late fall day. We certainly have been blessed by the weather." Pointing behind her towards the school, she continues, "Fifty years ago, our Freedom Elementary School was dedicated, and we are here today to renew that commitment to the education of our youth. I'm Cynthia Scabbot, and I'm your 5th District Representative in Richmond. It is my distinct pleasure to introduce a native Freedomite that I am sure most of you already know. His family has held a role of leadership in this community for five generations; please join me in welcoming Mayor Stanley Griffin Maynor, Jr."

Stanley doesn't bear much resemblance to his grandfather, Griffin, and his family no longer lives at Chestnut Hall. Mom told me that his wife, Becca, is a Pediatrician in Lexington, and that they have five kids ranging from two to fourteen years old. Stanley Jr's father bought farmland near Peyton Forge Road after Griffin died, and each of his two sons built homes on the property. Stanley's younger brother, Stapleton, is a broker at one of the mid-size Richmond banks.

Stanley Jr must have gotten his height from his mother because he is well over six feet tall. His hair is graying at the temples, but he has much softer features than his grandfather. As he steps to the podium, his smile projects a kindness and inclusiveness that I don't remember seeing in any other Maynor. Stanley Jr is an electrical engineer by trade, but appears very comfortable speaking with his constituents in his role as Mayor of Freedom.

"I really appreciate this time to be with you today. What a great occasion." His smile broadens, and the crowd claps genuinely.

"Representative Scabbot mentioned that we are celebrating the half-centennial of Freedom Elementary, and that is absolutely true. But we are also here to memorialize a woman that was responsible for many of our children becoming fine, upstanding adults, parents and grandparents. Ester Yoncey was principal of Freedom Elementary for more than fifteen years in the '50s and '60s. She tragically lost her life in the December fire of 1967, but her memory, and the success of her students, live on. As you know, we are opening a time capsule today that has been preserved in a vault located next to her likeness, right here behind the podium that I'm standing on now. When we reviewed the inventory listing the contents of the capsule, we found that one of the students had written a letter to Principal Ester Yoncey stating his appreciation and love for the administrator."

A significant round of applause begins in back of the crowd and spreads through the audience. It is clear that some of the older folks remember Ester, and many of the young people have seen her memorial.

"What better way to celebrate Ms. Yoncey today," Stanley Jr enthusiastically continues, "than to read this letter from one of her students to the audience. I have asked my youngest son, Chase, a fifth-grade student at Freedom Elementary himself, to perform this honor for us today. Chase."

As young Chase Maynor moves from his mother's side at the back of the podium, I begin to step towards my car in the Ruritan lot. The youngster looks sharp in his three-piece brown corduroy suit and stiffly starched white shirt. His bow tie looks to be hand tied and not clipped on, and his brown leather Florsheims are spit polished so glossy that the afternoon light is reflecting off of them. He brushes the neatly trimmed blond hair back from his forehead with his right hand, and hugs his dad with his left arm. Taking the envelope and note that I created fifty years ago, Chase Maynor confidently steps to the podium as I arrive at my car.

The same guy in the faded jeans that turned on the microphone for Representative Scabbot, lowers the mic so that it drops to face level for Stanley Jr's son. Chase covers his mouth, coughs lightly and shows the envelope to the crowd. With reverence, he begins, "As my Dad said, this letter was written in 1969. To, Principal Ester Yoncey. From, Bubba Armentrout. With love."

A number of the more senior audience members look from side to side, either recognizing the name from my parents, or trying to see if a fellow named Bubba Armentrout is going to make himself known in the crowd. When no one steps forward or is indicated from the podium, the audience's attention shifts back to young Maynor. Chase unseals the envelope and grins at the crowd.

"The letter reads, 'I been living with a secret for almost two years, and I gotta find some way to share it. Telling the secret ain't to benefit me, but it's a story that a great woman wanted told. What I'm about to tell is the whole truth, so help me God. I'm sure that you've heard about Louise Maynor poisoning Betsy Mae Byrd. Most of what's been said about that happening is true. I want you to know what ain't been told."

The crowd appears dumbfounded by the reading of the note, but mesmerized, nonetheless. Stanley Jr and his wife rush forward to remove the microphone from their son's hand with looks of sheer fright and embarrassment on their faces.

Chase, oblivious to what he is reading, continues, "In December of 1967, I got stuck in the old Freedom Elementary during the Town Council Meeting."

Stanley Jr pulls the microphone from his son's hand, as Chase's mother leads him off the stage. Poor kid, he probably thinks that he did something wrong. Maynor raises and taps the microphone, and reluctantly addresses the audience, "I'm sorry folks. I don't know if this is a mistake or a practical joke, but let's continue with the celebration."

"We wanna hear what the note says," yells one of the spectators.

"Yeah, that sounded pretty damn interestin'," another pipes in.

Soon, what seemed like half the crowd was urging Stanley Maynor Jr to continue with the reading.

"Look folks," the mayor says shakily, "I've quickly perused this letter, and I don't think that it's appropriate to read aloud to the crowd."

As I start my car, I hear one last question from amongst the crowd, "Mr. Maynor, Rico Hill from the Bankston Post and Courier. Would it be possible for me to review that note with you?"

I'll bet that Rico never thought that he would be getting a scoop like this one when he was assigned to cover a school dedication ceremony. After I called the newspaper and told them that it would behoove them to attend.

****

232

On my drive back to South Carolina from Freedom, my cell phone rings about the same time that I reach the Charlotte city limits. Mom tells me that she had gotten about thirty calls asking for me. The last one was from the Bankston Post and Courier.

****

Rico Hill calls my cell, as I pass through Columbia, South Carolina. We decide on a time to talk tomorrow.

Justice is served, Ester Yoncey. Rest in peace.

CPSIA information can be obtained
at www.ICGtesting.com
Printed in the USA
BVHW042319161121
621779BV00009B/271